As I stood over that table, looking down at their four pretty faces, their slender necks and graceful arms, their delightfully budding breasts, swelling out the thin cotton of their frilly blouses, I wondered how on earth I was going to choose one or even two from among them. No — actually, *choosing* wasn't the problem. I wondered how I was going to be able to turn two or three of them down. Then this insane voice inside me said, 'Take all four!' And before I could have second thoughts, there I was haggling over a price for the four of them for the night.

Willing Girls

Faye Rossignol

HEADLINE
DELTA

Printed and bound in Great Britain by
Cox & Wyman Ltd, Reading, Berkshire

HEADLINE BOOK PUBLISHING
A division of Hodder Headline PLC
338 Euston Road
London NW1 3BH

Introduction

I met Mr 'Riley,' as he wishes to be known, through a high-class, English-born courtesan called Holly, whose association with him he describes in the closing section of this present volume. It was some years ago that I put out the first tentative feelers for girls on the Game to tell me the stories of how they began in the Oldest Profession in the World. I published the responses last year in *Beginners Please* — available from all good bookshops, of course. In the introduction to that book I explained that Holly, then working from her own luxurious apartment in Paris, was one of the first to reply, though her account was extremely, indeed, devastatingly, frank about her first day working as a 'model' in Soho. It almost put me off the project entirely. Fortunately, the other girls who responded gave me the sort of material I was hoping for and the project was, in the end, highly successful.

But one part of Holly's letter intrigued me. In it she mentioned the aforesaid Mr 'Riley' and described him as the boyfriend of Holly's girlfriend, Joy. This man, she said, was a consultant in the field of heating, cooling, and air-conditioning. His business took him to all four corners of the globe and, in those days when the telex was considered to be the zippiest form of international communication, it left him with a lot of spare time in all sorts of exotic places.

Well, we all know what healthy young males do with
their spare time when stranded with lots of money in
exotic places!

So I asked Holly to broker a meeting between me
and this 'Riley' — at which I asked him if he would
kindly share his erotic adventures with other healthy
young males, and, indeed, females, most of whom do
not have the privilege of visiting those exotic places.

At first he demurred, not out of modesty or shame
but because he feared his literary skills just weren't up
to it. I pleaded. I cajoled. At last he agreed to try to
describe just one episode — the one that begins this
present collection, set in Perth, Australia. The worst
hurdle in any piece of writing is a blank Page One; as
soon as he had filled it he was away at a gallop — and
did not stop until he had rounded off his story with *his*
account of Holly's entry into the profession. (Readers
of *Beginners Please* will enjoy many a chuckle comparing
it with hers.)

And now, to continue the galloping-horse metaphor,
he has the bit between his teeth and will, very soon,
deliver his second volume of erotic memoirs, *More
Willing Girls of the World.* Don't miss it!

Faye Rossignol
Effingham

PERTH: Jill and Susie

Three of life's significant secrets have been revealed to me during international flights at over 30,000ft. Two of them I owe to a Japanese chicken sexer with an excellent command of English: how to tie a shoelace with a single bow that will never come undone; and how to hang trousers so they will never drop off the bar of the hanger. The third I owe to an Australian, a citizen of Perth, which was our destination on that particular flight. As we joined the landing stack and circled over the city he turned to me and said, out of the blue, "You know that brothels are legal down there?" Well, it wasn't quite out of the blue, actually. I was watching the way this air hostess moved at the time, and he was watching me.

He went on to explain how, although brothels were strictly illegal in the city, as they were then in the whole of Australia, the police had come to an accommodation with a number of houses: As long as they shunned brawls, drugs, liquor, and girls under twenty-one, they'd be left alone to ply the world's oldest profession.

The significant thing about this third 'secret' is that it changed my life.

I don't know why that particular bit of information tipped the balance for me. I mean, I'd been visiting foreign cities on business for the previous two years and, though I'd often toyed with the idea of renting a girl for the night, I'd never actually done so. Perhaps it was the thought that, in Perth, it would be perfectly legal, or safe from the police, anyway. I'd always promised myself that, if ever I got a contract in Nevada, I'd go to the Mustang or the Chicken Ranch or one of those other, equally legal houses I'd read about in *Hustler* or *Penthouse*.

Or maybe it was a dream that had ripened anyway, one whose time had (to coin a phrase) come.

I'd better explain what I do. I'm a whizz at solving all problems connected with the heating, ventilation, and air-conditioning of buildings: factories, office blocks, hotels … no job too large. I'm especially good at rescuing systems that other engineers have bungled. I'm the Red Adair of the air-conditioning world, you could say. Back in the years I'm now recalling — the early eighties — I'd arrive the day before I was officially due and run my eye over the problem building so that I'd go in with a pretty good plan already formed in my mind. Then I'd spend a day or so taking the necessary soundings and measurements — all of which I'd turn into code and telex back to my home office in London. Yes, *telex!*

My partner and assistants would number-crunch the data on our mainframe and, three or four days later, a courier would deliver the results — based upon which I would then hand in my quotation. Nowadays, of course, I carry more computing power in my laptop than my office would have had in half a dozen mainframes — such is progress!

In short, back in those dear dead days, I'd arrive at some exotic foreign location, work nonstop for up to thirty-six hours, and then take several days off to enjoy … well, until that visit to Perth, I'd enjoy the sights, the beaches, the hills, the hot springs, the shows … whatever the place had to offer the respectable tourist.

So, though a seasoned traveller, I felt distinctly like a first-timer when I said to the hotel porter, "I hear the local police have come to an interesting arrangement with the ladies of the town …?"

Five minutes later, and five dollars lighter, I was on my way, fearing that if I hung back and thought it over too long, I'd get cold feet and never break my cherry. But I might as well not have bothered. An American aircraft carrier and several escort vessels were paying a courtesy visit to the port, which meant that there were upwards of two thousand randy sailors ashore that night, all looking, like me, for the Cairo Bazaar. I was still four streets away when I saw them, moving in small, purposeful groups across my path in the street up ahead.

I stopped and stared in dismay.

Behind me a female voice said, "Looks like you picked the wrong night, mate."

I turned and found myself staring — be honest, *gawping* — at the sexiest young girl I'd ever seen: a tall, leggy blonde with a long ponytail, sparkling eyes, full of challenge, breasts like small melons, a waist both your hands would almost meet around, and … well, I'll come to the rest of her in a moment. I didn't see the rest, anyway. I was having trouble enough taking in what I've already described.

"Were you hoping for a nice long time with someone like us?" she asked.

In the shadow at her side I saw a brunette who, in any other company, would also have held the male eye in a trance.

"Someone *very* like you," I replied.

"Forget it," said the blonde. "These last three days it's been murder."

The two of them started walking again. The brunette took my arm as they caught up with me and passed on by. "Come see for yourself if you don't believe us," she said. "I'm Shirleen, by the way. She's Babysoft."

"Riley," I told them.

"Two thousand men ashore each night," Babysoft said. "And thirty full-time girls, twenty part-time, and who knows how many good-time sheelaghs to look after them. Believe me, ten minutes is a long time tonight!"

I did a swift calculation. "But that comes to …" It sounded too absurd to say.

But Shirleen said it for me: "Yep! Thirty or forty apiece for us between now and midnight! That's curfew."

I halted in my tracks. "But that's not possible! It's six o'clock already."

They walked on, laughing an old trouper's laugh.

"How d'you manage it?" I asked, trotting to catch them up.

"We close our eyes and think of the honour of the Empire," Babysoft told me.

"And keep telling ourselves tomorrow is their last day," her companion added. "So if you want a nice long time with one of us, give us a day to rest up and come back on Thursday. Ciao!"

And they swept on ahead of me into the crowd of R&R sailors who were now thickening up around the entrance to the Cairo Bazaar.

Here's the layout. The brothel had once been a

dance hall, then, briefly, a cinema. The entrance was about five feet above street level, it being reached by two ramps, one at each side, leading up to a tiny forecourt measuring about 10ft by 6. These arrangements must have had something to do with crowd control — well, they certainly did on that night. The street before it was narrow and, at that moment, choked to a standstill by at least fifty sailors.

They all had their eyes fixed on the doors to the Cairo Bazaar, which bore a tattered, handwritten sign saying CLOSED 5.45−6.00pm.

For fumigation, I guessed.

Few of them spotted the two girls until they were well in among the crowd. Then Babysoft did something that certainly made them take notice. She was wearing the shortest miniskirt I'd ever seen and, as she and Shirleen walked away from me — just as they were swallowed up in the crowd — she rolled it up behind her, exposing the cutest, tightest, most glorious pair of naked buttocks.

A stunned silence fell around them and then cut like a swathe through the crowd ahead. Sailors fell back to give them room for a progress that was more royal with every step. Those two firm, muscular buttocks jiggled as her hips rose and fell to a great, collective holding of breath. And *not a single hand reached out to pat or fondle her there!* Such was the measure of her power over them. She must have known every last peculiarity connected with male lust — and played it like an angler with a marlin on the hook.

Yet it was not enough for her. As she went up the nearer of the two ramps she let the skirt fall back to its full five inches. A jocular groan went up from scores of throats that had almost forgotten how to breathe. She quelled it by turning toward them the moment she gained the little raised forecourt in front of the doors. It was guarded by two horizontal iron railings. She pressed her belly against the upper one — actually her Venus mound protruded just below it — and slowly, teasingly, she drew the front hem of her skirt up until nothing was left for the imagination to do except indulge in the usual fantasies.

I was obliquely in front of her, about fifty yards back up the street, but even I had a high-tensile erection at the sight of her lightly tufted Venus mound bulging out beneath the bar. What havoc it wreaked among the men immediately in front of her, heaven only knows.

Then she repeated the tease with the front hem of her blouse — lifting it slowly-slowly up until she could lay it to rest along the top of her naked breasts. Two beauties! A vast collective sigh of wonder rose up around her as she entwined her hands behind her head and smiled down in triumph at us all.

There is a line in *Othello* where the Moor says Desdemona is so fair that 'the senses ache' at her. Well let me tell you — Babysoft was the kind of girl to make *everything* ache at her.

"Ask for Babysoft or Shirleen," she called out — and then skipped through the entrance door, which opened and closed in one smooth movement to let them through.

I turned and made my disconsolate way back to the hotel. As I went I tried to picture the scene inside the Cairo Bazaar once they opened their doors. If the girls hadn't been pulling my leg, they'd be opening theirs to at least half a dozen men every hour for the next six hours. I tried to imagine what it must be like to lie there and let three dozen men lie on top of you, one after the other, and pack your hole with their meat. Thrust-thrust-thrust ... squirt-squirt-squirt — all that tidal wave of sperm. I knew I could never go back to the place.

Then I thought of Babysoft and I knew I could, actually.

My chagrin must have shown in my face because the moment I entered the lobby, the porter came up to me, full of apologies. "The moment you'd gone," he confessed, "I remembered those damn Yankee ships in the bay. I could have kicked myself." He looked all around and lowered his voice. "If you're still interested, I could suggest an alternative — an escort rather than a straightforward prossy."

"What's the diff?"

"Well, the one I have in mind — name of Jill — she'll only ever go with one man per night. She reckons that's very high class. You wine her and dine her for a straight hundred-dollar fee to her escort agency. After that, any other arrangement is strictly between you and her."

"For how much?"

He shrugged. "I reckon two hundred would cover it."

"On top of the hundred?"

"Sure. Shall I give her agency a ring?"

I shrugged, too. "If I say no, I shan't sleep."

Jill was about twenty-three, blonde, well groomed, and handsome rather than pretty. I could imagine her looking good in the saddle or crewing an ocean racer — something outdoor and vigorous, anyway. But tonight she was dressed like a model straight off the catwalk —

in a superbly tailored black dress, diamond earrings and a diamond necklace that, if real (and I'm no judge of that), must have cost over £20,000. A shame, though, because all this finery definitely wasn't *her*.

However, she had all the experience in the world and put me so much at my ease that, by the time we were finishing our steaks, she said, "We don't belong here, either of us, do we? You'd rather be in short sleeves and sandals and I'd much prefer a teeshirt and jeans. And we ought to be eating these at a barbie down on the beach. Yet here we are pretending to be two stuffed shirts. Are we crazy, or what!"

"Perhaps tomorrow night?" I suggested.

She pulled a guilty face. "Thanks for the reminder, Riley!" And she made a sign to the waiter to bring the telephone — no portables then.

She took out a little book and looked up a number, memorizing and then dialling all nine digits in one, which was impressive. "Hallo," she said. "No, I'm afraid I can't … yes, I have. I'm at the hotel now … yes, it would have been super. I really enjoyed it, too …" Then she winked at me and grinned as she said, still to the guy at the other end: "He is, rather — since you ask. 'Bye!"

"My reserve date for the night," she said as she cradled the handset again. "I hope I've done right. We haven't talked about you-know-what yet, have we."

"Was he your last night's date?" I asked.

She nodded. "You're quick."

"Not in everything," I promised.

She laughed. "I hope not! I always take a contact number for dates I enjoy — just in case I can't face the one I'm landed with on any particular evening."

"Does that happen often."

"Oh yes," she assured me earnestly. "Several times a year."

She wasn't joking but she could see I found it amusing.

"Well, I'm pretty tolerant in my tastes," she said.

"I'm sorry. I should have asked how many dates you have in a year."

"Two hundred and seventy-five," she replied at once — and again she clearly wasn't joking.

This time I didn't give away my surprise.

"Twenty-one days in a row," she explained. "Then seven days off — for obvious reasons, I hope. I need sex every night — except those seven days. I can hack it through them. This is a very good way of getting it. I tried it the amateur way but I kept falling asleep over the typewriter. Then I thought of being a prostitute but decided against it."

Again I thought I did an excellent job of hiding my surprise. Having sex with two hundred and seventy-five men a year and charging them two hundred dollars a time *wasn't* being a prostitute? "Very wise ..." I began.

"*I* think so," she cut across me. "So does my boyfriend. We're saving up for a farm. I only charge him half price to have sex with me, so he doesn't grumble. In fact, he says I should go on charging him even after we're married."

"He sounds very ... tolerant."

I saw little point in trying to steer the conversation. Her unstoppable stream of consciousness would still carry us wherever she wished to go.

"You've never done this before," she said next.

"How does it show?"

"Because by this point in the meal most men are trying to tell me of all the wonderful things they'd like us to do. You must have some ideas yourself in that line?"

"Of course I do. But look — if we were going to dance ... would you like to dance, by the way?"

"Sure." She stood up eagerly and half turned toward the tiny dance floor.

But I caught her wrist and pulled her back. "Just a mo," I said. "We'll start with a chassis glide, then a reverse turn, a hesitation, a half sashay ..."

I was making it up, of course. I don't know one step from another, though I'm a fairly good natural dancer once the music and the mood takes me.

"What are you on about?" she asked angrily.

"I'm trying to point out that one doesn't need to *talk* about something in advance in order to enjoy it. Now, d'you want to enjoy a dance or two — or the other sort of jig?"

She threw back her head and roared with laughter, turning many amused eyes in our direction. "That's a good one," she said. "I must remember that."

As we took the dance floor she pressed herself against me, wriggled eagerly, and whispered huskily in my ear, "I like you, Riley — a lot. We're going to have a bundle of fun in bed, you and me."

She did it to give me an erection, of course, and enjoy my discomfort as I tried to control it, her wriggling body, and my own lead in the dance. Just when I thought I had it under control she said, "Could we have sex right here on the dance floor, d'you think? Would you like that? I could get them to turn down the lights for us."

She gave another peal of laughter when she saw I took her seriously. "Come on," she said as the dance came to an end. "I'm more than ready for it. Let's skip the pudding and go straight upstairs. I can give you until midnight."

It was then just short of ten o'clock. *Two hours!* I thought giddily.

We shared the lift with two elderly American ladies. She tried to shock them by asking me if I could keep it up for two hours. "Or can you come twice? Or" — she pulled an encouraging face — "three times?"

I wouldn't have minded much if the floor had opened up and sent me plummeting. But the Americans just laughed and one of them touched my arm. "Twice is enough, dear," she said. "But don't hurry."

Jill, realizing these two 'old dears' were unshockable, smiled sweetly at them but said no more. If anyone was embarrassed by the time the doors opened and let us out, it was she.

The moment we were alone together, however, she became a different animal — in fact, that is precisely what she became: an animal. I'm sure many men had spent their time at dinner with her, describing in lascivious detail all that they hoped to do with her when this moment arrived. But I'm equally sure that, once the door closed behind them, they might just as well have described the last seven cricket matches they'd attended for all the good it did them. The stream of consciousness that had impelled her conversation forward down there now turned into a mighty flood of unbridled desire, which caught up both her and me and carried us wherever it wished to go.

She fell to her knees in front of me and started

fiddling with the zip and waistband of my trousers. I'd had a continuous erection since the beginning of our time on the dance floor — weakened for a mere second or two by my brief embarrassment in the lift. Now he was back again at full power, throbbing inside my briefs, trembling to be free like an unslipped greyhound.

(I know it's a bit coy to speak of my own erection as 'he' but it's psychologically accurate, too, for *he* can have a will of his own, a blind, mindless will that often gets *me* into trouble.)

Her skilled fingers soon liberated him, at least to the extent that he thrust a great triangular, polka-dotted sail out toward her. The caress of a young woman's fingers on that sensitive gristle is one of the seven wonders of the world. I just stood there, closed my eyes, and prayed for it never to stop.

It did stop, of course, but only to be replaced by something better — her slim, skilled fingers plus glorious, sudsy soap and warm water. It brought me to the brink of a premature crisis.

"A shower?" she suggested as I pulled hastily, though reluctantly, away.

"On one condition," I panted.

"What?"

"That you don't wash certain parts of you too scrupulously. I want the taste of woman, not Yardley or whatever this is."

She touched the tip of my nose and gave a low, earthy giggle. "I like *you!*" she said. "No shower at all."

"Was that some kind of test?" I asked as she led me to the bed.

"Uh-huh."

"And if I'd failed — if I'd agreed to take a shower?"

"Oh, I'd still have fucked you but not so wholeheartedly. I'd have pleaded a headache or something and left at eleven. Did I make a phone call earlier?"

"You did."

"Good." She lay back on the bed. "I'm all yours. Let's get the most out of the next two hours."

"Or put the most in." I undressed her slowly and made a great fuss of each new revelation, caressing and kissing and sometimes licking the flesh laid newly bare. Girlflesh is so wonderful, so rich in sensuous possibilities. I don't know what it is — whether it's smell or texture or something altogether mystical — but if you covered a naked body with a sheet that had a two-inch hole in it, and you put that hole somewhere sexually unrevealing, like halfway down the thigh or in the middle of the back, and let me sniff and kiss and lick that meagre portion of flesh laid bare, I could tell you, a hundred times out of a hundred, whether it was manflesh or girlflesh.

Jill was girlflesh raised to the *nth* power. I mean, that girl just adored sex — her own and mine. Or her own and almost any man's, to be honest. There was no fake morality to get in the way.

Every age has its sexual puritans. In Victorian times they said all sex was abhorrent, and maybe people who knew better winked and smiled at one another behind their fans but nobody raised a peep of an objection. Today, of course, they can't get away with that. Too many people know better. So they trim their sails and tack with the new wind. Sex *without love* is abhorrent, they now tell you.

Hogwash!

No one denies that sex with love is pretty wonderful.

But so is straight sex all by itself. It's like saying that plain ice cream laced with Grand Marnier or Advocaat is fabulous — which it is — but that doesn't mean plain ice cream on its own is too awful even to contemplate. It's the same with sex on its own — and I've now had more than three hundred sessions with girls all over the world to prove it. Anyway, back to Jill, who was the most natural exponent of this philosophy I'd ever met.

Really, I suppose, she had what most people would think of as a man's attitude toward sex. Most men could make it quite easily with most women. I mean, we're loaded guns ready to fire at any good opportunity. I know it from my own experience. I've walked up some stairs to rooms with a bright red sign in the window saying MODEL or LOVE or, more honestly, GOOD SEX and then I've seen the 'girl' making these claims and my heart has fallen into my boots. And I've said to myself, 'Oh no — I just can't make it with a dog like *you!*' ... and ten minutes later I'm poking away with a will, thinking, 'A vagina is a vagina is a vagina ...'

Women are more selective. Or most of them are. Or they've kidded themselves into thinking they are. Hell, that's no secret.

But not Jill. She'd turn up each night at some posh hotel or restaurant, look her escort over, the way a man will look over all the beddable women he meets, and she'd think either, 'Wow!' or 'Unh-huh' or 'Why not?' — just the way a man would — and then, when the meal was over, she'd skip happily upstairs with him and spread her legs just as joyfully as he would thrust his ramrod up between them.

She did it for me as soon as I had her down to her stockings. "Did you ever see anything as pretty as that?" she asked archly as she spread her thighs wide.

And it was pretty, too. I'd seen young mossyface before, of course, but I'd never just sat and stared at her so frankly — and by invitation, too. I've gazed in equal rapture at hundreds of them since — thousands, if you count striptease girls and gogo dancers in bars — and their infinite variety never ceases to amaze me. In fact, I once had the same girl twice in Saigon — when it was still Saigon. The incidents were a year apart but I didn't recognize her until I got her pants off and settled between her thighs for a long, loving, lingering gloat over the pleasures in store.

Jill's precious commodity was like some decadent tropical flower. I know what the anatomy books say — fleshy outer labia, slim inner ones, rising to a little cowl around the tiny button of the clitoris … and buried somewhere in among it all, the little puckered cat's arse that marks the entry into paradise. Well, whoever made Jill must have thrown away the book. She had labia that divided in two, and subdivided again, and curled upon themselves like burr walnut. The only place you could call them typical labia was where they tucked up into her beaver, reaching like two slim fingers over her mound. But what was that poking out between them, like the tip of a little finger, or a prize-winning broad bean? Her clitoris? I couldn't believe it, though it was only inches from my eyes.

I leaned forward and wrapped a big, wet tongue softly around it, glorying in the nectar of an excited woman and basking in her sighs and whimpers, her moans and little tremors.

They grew in intensity and depth until at last she grabbed me by the hair, above my ears, and pulled me urgently up, the full, fabulous length of her glorious body, and, with desperation in her eyes, whispered, "Quick! Go in, go in! I can't wait any longer."

There is no other warmth in the universe like the warmth of a passionate young woman's vagina. There is no moisture half as stimulating as the heady juices that lubricate a randy young woman's vagina. There is no clench that can match the welcoming squeeze of a lecherous young woman's vagina as she receives the ultimate instrument of her pleasure. There is no ecstasy to equal the repeated experience of that warmth, those juices, that squeeze as the questing gristle thrusts majestically in and out, in and out, on that old, unstoppable ascent to orgasm.

Orgasm? I didn't know the meaning of the word until that night with Jill.

You know how it usually goes (I think of it as a kind of male lie-detector trace — because, of course, we can't fake it!):

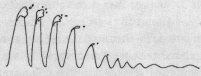

It lasts for about thirty seconds.

And with each squirt there's a sort of muscle spasm like when you nip off a piss. But not with Jill. Halfway through each squirt — certainly with the big whammies at the beginning — it was as if a piston came from out of nowhere and rammed its way up that tube which stretches all the way along the underside of an excited priap, really splatting each gobbet of sperm against the top of her vagina. And it *hurt!* I never knew that intense pleasure and pain were so close to each other before.

But I stayed stiff inside her, which she was quick to feel. And then, when she'd exhausted her own considerable jollies, she purred, literally, and stroked her fingertips up and down my back and murmured, "Now take all the time you want, lover-man!"

"As long as I don't want beyond midnight, eh?" I replied.

She bit the lobe of my ear, sending shivers through and through me. "Don't be pedantic," she said.

When she left, only a few minutes after midnight, she explained that she hated going home to the suburbs at eight or nine in the morning, still in her evening dress. It wasn't true, of course. She'd had two hours of the most intensely pleasurable sex *I'd* ever enjoyed — and I don't think she was far behind me, either — and that was enough. Tomorrow was another day. Another man. Easy come, easy go. She went.

Actually, tomorrow *was* another day in every sense of the word, for I met her quite by accident out at the beach, where we had both gone, independently, to swim and bask in the sun and, in my case, to cherish the memory of the best sex I'd ever had in my life.

And I'll tell you the oddest thing: We spent most of the day together, from about eleven in the morning to five in the evening, and we didn't talk about sex once! When we changed into our cossies, as she called them, she went behind one sand dune, I behind another. We shared our lunches. We lay side by side and dozed in the sun. We talked about life like two casual acquaintances (which, in all ways but one we were). But talk of sex never passed our lips — until the very end, that is.

And in a way the day was over, for we were already

strolling off the beach. I asked her, offhandedly, if I should sit by the telephone tonight and if so, for how long.

She said she didn't think so. She'd arranged a date with an officer on one of the US ships in the port. Then, after looking all around us, she lowered her voice and said, "He's asked me if, after fucking him, I'd fuck two other officers as well." And she stared at me, almost as if she were asking my permission. Certainly she wanted to know what I thought of the idea.

I hedged. "It'd mean more money," I said.

She appeared not to hear me — or, rather, she had her own bizarre justification for even considering this proposition. "I've often wondered what it's like to be a prostitute," she said. "You know — letting one man after another fuck me."

"Why the passive tense all of a sudden?" I asked.

"Because it would be just that on my part, you see — passive. I couldn't possibly enjoy sex with three men — bang, bang, bang — just like that. Could I? It'd be obscene."

"You did last night," I reminded her. "Not three men but three bangs!"

"That's right!" She grinned as if I'd unearthed a truth she'd never have discovered on her own. "Maybe I can do it, then."

So I waited by the telephone but I waited in vain. And I went alone to bed and tried to imagine Jill being fucked by three Yankee officers — bang, bang, bang! Or was she fucking them?

I should have called her agency next day and arranged to meet her for drinks, if nothing else, just to hear how it went. But my office came up with the calculations in record time and so it was a long, working day for me.

I was so randy by the end of it that I had a quick hamburger and went directly to the Cairo Bazaar, where, of course, I asked for Babysoft.

It was a mistake. I should have waited until the backlist of regular clients, squeezed out by the Yankee invasion, had slaked its thirst. Every single girl was *occupied* — the cashier told me, with a leering stress on that word. Even as he spoke, however, a girl came back down the corridor from her workroom.

"Ah," he said. "Susie's free — or, at least, she's available — if you're interested?"

She was a good-looker, all right. They were supposed not to take any girl under twenty-one, but I don't think she was even that old. She had dark hair, dark eyes, a rather flat face but she had sharp, pretty features. She didn't seem to know how to smile, but that was understandable after the time they'd all had. She was wearing a black lace bra, bikini-size panties, also in black lace, a black suspender belt, black fishnet stockings, and a black gauze negligée that covered her — or, at least, reached from her armpits to an inch below her mound. Little whorls of her bush peeped out over the top of her panties.

I stepped forward and held out my hand. "Riley," I said.

This courtesy took her by surprise. "Oh! Er ... Susie," she replied, shaking my hand awkwardly.

"Do I pay you or Susie?" I asked the cashier. "I've never been in one of these places."

It wasn't news to him. "Susie will take you to her room and show you her menu. You make your choice, pay her, and then you get comfortable while she brings the money to me and I start the clock. You'll get one short ring when five minutes are left and a long ring when time is up."

So Susie took me to her room.

Now I'd always imagined a whore would walk like a whore and talk like a whore. I'd had fantasies in which the girl of my choice would do both those things so provocatively that I'd be halfway to orgasm by the time we reached her room. I don't know what fantasies Susie had, if any. I won't say she walked like a prison wardress showing a new inmate to his cell but female secretaries with no thought of sex in their minds at all have shown me into their bosses' offices with more of a come-on than Susie possessed that night. From that moment on I should have known it was going to be a disaster.

But I remembered how randy I had felt only five minutes earlier and I thought the touch of her fingers or the sight of her nakedness would bring it right back.

"The menu," she said woodenly, pointing to a bit of cardboard with awkward handwriting on it, stuck to the wall with barrel pins. As near as I can recall it read (at one item per line): QUICKIE, ORAL, 69, POSITIONS, LONGER TIMES (20, 30, 40 minutes), DOMINANCE, FANTASIES. The quickie was five pounds sterling for ten minutes in one position. (I always translated foreign currencies to sterling, not just for sex but for everything.) Oral was five for five minutes. *Soixante-neuf* ten for five. Positions was not a separate option. It went with 20, 30, and 40 minutes, which were 20, 30, and 40 pounds. I didn't ask about dominance and fantasies. I mean, Susie's lacklustre recital of what ought to have been the most exciting goodies didn't encourage that sort of curiosity. "I suppose I'll go for twenty minutes in various positions," I said, starting to take off my clothes.

"Could you give me the money now?" she asked, holding out her hand patiently.

I undressed completely while she was gone. Then, ashamed at my lack of an erection, I put my shorts back on again.

"Oh," she said when she at last returned. "You want *me* to take them off, do you?"

"Why? Is that an extra charge?"

"No," she sighed. "Are you going to lie on the bed?"

"I thought we'd start standing up — with you bending forward over the back of this chair."

"But you haven't got an erection yet."

"I'll get one if you bend over the chair."

She just stared at me uncertainly, as if this sort of thing had never come up in the two years she spent training for this highly skilled work. "Okay," I said. "I'll sit on the bed and undress you first. That'll surely give me an erection."

I sat on the edge of the bed, thighs apart, and she came and stood between them. That was it — she just stood there.

I kissed her breasts as I fiddled round the back with the hook of her bra. I was all thumbs suddenly. You'd think I'd never unhooked one of those things before. "You should wear a front-opening bra," I said. "Or what women call a front-*fastening* bra."

"Perhaps," she said.

All right — it was the way I told it.

When I at last got her unhooked I held the straps together with my left hand while I slowly peeled the cups downwards with my right, feeling inside for her nipples, which were like two little cherries in there.

In fact, she had lovely little breasts, round, firm, and silky-smooth. All her skin was silky-smooth. I didn't find a single blemish on her. But it wasn't a lascivious smoothness, if you follow. It was the fine-textured, slightly waxen smoothness of a magnolia or lily petal.

You've seen the way young children go tense and hold their breath when a parent says, "Kiss Great-Aunt Maude goodbye, dear!" — how they do it with barely concealed aversion. Well that was how Susie leaned her body in toward my caressing fingers, my would-be hungry lips. It was just the same when I eased her panties down and rubbed the backs of my fingers lightly over her mound and bush.

"Anything happening?" she asked.

"Give it time," I said.

Absolutely nothing was happening. The last time I'd felt so lacklustre was two nights previously — *after* three of the most magnificent fucks I'd ever enjoyed.

"Let *me* have a go," she said, pushing me back on the bed, which, I forgot to say, just had a bottom sheet, half covered by a towel; also a pillow and a small round cushion.

I lay there while she used her wardress training to take my shorts off. Then she took my limp little winkle in her hand and applied what I have to admit was fairly skilled massage to its shrivelled parts. She knew more about the care and feeding of the male member than any amateur I'd ever let handle it.

But it did no good. From that moment on I *knew* it was going to be hopeless. I told her so. "I should have known better," I said. "I had the chambermaid at the hotel before breakfast and a girl I met on the beach this afternoon — and I thought my lucky number had come up. I should have quit while I was ahead."

She didn't believe me but it papered over the worst of our embarrassment and it let her salvage what professional pride she may have had (which she had so far kept well hidden from *me,* I may say).

"Can we just lie down together and talk for the rest of the time?"

"Sure," she said, though even that didn't seem to please her.

I got her to lie on her side, facing away from me, while I tucked myself in against her back, cradling those beautiful little breasts in my hands.

"How old are you?" I asked. "If that's not too personal."

"Nineteen."

"And have you been doing this for long?"

"Three months."

After a silence I said, "How many men would you see in a day?"

"Oh, I never count them." She glanced at me as if to say, 'Don't you understand? You'll never get honest answers to these questions out of us!'

That was the message I read there, anyway.

"How did you get into it to start with."

"Through friends and that — talking."

"What? Telling you it wasn't so bad, really, once you'd got used to it?"

"Something like that."

"And were they right?"

"Sometimes."

"I suppose you get some men who are abusive or very demanding?"

"A few." She half-suppressed a yawn and said sorry — the same message repeated in stronger terms.

"Can I just *look* at your body, then?" I asked.

"Sure." She knew what I meant.

I sat up while she wriggled past me, lay on her back, and opened her legs wide.

She had a sweet little pussy, very neat and clean. It had no girl-smell at all, but a faint, lingering odour of sperm — though that could have been off the mattress, of course.

I flattened my hands against the insides of her thighs at the top, to keep them spread like that while I explored with my lips and tongue. At once she put her hands on mine, pinning them there. "You mustn't touch me down there with your fingers," she said.

"Not *touch* you," I echoed. "A big stiff prick would be all right but not a teeny little finger?"

"A prick doesn't have a fingernail that could tear me." She lay back again and stared at the ceiling.

I wondered what was really going on in her mind — lying there, spreading her pussy-lips wide like that, with this total (and totally impotent) stranger staring at them. She was probably thinking of her next holiday, or the new dress she'd buy tomorrow.

"Let's have one last try," I suggested, straddling her in the missionary position. "You caress my nipples while I try and work it stiff."

She did as I asked though she kept her eyes firmly on the wallpaper or the ceiling. I was still trying when the five-minute bell rang.

What a farce! I thought. *I've forked out twenty quid for the privilege of tossing myself off in front of a girl who learned her trade while lying on a butcher's slab — where there was obviously a television in the ceiling — and I can't even get an erection!*

When I got dressed I heard myself saying, "It's not your fault. You're a beautiful young girl and, whatever you may think, I've still enjoyed it. It's just that I should have known better."

"Sure," she said.

But I'll tell you a funny thing about Susie. She stuck in my mind far longer than many another girl with whom I had much more enjoyable sex. I had never been impotent before, except, to be sure, in post-coital exhaustion. It really rocked me back on my heels. For months after that, I had fantasy after fantasy about Susie in which I corrected the historical record. Typically I got stiff when the five-minute bell rang and, promising her another forty quid, fucked her senseless in an orgy of sexual abandon — in which she at last joined in, begging me to go on and never mind the bell. But the most satisfactory one was quite different. In it I returned to Perth a year later, met her on the street, and was just about to walk tactfully on when she stopped me. "Hallo!" she said. "It is you, isn't it?"

"To my shame," I confessed.

"Oh, listen! That wasn't your fault. I was entirely to blame. I just wasn't cut out for that work. That was my very first day — did you know?"

"Well," I mumbled, "I did sort of wonder."

"You did me a favour. You showed me I wasn't suited to the work at all. I quit right after you left. But I'm so glad we met. I've had such a guilty conscience about you ever since!"

Indeed, I've enjoyed that little fantasy so many times, I'm not sure it didn't, in fact, happen after all. On the night in question, however, I went back to the hotel and — singlehanded — proved there was nothing intrinsically wrong with the basic tackle.

The following night I was just about to call Jill's escort agency when she called me.

"Are you alone?" she asked.

"At the moment, yes. How did it go last night?"

"That's what I want to talk about."

My spirit soared. "Join me for dinner."

She hesitated. "But *only* for dinner. Well … maybe for more — but not what you think. I'll explain when we meet."

Which she did — immediately. I mean, even before I'd had a chance to ask what she'd like to drink. "Listen," she said nervously. "You're going to think me crazy — and do say no if you've got the slightest reservation — I know I have no right to ask this — I mean, I know we've only met the once — and yet, in a way …"

"Twice," I said. "On the beach — remember?"

"That's the *once* I was talking about. Oh, I see what you mean."

I laughed. "Just ask!" I took her hand and gave it an encouraging squeeze.

She licked her lips, drew a deep breath, looked away over my shoulder, and, in a trembling voice, asked, "Could we sleep together tonight — all night — and *not* have any sex? Oh God!" She closed her eyes and lowered her head. "What am I asking!"

"But I would love that," I said. I don't know why but, the way she put it, it sounded like a nice thing to do.

"You would?" She eyed me suspiciously. "Why?"

I busked it: "Because it's something I've never done before — and I can't think of anyone I'd rather do it with. Or *not* do it with, as the case may be. We ought to decide what we do about farting, though. Do we go to the bathroom to do it or just let rip?"

Her laughter verged on the hysterical but the humour of it reconciled her to my easy acceptance.

We enjoyed a leisurely meal and plenty of wine but I wasn't trying to overcome her resistance. I really was more interested in seeing if she truly meant it and, more importantly, why it was important to her.

Throughout the meal we spoke not a word about her experiences with the three naval officers two nights previously. I guessed that that was what she wanted to talk about in bed — and why she had made that strange condition, which we also kept silent about while we ate. Toward the end of the meal I decided it was time to break our silence on the subject. I said, "Actually, it's quite uncanny you should set such an unusual condition for spending the night with me — because, quite unwittingly, I spent last night *practising* for just such a contingency!" And I told her the full, ghastly story of my impotence with Susie.

If I was expecting sympathy, I'd be waiting for it still. I might as well have said, "Last night I had a slight sniffle. Not what you'd call a cold, just a sniffle. But it's gone now."

"It's quite common," she said matter-of-factly. "Two out of ten of the men I go with can't get it up. Well, maybe not *two* out of ten, but certainly more than one."

I felt crushed. Not even the heroism of my confession impressed her. "What d'you do with them?" I asked.

"Play cards. Talk. Actually, I don't give up that easily if I really like the man and he has a good body. I say,

'Well, you must have some favourite positions you've enjoyed in the past. Why don't we just keep the memory of them alive and wait for better times to return?' And then I get into all sorts of sexy positions with him and encourage him to simulate sex with me — the way they do in the soft-core movies." It was movies in those days, not videos. "And pretty soon I feel the hot tickle of something waking up for a closer sniff of pussy …"

Of course, my erection was threatening to over-balance the table by this time. She sensed it and reached forward to squeeze my hand. "Sorry," she said. "Thoughtless of me. But you shouldn't have asked the question."

I was back in control by the time we went upstairs. We undressed and washed and brushed our teeth in the mood in which, I imagine, married couples do such things on a night when they both know they aren't going to make love. She put out the light as soon as we got into bed. We were both naked but, incredible as it may seem, I had no erection and did not feel in the least bit randy. I felt very warm toward her, almost loving — certainly protective. She was upset and I wanted her to be free of whatever it was that disturbed her. I wanted that more than I wanted sex with her. So I cradled her in my arms and said, "Tell me. I'll listen as long as you want."

I guess my lack of an erection heartened her, as if it were some kind of barometer of my sincerity — which, in itself, is a thought to curb the unruliest member. And here's her story — not quite in her own words because I did, of course, ask the odd question now and then. But I've woven her answers into the tale:

Jill's Story

Well, you know I met this officer through my agency —
I'll call him Bill — and he asked me if I'd dine with him
on board ship and then have sex with him in the usual
way, which he understood would be from ten until
midnight. And I said yes, of course, which sort of
committed me to go on board at least. So then he said,
well, actually, would I agree to have sex for the same
two hours but with him and two brother officers —
forty minutes each — the same amount of work, see,
but they'd pay me double. Did that seem fair?

So I don't know why I said yes, except that — as I told
you — I've often wondered what it's like to be a
prostitute — you know — do one man after another —
bang, bang, bang! And this seemed like an ideal way to
find out. I mean, it wouldn't be *too* unlike my regular
work and it also wouldn't be *too* unlike being a regular
prostitute. So anyway I said yes.

And then he said — of course, he had all this planned
out before he opened his mouth — he said, what if I
came an hour earlier and gave them an *hour* of fun and
games each — and they'd triple my usual fee.

Well, I've never done three hours of sex like that. I
mean, I've slept all night with my boyfriend and we've
done it three or four times — but with hours of sleep in
between. (He pays me for it, too, by the way, because
we're saving it all up for this dream house I'm going to
have in a couple of years.) [I didn't tell her it was a farm
last time. Now I began to wonder if the boy existed at
all.] But three hours of non-stop sex, and with a freshly
charged young man every hour on the hour — that
really would be like being a prostitute, eh? So then I
thought, *Jill, my girl, you're never going to get a better*

chance to try it out than this! So I said yes.

It's funny. For almost two years now I've been sitting opposite different men at the dinner table, almost every night, knowing that in a short while I'd be going upstairs with them to fuck every last drop of juice out of them before midnight. And that's often the most exciting part — sitting there all dressed up and civilized and wondering if he's already got a hardon, and what's he going to be like. And table manners are no guide — believe me. Nor is height, nor waistline, nor looks, nor age, nor smoothness of tongue. Little pigeon-chested men with dandruff have fucked me senseless, and big, beefy lifeguard types have left me cold. And vice versa. So you never can tell but it's fun to guess.

But that's with just one man. I tell you — to sit down to dinner, all very formal as you'd expect in an officer's mess, with *three* men — all good-looking in their way, all young, and all as horny as hell under their tropical mess kit — and to know that *all three* of them are going to try to knock the stuffing out of you, well, that's something altogether different.

I often think I'm two people, you know. I mean, tonight I'm definitely the *other* one — playing this mean trick on you, no sex, and all that. [I assured her it wasn't mean but she ignored me.] So I'm sitting there and half of me is as horny as all three of them put together. You know what my clittie's like? You've seen her, haven't you? She's a big girl, right? Well, last night she excelled herself. She was *aching!* And I just couldn't wait to be naked in bed with Bill — and then, having exhausted him, to leap onto a fresh … what did I call the other two?

I didn't? Okay. Well — Bob and Ted, say. I couldn't

wait to leap onto a fresh Bob and bob the spunk out of him. And then onto Ted and drain him, too. I was ready to take on the whole US Navy! At least, that was one half of me, like I said. The other half just sat there appalled at what I'd agreed to. She couldn't do a thing about my *physical* body, which was all wantonness and lust. But she fought for my mind. She wanted to lie there, rigid, disconnected, counting the minutes until it was over. She wanted it to be over already. And then she never wanted to dabble in the life of a prostitute again.

Well, you can guess which half of me won as soon as I climbed on Bill's magnificent body and felt his horn slip up and start getting acquainted with my pussy! Those three hours were some of the best sex I ever had in my life — which means I still don't have the faintest idea of what it's like to be a pro, right? Because if they went through each day's work like that, they'd go mad. That's the thing I don't understand, see — how I could ever turn off my sexual desire when there's a man inside me doing his best to turn it on!

So — okay — I'm in a mess, as you see. So I *need* this night alone. I need to spend it with a man I like, just being me. Not his partner — I mean *your* partner. D'you understand? Don't lie! Even *I* don't understand me, so how can you!

So that, more or less, was Jill's story. The mood lasted until about four o'clock that night, when I got a hardon (the hundredth of that night, I should think) and she became aware of it. While pretending to be asleep, she managed to wriggle her cleft down over my pride and joy. She relished the situation for a minute or so and then, pretending to cough in her sleep, used the convulsions to disguise the extra wriggles necessary to get me inside her — whereupon … "Oh! Oh! Surprise surprise! You naughty man! Oh well — go on — might as well — now you're there!"

Only one bit of me was proud — the important bit, of course. The rest was humble enough to accept the sweet warmth and succulence of her vagina on any terms. And then again in the morning, before we rose for breakfast, I didn't have to swallow my pride — she did it for me!

BANGKOK: Phuc Mi and friends

My first visit to Bangkok came just after the American withdrawal from Vietnam and just before the city's fame as an international centre for sex tourism started to spread. Prices were low because the Yanks were no longer there and there were four girls to every man with nookie on his mind. I have to point all this out in my own defence, otherwise I'd never have gone over the top, the way I did.

This time I'd been commissioned to redesign the antique air-conditioning and heating system at the Rose Bower, a regular tourist hotel that, for half an hour each evening — and only for those thirty minutes — became a brothel for those of its male clientele who were too lazy, or too impatient, to go out and pick up some of the local talent for themselves. Actually, they would have found the same talent out there in the nightclubs and bars at any other time, but at half past seven of an evening, right after dinner, the girls left their bar stools and came flocking to a back room at the Rose Bower, where the male guests made their choice(s) for the night.

They were all there, as usual, at seven o'clock on the night of my arrival. (I was, of course, staying free at the hotel and, in fact, had been given one of its four penthouse suites, the only rooms in the building that did not need air-conditioning on that sweltering July night.) And we males were all there, too — Arabs in their sensible robes looking the coolest. And the smuggest, for this was after the oilshock and everyone knew they had money to burn. Also Germans, French, Scandinavians, Japanese, Australians, and even a scattering of those once numerous Americans.

The room where the girls were assembled and waiting was — appropriately enough — the ballroom. We punters were, for the moment, all penned back in the corridor behind three large folding doors. At precisely seven o'clock the entertainments manager blew a whistle and six of his flunkeys pulled the doors wide open, allowing something like sixty horny men to erupt into the ballroom within seconds — and so stand a more-or-less equal chance of picking a good 'un. Anyway, as I said, even the last man in there was still spoiled for choice.

I knew a thing or two about Oriental ways by then. I knew, for instance, that they respected age far more than we Occidentals do, even when it comes to whoring, where age is not usually at a premium. And sure enough, despite the rather dim lighting in the ballroom, I saw at once that the ladies standing near the front were rather longer in the tooth than those in the shadows at the back — that is, they were in their early twenties, while the ones behind them were in their mid-teens. These differences were not immediately apparent to most of my fellows for, while they chatted and haggled with the geriatric front line, I slipped among them and approached a table where sat four of the most delectable samples of jailbait you ever saw.

They told me their names but I have, of course, long forgotten them. I remember them as Gazelle (she had the most beautiful doe eyes), Nipples (she had ... well, work it out for yourself), and Venus (for the size and softness of her Venus mound). The fourth kid I still think of as Phuc Mi, which (I discovered later) was what someone had written in four-inch capitals across the tops of her delightfully curvaceous buttocks. When I first saw it I thought the letters were tattooed there permanently. But closer inspection, which I conducted both eagerly and thoroughly, revealed it was only indelible ink, already beginning to wear off against the sweating groins and clutching hands of the dozens, if not hundreds, of men who had leaped into the breach before me, eager to obey such an amiable command.

As I stood over that table, looking down at their four pretty faces, their slender necks and graceful arms, their delightfully budding breasts, swelling out the thin cotton of their frilly blouses, I wondered how on earth I was going to choose one or even two from among them. No — actually, *choosing* wasn't the problem. I wondered how I was going to be able to turn two or three of them down. Then this insane voice inside me said, 'Take all four!' And before I could have second thoughts, there I was haggling over a price for the four of them for the night. Phuc Mi was their spokeswoman and she drove a mean bargain — bidding me up to fifty quid, which was almost as much as one would pay for half an hour with one girl in Soho.

The deal was we'd have fun for a couple of hours, break for a meal between nine and ten, and then go back to our fun for the rest of the night. When they heard I had one of the penthouse suites, they started acting like the queens of the establishment, sailing up the passage to the lifts with a regal mien and favouring the other girls with pitying looks.

Two men were waiting at the lifts by the time we arrived — an Arab and a German. The Arab had three girls in tow; he had been looking condescendingly at the German, who had only two — until I came along. Then they both looked sourly at me — an expression that intensified when Phuc Mi pressed the top button and said loudly, "Penthouse!"

One little-proclaimed advantage of the penthouse was that we got given a towel each; patrons in ordinary rooms got no more than two towels no matter how many girls they took upstairs. How the Arab and his three houris managed to bathe and dry themselves in that heat and humidity I cannot imagine.

The air-conditioning wasn't working (of course, or I wouldn't have been there in the first place) but there were electric punkas and several three-speed portable fans. As soon as the penthouse door closed behind us the girls eagerly switched them on and set them out strategically around the open space near the bed; the atmosphere in the lifts and corridor — and, naturally, in that meat market downstairs — had been stifling.

They began undressing at once, not so much for sexual reasons as to enjoy the waft of cool air around their naked bodies; but I stopped them, saying, "Slow! Slow! No hurry!" I don't know if they understood even that much English but it hardly mattered. They weren't hired for their conversational skills.

For me, the act of undressing a gorgeous young girl, knowing I'm about to enjoy the pleasures of her sex for the next twenty minutes — or hour, or entire night — is one of intense delight. I'd never before undressed four of them, one after another, and I intended to make the most of it.

As far as I could see, they were wearing high-heeled shoes, stockings (two sheer, two fishnet), visible suspenders (and, presumably, a suspender belt), miniskirts short enough to qualify for the title 'fan belts,' and flimsy cotton blouses, two plain, one floral, one gingham. Patterns and colours apart, it was a kind of uniform. They were all short-sleeved and low cut — just three buttons separated me from whoopee time with each girl.

I lined them up before me in a giggling semicircle; I'm pretty sure they'd never been four-on-one before, either, and were unsure how it was going to work out — which made five of us. I undid one button of each blouse and then invited them to return the compliment. I had more clothes to shed than they, so it was going to work out about right, I reckoned.

Then I loosened their second buttons. Standing above them, peeping down inside their blouses, inhaling the fragrance of their hot young bodies, I thought, *There are a lot of happy men in Bangkok tonight but none could possibly be happier than me!*

Phuc Mi was still their leader; they took their cues from her. So when I undid the third and final button of her blouse and she tweaked it open to show me the lovely buds of her breasts, I let out a gasp of admiration and gingerly reached my hands toward them ... softly caressed her nipples with the backs of my fingers, and generally behaved as if I had never seen or fondled anything half so beautiful before — which, in the erotic passion of that moment, I'd even have sworn was true. When you're buying sex from a lovely young girl, and perhaps she's the hundredth one of your career, a merciful oblivion clouds your mind to the other nine-and-ninety. And the glory is virginal once again.

Also I don't care how hardened in the trade a girl may be, she still has the normal human responses to simple admiration. The sexual response may be dead or on ice but everyone likes to be prized, honoured, and valued. And I valued that girl's beauty with my hands, I honoured her with my eyes, I prized her with my shivering breath and limbs. And she responded, emotionally if not sexually.

Of course, she made sure it showed as a sexual response — with her slackly open lips, her upraised face, her half-closed eyes, her fluttering eyelashes, the panting and heaving of her bosom, the formless, almost whispered cries ...

The other three followed suit and, slipping off their blouses, pressed their naked torsos to mine, clung to me, sighed, whimpered, rubbed their swelling nipples all over me, bit me, licked me, dug me with their nails.

I do not remember shedding the rest of my clothes, nor relieving them of theirs. Our little orgy fell into confusion as, like a pack of hunting maenads, they bore me to the carpet and fought each other for the possession of the largest share of my nakedness. At least, that is what it felt like to me. In her own mind each girl was probably struggling to give me the best whole-body massage she could, in rather uncomfortable circumstances. Who cares? The result, for me, was utterly mind-blowing. Press PAUSE and imagine it:

Venus is massaging my right forearm with the fuzz of her generous mound; her breasts, by my head, are competing for licks and kisses with the lips of Gazelle, who is also trying to slip the hot, moist flesh of her vagina down over my left thumb, which is vying for my attention with my right hand, which is fondling happily away in the fork of an excited Nipples, who, lying north to my south, is doing unimaginable things to my toes with her lips and tongue — and occasionally teeth. And that would be lifting my scalp off if it weren't for what Phuc Mi is doing with *her* lips and tongue and teeth — and throat — to that stiff tyrant between my legs whose outrageous appetite has forced me into this grotesque and glorious escapade!

Whew!

And that's just one freeze-frame moment plucked at random from a thousand.

When I felt myself teetering on the brink of that unstoppable rise to spermspouting time, I sat up abruptly and sent them sprawling away. They *knew*, of course, veterans of a thousand thar-she-blows. They just giggled and threw themselves back upon me, determined to bring me to a conclusion so that they could shower and rest. It was a tough struggle — and a bizarre one in many ways: four naked girls, probably not sexually roused, all fervently looking for an orgasm (admittedly not their own) and one naked man, paying for that very pleasure but determined not to take it, to hold out against it for as long as he could!

To restore some semblance of order to our romping I cajoled and bullied them over to the edge of the bed, where I made them kneel as if in prayer — not literally with their hands together, of course, but with their four delightful young bottoms facing me invitingly.

But that, I'm afraid, is where fantasy and reality part company. I don't think I had ever actually fantasized about poking four girls at one session, but certainly I'd often imagined enjoying *two*. In fantasies, however, you have no weight. And you don't have knees that object to carrying you for long. And when you waddle on those same protesting knees — as you must if you want to poke, in quick sucession, four giggling girls kneeling side by side and bent over the edge of a bed — you don't spend ninety-nine percent of your time sorting out whose knees are whose and trying to avoid crushing them … which doesn't leave much time for worshipping those darling fuzzy lips and fleshy folds which that provocative pose spreads for your delighted eyes to explore.

In short, from that mad moment when I decided to take all four young beauties up to my room, a strong element of farce was built into the very situation. Of course it's marvellous to plunge your gristle into a willing vagina and take full measure of her glorious length, and I can't pretend I didn't enjoy it four times over, relishing the different warmth and softness and grip and texture of each. Indeed, I enjoyed that fourfold delight many times over as I passed up and down the row. But the tangling of ten damned knees, and the pain from my own as the weight began to tell, at last outweighed even that pleasure.

I collapsed exhausted on Venus and panted, "This isn't working out."

Phuc Mi understood the sentiment if not the words. "So!" she said, laying herself down on Venus, who was kneeling beside her. She added a few words in Siamese, which always sounds to me like Muppets fucking, and then Nipples lay down on Gazelle. In the language of an American pancake parlor, I now had two two-stacks to enjoy, side by side, over the edge of my bed.

That was fun, too, but not quite perfect. Each pair of vaginas was now almost a foot apart and the struggle to get out of one and into the other, and then back again, and then again, was just too ungainly.

Nipples and Gazelle saw this and, after a bit more Muppet-fucking, Nipples lifted herself while Gazelle turned over to lie on her back with her legs out straight and spread wide. Nipples lay down again, facing her, girl on girl, and spread her thighs even wider, resting them outside Gazelle's. Giggle, giggle, giggle.

Now their two holeys-of-holeys were only inches apart. In fact, when Nipples tightened her buttocks, like a man on the job, their twin crevices formed one beauteous furrow of glistening enticement that just begged me to explore it.

Venus and Phuc Mi had meanwhile disentangled themselves and were watching in fascination. But their passivity did not last long. "So!" Phuc Mi said again as she reached out, grabbed my best friend by his root, and started running the tip of him up and down in the sticky juices of that delectable combined groove. Her expression was one of intense concentration. She looked as if she feared my gristle might break off in her waggling grasp — the way it certainly would have if I'd been made of some malleable metal.

But there was no fear of that. At the appropriate places, one below and one above, I gave the elemental thrust of life and took full measure of each girl's dainty hole. Every jab was a whammy to my senses, but I had to stop and cool off, yet again, when Venus reached in below my buttocks and did the gentlest, sweetest things to my balls with her fingernails.

Then she and Phuc Mi had to experience this novel form of copulation while Nipples and Gazelle assisted — all doing their utmost to finish me off. Farce ruled once more when they tried to lie in a four-stack, with a gasping, protesting Venus at the bottom and a lissome, wriggling Nipples at the top. All I can say is that every man should try it — but only once and not for long.

We collapsed in a laughing melée on the bed and would have resumed our free-for-all if I had not decided it was time for the adagio movement — *molto lente*. With a certain amount of physical persuasion — mainly by grasping each girl by the waist and laying her face-down on the bed, side by side with her sisters. When they were so arranged, hips touching, thighs together, it needed only a few tender caresses and a couple of slaps on the buttocks to get them to lie still and silent.

It was a sight to revive even the most jaded roué — which I certainly was not: four pretty girls lying stark naked on their tummies with their soft, svelte bodies pressed together and their lovely little rounded bottoms pouting an unambiguous invitation at me ... and their eight sparkling eyes glancing at me over their slender shoulders or smiling into each other's as if to say, 'This beats bending double in a rice paddy all day for fifty cents, eh!'

In a gentle, almost ceremonial mood, I lowered myself across all four of them and began wriggling like a snake — slowly, sensuously, like a *lazy* snake — taking time to relish every point of contact between my flesh and theirs before moving on the merest inch or so and enjoying it all over again.

The gentle slowness of it, and the spreading of my weight over all four bodies, worked a subtle spell on their mood, too, which turned from frolicsome and giggly to contemplative and deep. Again, I don't kid myself that any one of them was sexually aroused, but they were aware of being in touch with a rarer form of pleasure than they usually delivered to their clientèle. Indeed, they were more than 'in touch'; they were its very cause. Collectively they were transcending their usual professional selves and providing something none was aware of possessing before that night. And thus, in our different ways, we were all launched on an unknown adventure; the landscape might look familiar but none of us had been exactly here before.

After heaven knows how long at this magnificent diversion I found myself lying exclusively on Phuc Mi and in perfect alignment for you know what. And she knew what, too, for she lofted her derrière a mere inch or so, pressing her firm young buttocks against the base of my stomach and, by curling me round her there, bringing hard and soft into splendid conjunction. And I slipped inside her as slick as oil on grease. And there I wallowed in her warmth, lying perfectly still while she gave me one long, slow squeeze after another. In return I gave out a whispered moan each time to let her know how much her efforts were appreciated.

So it was with each girl as I passed from one to another, luxuriating in the novelty of each fresh vagina — Gazelle's, firm and tight ... Nipples's, also tight but strangely yielding ... Venus's, soft and succulent ... and so back to Phuc Mi's, lithe and active.

It was, inevitably, she who took the first mighty broadside from my throbbing, leaping spermspouter when I could hold myself back no longer. I mean — if a girl flaunts a message like that in four-inch capitals all over her gorgeous derrière, what's a mere man to do?

So, with the edge taken off my lust, memories of how we five had teetered between glory and farce came flooding back and I realized I had to reduce our numbers by at least two if I was to get any sleep that night. No way could five fit that bed, generous though it was. Four would be a sweltering squeeze. But three might be okay.

Therefore I kissed Phuc Mi tenderly on both cheeks and told her she could go. A generous tip persuaded her — plus, I suppose, the realization that the night was yet young and she could still sell a lot of tail down there.

Randy once more, I got back into bed with Gazelle, Venus, and Nipples. When I said four would be a squeeze, I meant lying side by side, trying to sleep. But with *three* lying on their backs, side by side, and the fourth on top of them — and none of them thinking of sleep — it was the squeeze of heaven itself. We didn't make a big production of it — nothing athletic — in fact, nothing that would get you beyond page three of your average how-to-make-love book. I simply passed from one to the other with steadily mounting excitement until the frenzy seized me and I came again, not so copiously, of course, but with a sweeter, sharper pleasure. And that was when I said goodbye to Nipples.

Venus and Gazelle were sharp little cookies. They knew we'd be eating our dinner soon, followed by a natural pause to let it settle before going back to bed for more of the four-leg frolic — or six-leg frolic in our case. After which, if they went back to their bar stools, their clients would all be drunks or men whose eyes were bigger than their pricks.

"We stay all night?" Gazelle fluttered her gorgeous eyes at me.

"We show you much nice things," Venus promised.

I had to agree.

We enjoyed one of those subtle, spicy dinners they do so well in Thailand. There wasn't much conversation but lots of smiling and a general atmosphere of relaxed goodwill.

"How much time you fuck?" Gazelle asked at one point.

"How much time or how many times?" I replied. They have difficulty with much and many.

"How many time?"

"In all my life?"

She giggled. "No — tonight. How many time you want fuck Venus and me?"

(She used Venus's real name, of course.)

"How can I say? Maybe two times. Maybe more." I could see her winding up to pursue the point. "Listen," I said. "Two *good* fucks, then I sleep." I mimed a deep post-coital coma. "Two *not*-good fucks, then I want more, more, *more.*" I rammed my index finger viciously in and out of the tunnel of my other fist. "Understand?"

They laughed. They understood.

"So, you give me two *good* fucks, yes?"

"No. We three *all* have good fucks. You give us good time, too, yes?"

Well, I didn't say no.

We took a shower together.

There was lots of vertical, whole-body massage at which Venus, especially, was excellent. I was iron-hard and hot for it by the time we stepped out into the balmy warmth of the tropic night. I started using my towel but they walked out onto the terrace and did a slow, sensual dance until they were dry. I followed them out and sat near them. Their slim, restless young bodies, swaying uninhibitedly so close to me ... the memory of our earlier intercourse and the prospect of even greater thrills, which we were about to share, soon reduced me to a quivering mass of sexual hunger.

"Now!" Venus took a step forward and pulled me up from my chair. As soon as I was upright, she leaped upon me from the side and clamped her legs around me, with her moist little oyster pressed against my left hip and the softness of her breasts against the side of my chest. She was still laughing at my shock when Gazelle did the same on my right side. At least they balanced each other as I started a ponderous walk through the patio doors and back into our bedroom. From the way they clung, slowly gyrating their hips and torsos to massage their more sensitive parts against me, kissing my neck and ears and cheeks, and sighing, they left me in no doubt of their determination to have a good time, too.

To encourage me to provide it, Venus clamped her thigh tight to me, pressing my erection against my belly but leaving the fiery knob of it free — free, that is, for her dainty fingertips to dance in feather-light strokes all over it. How I made it as far as the bed without spouting a whole blancmange I do not know.

The moment we lay down, however, an extraordinary change came over us — or over me, anyway. The urge toward sexual athletics, prompted by their dance on the terrace and my antics in carrying both of them indoors, was lifted from me, and in its place came a sense of golden, glowing lassitude, promising infinite pleasure for infinitesimal effort. It was as if the very air we breathed was, of itself, aphrodisiac.

Perhaps it was. Within the walls of that one hotel, upwards of a hundred men were enjoying that same wanton sweetness with some of the sweetest, most willingly wanton girls in the world. It's hard not to believe that all that intensely focused energy and desire does not combine to produce an aura, an enchantment of some kind, which grips all who come within its range and locks them into a single, collective being, sharing its sensations, each with each. Now I'm a scientist, an engineer, a man trained to scoff at such notions, yet I find it hard to avoid the idea that the intensity and duration of the pleasures I enjoyed with Venus and Gazelle that night were not part of a far greater mass orgy that held us all in its omnipotent grasp.

The three of us lay together, naked and uncovered, for the night and our exertions, gentle though they were, made even the flimsiest covering unthinkable. We writhed together as in a slow-motion dance while I passed from one exquisite body to the other, not knowing whether I was slipping gently into them or they were sheathing themselves delicately around me.

At last, even the boundaries beween 'me' and 'them' began to dissolve, so that when, for instance, I ran my fingernails delicately up and down Gazelle's back, the long moan of female pleasure it provoked from deep in her throat and the little shiver from her head to her toe was as much my response as hers.

Whether by luck on my part or consummate skill on theirs I cannot say, but I rose to the threshold of orgasm quite soon during our languid sport — and simply stayed there. I neither went forward into climax nor slipped back off the boil entirely but lingered for what must have been almost half an hour in that wonderful twilight between *Yes!* and *Oh-oh-oh!*

But it was *Oh-oh-oh!* at last, deep in the softness of her, Venus or Gazelle, I do not recall, even if I knew it at the time. She let me soak it to the last tiny twitch but then, the moment she felt it begin to shrivel, she leaped off me and began a frantic attempt to suck some life back into it. The other meanwhile knelt above me, hanging her breasts over my face and sucking my nipples. I was amazed, first that they could want yet more sex so immediately, then at their obvious belief that a prick that had given so much already had anything left to offer even two such provocative and thrilling young creatures as they ... and finally at the realization that they were, indeed, correct.

My fellow seemed to have developed a life of his own. No matter that I was in the final stages of exhaustion, nor that the pain of this new erection was almost as great as the pleasure, he swiftly joined in their conspiracy to milk me one more time. I could do nothing but lie back and think of England. I was superior blow-up doll for *their* sporting pleasure they took full advantage of my torpor and my fellow's rampant eagerness to please. I slipped in and out of consciousness while they took turns to slip down over me, get him firmly lodged inside them, and indulge themselves without the slightest need to indulge me.

I remember little in the way of detail — not even how long it lasted for I drifted off into sleep before they finished. It would have been nice to dream of herculean potency but, as far as I know, no dreams of any kind troubled me that night. I do have a vague memory that when Venus was lying on me, gasping and giving out little moans in the grip of her umpteenth orgasm, Gazelle took my hands and led them to Venus's breasts, whose nipples I then squeezed and caressed while she thrust her thumb in the poor girl's bumhole and waggled the tip of it about in a sensuous trawl for the ultimate thrills that might still be lurking there. I say 'poor' Venus because she burst into tears at the unbearable exquisiteness of those sensations. And for some strange reason I cried, too, though I was laughing and fighting for breath at the same time — a confusion from which sleep at last rescued me.

When I woke up piss-proud just after dawn the following morning, the sunlight was stealing over the terrace wall and reaching long fingers into the room, touching everything with gold. Especially, I noticed in the dressing-table mirror, the voluptuous derrières of my two nymphs, sleeping by my side. I enjoyed the sight — and the memory — of them for a while but, since a full bladder had already given me an erection, no outward sign of my enjoyment followed. I rolled away from them as quietly as I could and went to the bathroom, where I cured the prime cause of my condition. Then, thinking that the noise of a shower might awaken them, I had a good all-over strip wash, brushed my teeth, and returned to the bedroom as refreshed and full of vigour as I'd ever felt in my life.

My idea was to climb quietly back into bed and sit there, playing with myself and admiring their charms until they awakened naturally. I was proud again, of course, but now from the more usual cause. Alas, they were already awake, and only waiting for me to finish with the bathroom, which they then used as I had done, taking rather longer about it, though — probably not having quite as much incentive as I had for hastening back to bed.

When they returned at last they took one look at me lying there, grinning at them over an erection as hot and ardent as anything they'd seen last night, and Venus said, "Okay, man."

They returned to our bed, one each side of me, and Gazelle said, "Now we give you most good time of all."

At which she pulled my thighs even wider apart, stretched herself full length between them, and, grasping my fellow like a fat lollipop, began kissing and licking and sucking — and from time to time biting and swallowing — him. I'd had quite a few skilled suck-stresses go to work on me before Gazelle but she could have taught them all. I'll swear her tongue and lips somehow managed to link up with my nervous system, so perfectly did they anticipate each little throb and thrill. If I had had any idea of enjoying them in more regular copulation, I forgot it then and there. This was the ultimate of all sexual pleasures; last night's romps had been a mere curtain raiser to this.

And Venus, showing willing too, squatted over my

face and, with saucy wriggles and lascivious gyrations, teased me with the sight and tickle of her cleft and shrubbery. She tantalized me, too, for, every time I went to taste her with my outstretched tongue, she pulled away and giggled coyly. At length I could stand it no more and, grabbing her by the hips, pulled her down upon me — whereupon she relented and let me dine to my heart's content. I would have said 'to my prick's content' but for that fact that all *his* desires were being fully satisfied by Gazelle and her wondrous mouth. And tongue. And teeth. And throat ... oh, that throat!

Slowly, skilfully, she coaxed me up to one more orgasm, whose rhythm she caught perfectly. She took me as deep into her as possible — I mean to the hilt of *me* not to the limit of her — and made those gulping motions that constrict the throat so powerfully and, when timed aright, can turn an orgasm into a near-death experience. She timed it aright, let me say.

Later, when I could do no more than lie there in utter exhaustion, they draped themselves on top of me, one forked sensually over each of my thighs, their breasts like soft fruit on my chest and the three of us fell briefly back to sleep. It can't have lasted more than five minutes but I awoke with this brainwave. "Listen!" I said, twitching my thigh muscles where it would arouse them most — assuming they were still capable of arousal at all. "How much for you to stay with me all week? Six days. You be my girls all six days — how much?"

They looked genuinely crestfallen — or Gazelle did, anyway. "I go Chieng Mai today," she said. "Family in Chieng Mai. I must go."

"I be your girl six days," Venus said.

When I looked doubtful, for I really wanted two girls

each night — passing from one vagina to another was much more enjoyable than moving to a new position with the same vagina — she said, "You try me this evening, six o'clock. You no fun from me, we go down pick one more girl. I pick good girl, too. You see."

And I did, too.

At six that evening I came back to find her all ready for our promised orgy *à deux*. The equipment consisted of a large rubber sheet, spread out on the carpet by the bathroom door, and a bottle of something or other. "I give you body massage," she said. "Please to undress, lie down, take it easy."

I'd seen it advertised all over town, of course, and the guidebooks took care to stress that it was quite a separate service from full intercourse, by which they meant it was paid for separately, too, and the girl would charge a second fee if you wanted to go all the way with her after. It sounded like a rip-off to me — another way of milking the tourist cow, so I'd never looked into it.

How wrong can you be! Whole-body massage is as different from intercourse as a sauna is from a bath. It's a full sexual experience in its own right. No man should refuse one. No girl should pass out of her twenties without having given her lover at least one — and I'll tell you why. A lot of girls think nature has been more than slightly unfair, giving them an anatomy that forces them into the more passive rôle in bed. I've known several. One of them, when she felt frustrated enough to roll me on my back and take the active part, had a trick of tilting her hips while she pumped her bottom up and down. Jenny, she was called. I know why she did it, of course — it increased the pressure of my knob on one side of her vagina and it strengthened the contact down at the other end, too, between my root and her vulva. Unfortunately it became quite painful to me after the first half-dozen thrusts. If I tried to shift a little to one side, easing off the prick-breaking pressure, she'd move with me in her eagerness to grab those thrills. There was nothing to do then but to grit my teeth and bear it for her sake — and relish the extreme pleasure it obviously afforded her; and I do not deny what a pleasure it is for a man when a girl lies on top of him, panting and moaning in the extremity of her orgasm. But poor Jenny was crestfallen and bewildered when our splendid orgies petered out and I stopped calling her at last.

Jenny, if you're out there still and you ever read this: I'm sorry. I didn't know about whole-body massage. It would have given you everything you were looking for — and then some. Let me tell you:

When I was 'completely comfortable,' as the sporting girls all say, she laid me down tenderly in the middle of her rubber sheet, which measured about nine-by-nine. It was sold, I think, as a garden-pond liner. It had that blue-green colour, anyway, which set of her pale bronze skin to perfection. The first thing she did was to rub me all over with some kind of non-oily jelly, which was odourless and colourless — something like KY-Gel but with a little more body to it. She said it was made from seaweed.

Her English, by the way, had shown an amazing improvement over the past twelve hours; she said it would have been hurtful to Gazelle and the other two to flaunt her superior skill before them, by which I surmised that they somehow had more status than she.

Perhaps they had all been longer on the Game.

Anyway, she began by slowly massaging this stuff into my skin — or onto it, rather, for it didn't seem to be absorbed. She rubbed every part of me, front and back, except you-know-where — even though the old fellow sprang up at her the moment she rolled me on my back again and he just begged for the comfort of her touch. I tried, with comic eye movements and childish whimpers to indicate his distress but she seemed to have gone into a light form of trance, almost as if we were now embarked on a religious ritual.

The moment every *other* part of me was covered she filled her palm and smeared the jelly the full length of her front, from ankle to neck, especially over her breasts.

"And your back?" I asked. "Shall I?"

"Ssh!" was her only reply. So it was a solemn ritual.

She grasped my wrists and sat astraddle me, pinning my arms one each side of my head. She closed her eyes and sat rock still for a while, either praying or gathering her concentration. Her breasts hung enticingly close to my lips. I was about to try and kiss them when I noticed that her nipples were growing larger and darker, even as I watched.

She was turning on!

This was no religious rite, it was her private good time before she turned back into a pro and delivered the promised goods to me.

A moment later she spread her body flat upon mine and began the slowest, most sensual horizontal dance you can imagine — up and down the length of me at first, pushing alternately with her toes and hands. Any movement that touched my best friend down there was purely accidental; it was every *other* inch of our flesh which counted here.

For a woman the main pleasure of whole-body massage is that it frees her from the tyranny of being pinned, or pegged, in one particular place and dancing to the tune of that peg. The whole-body thing is not such a novelty, I imagine, since, if she gets excited at all, it is with the participation of her entire body anyway. For a man, however, it's a whole new experience. Our sexual pleasure is normally so focused on the few square inches of exquisitely sensitive flesh at the tip of our tools that the rest of us gets starved of attention. A reminder that we have other sensitive areas, too, is a blessing beyond price, especially when our attention is drawn to them by the slow massage of a lithe, sexy, naked young girl as she sprawls and writhes all over us.

And that lubricant jelly had the curious effect of making one feel skinned. If you can imagine, first, being peeled back to your bare nerves — quite painlessly, of course ... and if you can then imagine those nerves being free, for the first time in your life, to experience the world in all its raw immediacy ... and if that world is fillcd with a naked lover ... then you'll understand why I say it's not an experience *like* straight sex, nor any kind of substitute for it, but something quite unique and special.

And it's probably an activity in which the woman's experience and the man's most closely coincide, since each one's part duplicates rather than complements the other's. There is no doubt that Venus was enjoying it as much as I was — more, indeed, for it soon became clear that she was living through one of those enviably long multiple orgasms that the human female, uniquely among all the animals on earth, can enjoy when the mood is right.

It was nothing very showy. She did not writhe and thrash around and gasp and shiver and stuff like that. On the contrary, it was quiet, controlled, intense, and deep. She'd take a long breath in, hold it a second or two, and then breathe out again with a long, barely perceptible shiver, accompanied by the ghost of an occasional, whispered, 'Oh!' And all the while, of course, she was slithering quietly, this way and that, all over me. I just lay there and marvelled.

When she'd had as much as she could take, she flipped herself over and lay supine, still on top of me — both of us now staring at the ceiling. I wondered if this was my cue to give her more conventional massage with my hands, but the first movement I made to find out provoked a sharp 'No!' from her, whereupon she resumed massaging me, this time with her back.

I suspected she was taking a rest, so to speak, from the turmoil of her long orgasm — a concept so alien to a man that at first it seemed merely fanciful. However, I noticed a certain wiliness in her movements now in this new position, as if she feared she might have neglected my pleasure in the singleminded indulgence of hers. She hadn't, in fact, but she wasn't to know that.

Now she began to trap my erection between her thighs and give it a loving squeeze. I was, of course, harder and more eager than ever. She made it seem an accidental part of her continuing massage, but such an 'accident' had not happened even once when we had been face to face. Now and then she even managed to 'give the old ferret a sniff of the coney hole,' as an Australian colleague once put it. This, too, was in strong contrast to her earlier behaviour, when she had been most careful to avoid direct contact between her actual sex and mine — not easy when she was writhing and slithering around with them only inches apart at times. These fleeting contacts were her way of saying, 'Soon, soon, I promise!'

By 'her sex' I mean, of course, her actual cleft and hole — not her Venus mound, which, I suspect, was the source of all her pleasure. It was certainly prominent enough to be so. She was a clitoral pleasure seeker rather than a vaginal one. Moments later, having taken her breather, she was at it again, only this time she turned me to lie on my front. This time I, not being concerned to wonder if our sexes would touch, accidentally or otherwise, could focus my attention on her. And, sure enough, she was back on the peaks of her orgasm within a minute or so of taking up this new position. And again I could only lie there and marvel at its duration and intensity.

After about ten minutes of this I began to feel cramped and made movements to turn on my side. Her response reminded me of those cliché comedies where, for instance, a teenage girl expects her father to say, 'Go to your room without any supper,' but what he actually says is, 'Would you like chocolate or strawberry ice cream?' and she starts telling him how beastly and horrible he is and then does a double-take and says, 'What was that?' In just the same way, Venus started making a whimpering, complaining noise in her throat, but then, feeling my hip against her Venus mound and the delightful pressure it offered her clitoris, changed in mid-whine from complaint to purr. Her final orgasm, played out against my hip, was as wild as anything I've ever experienced with any girl, amateuse or pro, genuine or faked. And it certainly was not faked. At least, I don't know how any girl could acquire enough control over her autonomic nervous system to make the skin of her back and breast break out in hot rashes, and sweat break out on her brow and lip. And — most telling of all — her outer labia, which were normally engorged (as they are with most prostitutes who gratify six or more men a day), were as thin and bloodless as those of any virgin, while her inner labia were swollen and impassioned. *Those* are the signs no pro can fake.

I discovered them moments after her final convulsion, when she was too exhausted to protest and I went down on her, curious to see if I could prolong her ecstasy by the more active stimulation of my mouth and tongue.

It turned out that I could.

She begged me to stop but the moment I lifted my mouth from that sweet little fig between her thighs she grabbed me by the hair and pulled me back — and instantly begged me to stop again. You'd have thought my tongue was releasing ten thousand volts through her, the way she jerked and twitched under the merciless softness of its explorations.

At last she collapsed and lay utterly still. Perhaps she actually did pass out, or perhaps it was her only way of making me stop when, at last, she genuinely wished me to.

"Now we shower," she said when she came to again.

After that we went to bed and enjoyed the gentlest, most relaxed sort of copulation for about forty minutes before I spouted an ocean of sperm into her belly. She did not come again, nor did she even pretend to. Her attitude was that of the infinitely willing, skilfull, and cooperative houri toward her lord and master — anticipating my every desire and offering me the fullest scope of her sex to encompass it.

Later, over supper, I asked her about the body massage — did she offer it to many customers? How did she stop them from coming prematurely — because, presumably, she'd want to offer them full sex as an option afterward? And so on.

She was very frank. She said that Arabs and other Orientals seemed to understand it best; they hardly ever came. But westerners were more difficult (she thought I had done very well) and Americans the worst of all; she usually made them lie face down and didn't risk face-to-face massage at all.

We had no more sex that night but she fell asleep in my arms, which was a sensation just as beautiful in its own way. I cradled her glorious young body to me with a feeling more protective than possessive, and I thought of all the unsuspected pleasures (for me) that might still lie concealed within her. I knew then that I'd go whoring no further in Bangkok, not on that visit at least, but would instead ask dear Venus to stay with me for my remaining ten days.

The following morning I did so, and she accepted, and I never regretted it for a moment. She went down on me at once, and proved as good a suckstress as Gazelle had been the day before.

I came to know her well over those days and nights we were together and I'll swear her English improved by the hour. Unlike many of her sisters on the Game, she did not waste her money on drugs, clothes, drink, or trinkets. She was saving up to buy a small hotel on the seafront, about twenty miles east of Bangkok. She was actually quite rapacious for money and always expected a 'little tip' after each time she gratified me; but once I knew her purpose, I didn't mind so much. I felt I was conspiring with her to break the usual mould of vice, degradation, and despair. In fact, that was shallow sentimentalism on my part. Quite a lot of girls on the Game get out with enough money to start respectable small businesses — and run them successfully; more, certainly, than moralists would like us to believe.

I did not return to Bangkok for several years. When I did, I took the first chance I could to go to the resort she had mentioned and look her up. And she had, indeed, bought her hotel and was making a considerable success of running it, too. Neither of us even mentioned sex.

Nor did I look for a replacement for her — another girl with whom I could spend the whole of my time there. Indeed, I went to the other extreme — and again I blame a man I met on the plane on the way there. He was a stocky young ginger-headed Glaswegian — a little bull of a man who told me he was going there for one reason only: to see how many girls he could fuck in the course of a single twenty-four-hour day. Eight, he reckoned, might be about it.

There must be something about the Bangkok air that encourages me to lunacy. The first time it led me to take four girls up to my room at once. Now it challenged me to see if I could match, or even outdo, my randy young travelling companion.

I had the usual three days' intensive work, this time on a refrigeration plant for a meat-casings factory, followed by three days of waiting for my London office to crank out its figures and quotations. The first day I rested and went to see dear Venus in her splendid hotel. The second day I began on my challenge, right after breakfast. I saw no point in delaying my likely defeat; it would come better in the early evening than in the achingly small hours of the following morning. I met a pretty young girl out in the hotel corridor — just finishing her night watch with one of the other guests. I didn't even undress her. I just got her to take off her panties and lie on my bed. I finished inside six minutes — which was understandable, since I'd had no sex for more than a week, not even 'a little private outing with Madame Palme and her five fat daughters,' as that same Australian put it.

I was so pleased with this auspicious start that I went out and did the same again, catching another young girl down in the foyer. With her it took twelve minutes before I came — which was ominous if each one took double what the previous one had required: 6 minutes, 12, 24, 48, 96, 192, 384, 768 … that came to a grand total of 25½ hours for eight girls, with no time for anything else, not even breakfast, in between. I was never going to equal my Glaswegian rival. And if I couldn't even equal him, there was no point in trying.

I decided to abort the mission — or multiple missions (or multiple *e*missions, actually) — and go down to breakfast. The juice on offer was passion fruit. What's in a name? Nothing, maybe, but it seemed to put some lead back in my pencil — or, more to the purpose, it put some juice back in my balls. I even felt a twinge of desire for the waitress, who was twice my age and almost toothless. I decided to give it my best try — not so much in rivalry as in a straightforward scientific search for my limits. Every man should know his limits. If mine proved to be only three, okay, so it was three. I wouldn't make a fool of myself in any future situation where numbers were important.

At least I got one thing right. These were not to be gourmet-sex sessions in which I milked the situation for every last thrill. Who could eat eight gourmet dinners in a day? But most people could down eight hot dogs or eight pizzas if it was a matter of winning a bet or proving a point. So I continued with Girl Three as I had with the first two. She was tall for a Thai, well built and in her mid-twenties. I picked her up in the nearest bar and took her back to my room. She suggested lots of exciting things, which I was loath to turn down — though I did. I asked her just to undress and lie on her back with her legs slightly apart and move as little as possible. I climbed aboard, got well lodged in what proved to be a delightfully slim, soft vagina, and began poking away with long, slow thrusts and quicker withdrawals. I closed my eyes and concentrated all my thoughts and feelings on the few inches of glowing flesh at the tip of my tool. Amazingly, I came in only eight minutes! It wasn't much and it hurt more than slightly, but it was a definite notch on the bedpost. She was amazed that I tipped her for something so quick and simple.

In a daredevil mood I went straight out and picked Girl Four, also in her mid-twenties, prettier and slimmer than number three — so it was even harder to turn down the even naughtier suggestions she made when we were alone in my room. Again I got her to lie naked on her back and move as little as possible. The sight of her gave me a useful erection, all right, but the pain of it was quite severe. I couldn't call it excruciating, nor even intense; in fact, it was a kind of dull, sad ache all over my fellow. As soon as I got nicely snug inside her, though, the ache seemed to migrate to the swollen knob, driving out all the thrills that should be there instead. It didn't help that her vagina was softer and flabbier than any of the previous girls'.

In fact, those thrills *were* still there. I could *just* feel them, lurking, as it were, behind the pain. I realized that from here on it was a matter of willpower rather than of mere physical stamina — mind over matter. The thrills were there, I told myself. I just had to grit my teeth against the pain, concentrate on the pleasure, and show my tool who was master here.

It was uphill work at first. No matter how hard I concentrated on those tiny hints of pleasure, the pain increased with every thrust. My tool, it seemed, had a will of his own, too, locked in mortal combat with mine. My life versus his death. The death-wish consumed him. I felt him weakening with each excruciating thrust — oh yes, the word was quite appropriate now. Grimly I struggled and feebly he flagged. God forgive me, but I began to hate *her,* the poor girl beneath me who was innocent of my afflictions. But God bless her, for, at just the right moment, she coughed — which caused her vagina to contract in a brief squeeze.

She felt the effect it had on me and did it again, deliberately this time. I don't mean she coughed; but she caused some wonderful muscular contraction to occur down there — which, in turn, caused my fellow to forget his pain, not entirely but more than somewhat, and take a new interest in these new pleasures.

"Yes!" I encouraged her. "Do that — more!"

We settled to a new rhythm, in which she gave me one of those magnificent squeezes during the brief pause at the end of each thrust.

Pain? Where had all that pain disappeared to suddenly? A distant memory!

And this new pleasure was a distant memory, too, dredged up from my early teens. I remember when giggling, cock-tickling sessions with pals on the golf course ended with tiny pearly beads of spunk on the angry red tips of our hot little knobs … and how we could go for tickle after tickle. Four or five of them, one after another, and each one climaxing in an orgasm (though no pearly beads after the first or second, of course). Multiple orgasms were no difficulty to us in those days. But the thrill of each succeeding masturbation in such a sequence would change subtly between one and the next. The first was riotous and confused, like an eight-octave chord from a theatre organ with all the stops pulled out; the last was thin and clear, like a single note from a flute — a purer musical pleasure in some ways.

And that was the memory — and the revelation — which came back to me with clever young Girl Four in that Bangkok hotel bedroom, just before lunch on that unforgettable day. I felt I stood at the threshold of a purer sexual experience than any I had enjoyed before. Perhaps it was all that Zen in the air? Or perhaps this is something all men might experience if only they could manage to break through that barrier of pain and sexual fatigue which normally inhibits such multiple performances? I don't know. I never tried it again — for the same reason, probably, that I never climbed

Ben Nevis again, after doing it once.

Anyway, it took me twenty minutes to come with Girl Four. I suppose she, too, never understood why I tipped her so generously, but she had been responsible for a great revelation. The power of a single cough!

Girl Five took longer — just over half an hour — but at least there was no pain. A bit of a dull ache, maybe, but no twinges, no throbbing, not of pain, anyway. And as for pleasure, it was getting thinner, finer, purer all the time. And it was now almost entirely concentrated in the knob of my tool, which seemed to have developed a quite unprecedented sensitivity and tactile awareness. For instance, halfway through poking Girl Five I turned her over on her tummy and enjoyed ten minutes or so, lying on top of her in that position. And the nerves in my knob could actually feel the different texture of that front wall of her vagina.

Of course, it's well known that the front vaginal wall is less smooth than the back one, and is sometimes furnished with little corrugations. It's supposed to be a relic of our ape-ancestry, when all copulation was in the doggy position and the rougher texture of that front wall would be more stimulating to the underside of the male's erect penis — and, presumably, to the female, too. I'd been vaguely aware of it with many girls in the past but this was something quite different. No vagueness about it. You know the way your tongue can distinguish between the hundreds of different textures all around the inside of your mouth, whereas your fingertip can feel the difference between maybe ten or so? That was the sort of difference I'm talking about here. My knob had somehow become as sensitive as my tongue to the textures of a girl's vagina.

I explored Girl Five's with such excitement that it partly explains why I took so long to come. Indeed, my excitement was so great, even after coming, that I wanted to go out and bring back Girl Six at once. But I thought it might be good to pause while I still had an appetite for more, and, in any case, hunger of a more gastronomic kind was calling. I ate a light lunch of curried delicacies, fruits, and salads and then slept it off for an hour or so. Around three o'clock I picked up Girl Six and took her back to my room; the desk porter was highly suspicious of me by now. Was I a muckraking journalist? A religious snooper? A civil-rights inspector for some international agency? I was certainly no ordinary punter. No matter. The truth would merely convince him I was one of the above.

Girl Six was younger than the earlier ones — sixteen, perhaps, and very pretty. I hoped she had a tighter vagina for me to explore with my newly sensitive organ. For one ghastly moment, however — in fact, for almost two ghastly minutes — I feared I wasn't going to be able to explore anything as we both stared in dismay at my shrivelled, discoloured fellow.

"It's purple with embarrassment," I told her. And then quoted the old poem: "Poor Willie is a sad old boy, of that there is no doubt. For what was once his pride and joy, now's just his water spout."

But she had a trick or two of her own and, with the subtle application of her tongue and teeth, soon turned my simple water spout back into my pride and joy. The pain returned, too, but I knew I'd soon break through that barrier again.

And so it proved. Fourteen minutes later I was squirt-squirt-squirting my nothingness into a slightly bemused

Girl Six. And ten minutes after that, I was poking happily away inside Girl Seven. I was a little apprehensive when I brought her into the hotel for I saw that Girl Six was still chatting away with the porter on the desk.

However, I knew I was on a marathon run by now. I was well into my second sexual wind and going with an easy stride. There was pain, of course — all marathon runners will tell you that — but it released its own strange pleasure, too. By the time I was throbbing ecstatically (can't really call it 'coming' since there was nothing left to come!) inside Girl Seven, I was starting to feel I could go on for ever. Marathon runners and Channel swimmers will tell you that, too, but they'll add that it's amazing how the 'forever spirit' withers when the finishing line or farther shore is breasted. I saw that my problem now was not to keep going but to avoid setting a finishing line too low — in fact, to avoid setting one at all. The Olympic marathon is 26 miles and 385 yards long, not because that was the original distance in Ancient Greece, nor because someone once decided that was the limit of human endurance; it just happened to be the distance between Windsor, where the race started, and the White City Olympic Stadium back in the early 1900s, when the games were held in England. I told myself I must avoid setting any such arbitrary limit. If only I knew the finishing line, I could, like any good athlete, pace myself properly! I decided to press on regardless and let my body tell me when to stop. And so I went out in search of Girl Eight.

When I brought her back I was even more disconcerted to see that the porter was now talking to Girl Seven. Even more worrying, Girl Six had come back and joined them — and all three were looking at me in some curiosity. They quacked something at Girl Eight, on my arm, who then stopped, looked at me, and laughed.

"Is true?" she asked.

"Is what true?"

"You go for sex record — how many time you fucky-fuck girl?"

"Not really," I said, blushing. "Just curious, that's all."

Something in their attitude told me this was not the first time they'd met such a situation. It can't have happened every week — or the porter would have twigged at once. But it hadn't surprised them too much, either.

"Do lots of men try?" I asked. "To go for a record, I mean?"

"Happen all time," she replied dismissively.

"And what *is* the record?" I asked.

I wish I hadn't.

"Thirty times," the porter said. "A Norwegian. Last year."

Okay, so I'll confess my utter inadequacy right now: I threw in the towel at Girl Fifteen, shortly after nine that night when I still, theoretically, had twelve hours to go. I wasn't particularly exhausted. I was (let me whisper it) *bored*.

MEXICO: Chantal and Vanita

They probably had unpronounceable Mexican names but for professional purposes they called themselves Chantal and Vanita. They weren't lesbians but they shared an apartment and they usually worked together — that is, they went out on the street together and tried to work it so that they picked up a pair of men and took them back to the apartment, where they screwed them in separate rooms.

I spotted them on my first night in Mexico City when I went out, not looking especially for sex, in fact, more in search of a good meal than anything. I was sitting on the sidewalk terrace of this rather good restaurant, enjoying a superb meal but feeling less than enamoured of two male German tourists who were sitting a couple of tables away, slightly drunk, and more than slightly boisterous.

Just when I'd had it up to here with them, the taller and fatter of the pair called a waiter over and mumbled something I didn't catch. The waiter left his station, walked off into the night and, ten minutes later, returned with these two very attractive girls, both in their early twenties. The taller, whom I later knew as Chantal, had long, straight blonde hair tied in a frisky ponytail with a gorgeous ribbon of black velvet. The other, Vanita, had short black curly hair embellished with a huge silk peony, almost the size of a hat, over her right ear. The night was warm and both girls wore those off-the shoulder blouses with short, puffy sleeves and an elasticated gathering across the breast. In their cases it was very low down across their breasts, so that, even when they stood upright, the roving male eye was left in no doubt as to the size and shape of their charms. And when they stooped to sit down — as they soon did — the weakness of the elastic and the force of gravity combined to gratify that same roving eye as to the last detail of their professional equipment, or the upper half of it, anyway. The lower half was, a little surprisingly, hidden beneath voluminous skirts with a hemline halfway between their knees and ankles.

I was willing to bet that, just as they wore no bra above, so, too, they had no panties to hide what was below. I itched to find out, and thus had one more reason to curse those Teuton loudmouths who were now, quite obviously, filling the girls' ears with lewd, if incomprehensible, suggestions. Incomprehensible as to language, that is; I'm sure they understood the men's intentions to the last grope and squirt.

I nursed my chagrin and enjoyed the rest of my dinner while they knocked back a leisurely drink or two. Then, as I sipped my tequila and coffee, and tried not to look their way, they paid their bill, rose, and sauntered past me into the street, each with an arm around 'his' girl. Jealousy is an absurd emotion at the best of times, I know. It's ten times more absurd when squandered on a whore. But on that evening I was consumed with a jealousy I hardly knew how to control. I quickly paid my bill and hastened after them, though I can't imagine what I hoped to achieve by it — except to increase my useless rage.

I caught up with them two streets away, sauntering along and laughing. The guy with Chantal had his hand right down around her buttock and was squeezing and caressing her there quite brazenly. I'm a little ashamed of it all now, and, to be honest, I don't really understand why I felt so strongly at the time, but my jealousy grew so powerful that I was afraid it might entirely possess me and lead me to do something extremely stupid.

Fortunately, they reached the girls' apartment just about then. Once they were out of sight the provocation diminished and I became more like my usual self. Even so, I spent a restless night. Every time I woke up I got this picture of one or other of those two fatties squashing one or other of those lovely young women beneath him as he rammed away without finesse or style.

My contract in Mexico City was a small one — a follow-up to one my partner had made the year before, just to check that all was well before our guarantee expired. I was through by five the following afternoon and, in the normal course of things, would have caught the first plane back to Las Vegas, where a much bigger contract was waiting for me. However, I knew I couldn't leave now — not without enjoying *both* girls and purging their memory (that is, my memory of them) of the two men I'd seen them with the previous night.

I returned to the street where their apartment stood and, noticing a café opposite, sat there and drank a Coke while I composed the report on my day's work. My vigil was rewarded about forty minutes later when Vanita came across to the café to buy a pack of cigarettes. On her way back among the tables I caught her eye and beckoned to her to join me. I offered her a coffee but she said her friend was waiting for the cigarettes. She was, she said, a desperate smoker.

"The blonde?" I asked. We spoke in Spanish, then and later.

"Yes." She peered at me hard, trying to remember if she'd ever gone with me before.

"I saw you both last night," I explained and mentioned the name of the restaurant.

"That's it!" she crowed. "I knew I'd seen you before. Was it only last night, eh? Whew!"

"Easy come, easy go," I said. "I was annoyed those two Germans got to you first. Really I should be flying back to Nevada right now. But I stayed on in the hope that you and … what's your friend's name?"

That's when I learned both their names.

"I stayed on in the hope you'd both be working again tonight."

"Both?" she asked.

"I'd like to spend the night with both of you. First, though, I'd like to ask the pair of you to dinner — maybe at that same restaurant? Then go back to your place."

"We ask Chantal." She took me across to their apartment.

Chantal looked me up and down and said okay. Neither of them mentioned money. I was glad to see that either girl's bed was large enough for whatever threesome frolics we might enjoy there. I sat on one of them, Vanita's, while they undressed, washed, half dressed again, did their make-up, and completed their dressing. I felt like the man who broke the bank at Monte Carlo as I walked down the street with a girl on each arm — the very street where I had stood in impotent rage a mere twenty hours earlier. But the crowning moment — the crowning public moment, anyway — came as we took our seats in the restaurant, for the two fat Germans chose that same moment to arrive. There is no doubt they had hoped to engage the same two girls for another night because their faces fell a mile and, after a brief confab, they turned about and walked disconsolately away.

Neither girl showed the faintest sign of recognition. That would have been standard whore's etiquette, of course, but as soon as the men were safely away, Chantal made her attitude clear. "God be praised!" she said, miming the act of throwing up.

"Mine wasn't so bad," Vanita said, but with little conviction. She obviously thought it was also good etiquette to say nothing ill of one client in the presence of another. "But I prefer you," she added quickly, patting my hand. "It's much easier to speak Spanish."

I wanted to talk about them, their lives on the Game, how long they'd been at it, their clients, their hopes … all the usual things. But, since neither of them had even mentioned money yet — which was unique in my experience of prostitutes — it didn't somehow seem right. So our conversation meandered from one topic to the next, almost as if we were three strangers united by a mutual but absent friend, getting to know one another. In between the lines I gathered they were not so much prostitutes as good-time girls. They got fairly regular work as photographic models, tourist guides, crèche helpers … and they went out and picked up men when they felt like it. If they needed money, they'd ask the men for it; otherwise they didn't bother.

"Tonight," Chantal said, "you buy us a magnificent meal and some Coke. Okay?"

"If that's what turns you on," I replied, thinking it an odd combination of requirements.

They teased me, too, by leaning forward, far more often than was necessary, so as to offer me the most tantalizing glimpses of their adorable breasts; and what they did to me with their hands under the table would have got us thrown in jail if the cloth had not concealed it.

When we returned to their apartment Chantal turned to me and said, "Now for the Coke. I can get some good stuff for fifty dollars — enough for the three of us."

She held out her hand and I realized she hadn't been speaking of Coke but of coke; I had supposed that Spanish would have another word for it.

After she'd gone Vanita plonked herself in my lap and began kissing me, just like a lover. I hated myself for it but I just had to ask if she'd kissed the German like that the previous night. She pulled a face and said, "No!" but my breach of the etiquette brought on a brief coolness between us.

But, thankfully, it was only brief and she was soon kissing me again as if we were long-established lovers. I responded eagerly, realizing it was a long time since any girl and I had kissed so tenderly. When I tried to fondle her breasts, however, she pulled my hand away and said, "Wait for the coke, eh? It makes it even better."

"Ah," I said.

"No?" she queried. "Not for you? What does it do for you?"

"I don't know," I confessed. "I've never snorted the stuff."

"Never?" She stared at me wide eyed and only half believing. I think she'd have found it easier to accept that I was still a virgin.

"Never," I assured her again. "Why? What does it do for you?"

She grinned and stretched luxuriously, until she was almost lying at attention across my lap. She pointed toward her crotch and said, "It makes heaven down there."

"Ordinary sex can do that," I told her, adding with a leer: "If you do it with the right partner!"

She shook her head and corrected her earlier statement: "Coke makes a *seventh* heaven down there. We only brought those fat men home here last night because they had some really good stuff. It makes sex with such men possible. But with a man like *you* …" She curled herself tight against me once more. "You'll see. Then you'll understand."

"Okay." I shrugged. There was no point in spitting against this wind. "But I'm sorry *we* won't have sex, just you-and-me and me-and-Chantal …"

She didn't let me finish. "We will!" she protested. "You'll fuck me … you'll fuck Chantal … then me … then Chantal … many times. You'll see!"

"But there'll always be this third *thing* between us — this coke."

She laughed. "Now I know you've never snorted before! We live for it."

"Can I just touch your nipples?" I asked. "Very gently. Nothing else — just your nipples. Like this."

She permitted it. After a few seconds she surrendered to the pleasure of it. She was flushed and well roused — hell, be honest, we both were — by the time Chantal returned with the precious powder. She saw our condition and wagged a schoolmarmish finger at me. (Odd, isn't it, how women will always assume, when they see another woman sexually aroused, that the man is to blame! Yet they know damn well that most men are ready for it at any hour of the day or night. The go-ahead always comes from the woman. And the no-no.) Anyway, she was too pleased to have got tonight's fix to be really put out.

I watched the ritual in fascination — how they tipped out some of the powder onto a mirror, divided it in three meticulously equal piles with the help of a razor blade, and then invited me, the guest in their home, to go first. But then Vanita split some off my pile onto hers and Chantal's, telling her I'd never had the stuff before. She was met by the same scornful disbelief but eventually she accepted the truth and so agreed to show me the way.

"Got a bill?" she asked.

With a straight face I gave her another fifty, which she rolled up enough to get it in her nostril, where she let it unfurl enough to touch all round inside. Then, pinching the other nostril shut, she snorted the whole of her pile, which was about a small teaspoonful, I guess.

"The other nostril?" I asked.

"Later." She winked. Then she caught her breath, like a woman having a sudden, surprise orgasm. She closed her eyes and lifted her face upward, breathing in jerks. I watched in even greater fascination than before. It was *very* like an orgasm.

Meanwhile Vanita was snorting her share. Soon she, too, was showing off an ecstasy.

"Now you," they said when the explosion began to clear.

Let me confess it — I've only snorted coke four or five times in as many years, so I can't even claim to be an occasional user. It's not a question of my moral superiority. The fact is, it simply does not work with me. I don't say it has *no* effect — but I'll come to that in a minute. But I will say it doesn't have the *claimed* effect. You're supposed to get this rush and then you live on cloud nine for an hour or more and then you come down again, heavily or gently as the case may be — right? Well, none of that happens with me. No rush. No cloud nine. No let-down.

Those poor girls! was my first thought. They had wasted on me what would have kept them in heaven for a couple of hours longer. To spare their disappointment, I faked it. I, the customer, faked the nearest thing to an orgasm so as not to disappoint two near-prostitutes, who were close to experiencing the real thing! Lust can certainly lead one into the strangest situations.

The moment I'd convinced them I was high they tore off their clothes — and mine — and pushed me back on the bed. Chantal straddled me and, seizing my erection, waggled it round like a lunatic pilot with a joystick while she tried to position it in the entry to her vagina. The moment she had it right, however, she sat down heavily, plunging me to the very hilt inside her and letting out a little shriek of joy. Not so little, actually.

Vanita meanwhile squatted over me, lowering her sex to my face and making it clear she expected my tongue to do its best to match what my joystick was doing in Chantal's cockpit — which wasn't much. I mean in that position there was little I could do to compete with two excited and lively young lasses like that; *they* were doing all the work. Chantal was popping up and down on me like a pneumatic trench leveller, crying oh! and ah! and whoo! and other formless cries of ecstasy; and Vanita was doing the same on my face.

Twenty minutes — and at least double that number of orgasms — later, Chantal stopped. Panting and exhausted, she asked me if I was *ever* going to come.

"Soon," I promised, though by then I already knew I wasn't going to — perhaps not ever again. I mean, that's the effect coke always has on me, or, I should say, has had on me on the four or five occasions when I've snorted it. I still can't decide whether it's a good effect or a bad one. It enables me to sustain an erection almost indefinitely and it does not numb me to the pleasures of thrusting it in and out of the warm, wet vagina of a willing girl; but it does rob me of the power of climax. Until the effect of it wears off, I am stuck in the *allegro amoroso* movement of love's symphony; the *saltarello alla breve* of the climax eludes me.

It's very pleasant, of course. I certainly enjoyed it immensely on that first occasion. But it's not the name of the game. I don't think Chantal had ever encountered such a thing before. It nettled her. She seemed to take it as a challenge to her womanhood, and started going at it even more furiously than before — and giving herself yet more orgasms in the process.

Meanwhile Vanita had tired of being licked and was now sitting on my chest, legs wide apart, while I played around inside her with a big, wickedly curved vibrator she had given me. If anything, she was having an even more fun time than Chantal. And for my part, the sight of young mossyface smiling her lovely wet vertical smile at me, just inches from my face, only added to the pleasures I was getting down below.

At length, after we'd been at it for more than half an hour — or it could easily have been three hours … time didn't mean all that much to any of us that night — poor Chantal gave up in indignation. She flung herself down on the bed beside me and, staring me balefully in the eye, said, "You're no man!"

I just smiled at her, a heavy-lidded smile, and blew a kiss.

For some reason that was the last straw. She let out a gasp of anger and sprang from the bed. Quickly she gathered up her clothes and, trying to slip on her shoes as she went, hopped awkwardly to the door.

"What's eating her?" I asked Vanita as soon as she'd gone.

"You've hurt her vanity. She likes to feel a man exhaust himself inside her."

I chuckled feebly. "And she thinks I'm *not* exhausted?"

"You know what I mean. She likes to feel his cock explode — bang-bang-bang — inside her. You wait. She'll go out and find another man to bring home now."

"And what about you?" I asked. "Have I disappointed you, too?"

"Not yet." She grinned and slid down the bed until we were side by side.

But not for long. She slipped her arms around me and rolled on her back, pulling me on top. Either by luck or long practice she got male and female in perfect alignment, so that when she threw her legs up around me I slipped inside her in perfect synchronization.

"I still don't feel like I'll be able to come," I warned her.

"I can be patient," she replied, already breathing excitedly and letting out those little formless cries.

The outer door slammed shut.

"There she goes," Vanita said.

We continued screwing without a pause, at different paces and in different positions, for more than an hour. Halfway through we heard Chantal return with her fully performing lover. They screwed very loudly in her bedroom, which was separated from ours by the thinnest stud wall. My senses were still so heightened by the coke that I could hear the sticky little crackling noises his tool made as it butted in and out of her — even above her huge fake — or at least exaggerated — orgasms, which she was quite determined I should hear.

I was still screwing Vanita — or she was screwing me — when I fell asleep. I'm sure I had the weirdest, wildest dreams in those circumstances but they faded into oblivion even as I woke, which was about eight o'clock the following morning. I still had an erection, though now it was simple piss-pride. What woke me, I discovered through half a bleary eye, was Vanita using the pisspot.

That chamber music is the sweetest in all the world. I remember once sitting in the low-ceilinged parlour of a little four-girl brothel in Nevada, having arrived about ten minutes before their official opening time. And I heard one of the girls using a pisspot in the room above, just six feet over my head. I came in my pants. So, as you'll gather, the sound of a girl pissing in a pot is

one of the most erotic things I know. And as for the
heady aroma that fills the room shortly after … words
fail me.

So my piss-pride was immediately reinforced by the
more usual sort of stiffness and I had quite a job
emptying my bladder because of it.

Vanita was meanwhile washing her face and hands
in the ewer at the foot of the bed. I had to look away,
she was so sexy. I was still struggling to piss when,
having dried herself, she started rummaging through
one of her dressing-table drawers. She found whatever
she was looking for just about the time that I finished.
She came over to me and was delighted to see that my
old soldier was standing to attention again, ready to
drill for as long as she liked. She slipped her hand
around him — oh, those soft, cool, delicate, feminine
fingers! — and led me unprotesting back to bed.

With a final flourish she spun me round, still gripping
me there, and caused me to tumble on the bed. She did
not immediately join me. Instead, standing right at the
bedside, she turned her back on me and bent almost
double. At the same time she handed me the thing she
had been rummaging for earlier. It proved to be a jar of
cream. There was no doubting where she wanted me
to rub it.

There can hardly be a more beautiful sight to awaken
any man than that which now faced me. Those two fat
labia, inflamed and engorged with sexual excess and
softened by the black, velvety fuzz of her bush, nestled
invitingly between the provocative curves where her
plump young buttocks met the slender concavity of
her thighs. I did not hurry in my task of spreading the
soothing, lubricating cream all over them — and into

every tuck and fold and cranny hidden in between.

When I had excited her enough (and she, me — more than enough), she took the jar from me, capped it, and slipped into bed, all in one clean movement.

"Now!" she said, still with her back turned toward me. She wriggled her derrière against me, into my groin, and, with that uncanny skill of hers, slipped her newly lubricated vagina down over my fellow. "Now you can fuck Vanita, eh?"

"Can and will — and do." I suited my action to the words.

"With a big bang-bang-bang."

"Just wait and see!"

"I can wait quite a time," she warned me. "As I said last night — I am patient."

MALTA: Marina

Marina would turn any man's head in a crowd — which, in a way, is how I came to meet her. I was sitting on the terrace of this café in Malta, down near the harbour, where the sporting girls of the town parade their considerable charms, when she walked by. After that it was no contest. She was about eighteen, tall, dark, and well built. Her long, straight black hair was tied in a plait — high up, so that it bounced friskily with each step. So did her full firm breasts, which her fine cotton blouse did little to conceal. Or restrain. Her trim little waist swelled magnificently to a generous pair of hips and she needed no miniskirt to reassure you that her thighs were long, lean, and shapely; imagination could easily infer the fact from the alluring pair of calves that flashed beneath the hem of her ample skirt. Even her ankles and toes, which peeped seductively from her sandals, were enough to rouse a man, or that vital part of him which needs to be aroused in such encounters.

As I remarked: a girl to turn any man's head in a crowd. There was certainly a crowd there on that busy evening. And she certainly turned one man's head who should have known better, for he was cycling by with a short ladder over one shoulder! As he turned to ogle her, so did the ladder. It struck a lamppost and off he came. The girl turned, like everyone else, to see what the commotion was, and so failed to step out of the path of an oncoming priest. Since no priest would stand aside for a prostitute, he had been convinced she would step aside for him; and in any case, his attention was also fixed on the fallen cyclist. So he knocked poor Marina to the ground.

Had it not been a priest who bowled her over, she would have had a dozen willing helpers to haul — or maul — her back on her feet. The priest, of course, did nothing, and the other men hesitated just long enough to let me get to her first. I helped her back to my table and, noticing a few flecks of blood on her skirt, just about where her knee would have touched it, asked if I might have a look.

With an extraordinary coyness, considering her profession, she permitted my inspection, rolling up her skirt herself and holding it tightly against her thigh just above her knee. It was a small graze, looking worse than it was. The blood was already congealing.

Now here's the amazing bit. I had just come from the chemist, where I had bought — now get this — a bottle of Dettol, some Savlon antiseptic cream, gauze, lint, bandages, and low-allergenic sticking plasters of various shapes and sizes! Why? Well, when you're inspecting metal ducting in awkward places in old buildings it's horribly easy to cut yourself, no matter how careful you try to be. I get anti-tetanus boosters every six months and I never travel without at least the above-mentioned items — except that this time I'd forgotten to pack them. Now do I have a guardian angel or don't I? He must be quite a voyeur, too.

Marina must have thought that *I* was her guardian angel. Anyway, a few minutes later, we were upstairs in her workroom, where I bathed and dressed this minor wound with all the tender loving care a doctor would have expended on a deep, life-threatening cut. We chatted about this and that ... no, actually, we chatted about everything but *that,* strangely enough, or not about *me* as part of *that.* She treated me as a good samaritan, someone in quite a different category to a punter, actual or potential. And while she rabbitted on, I wondered if it was quite the right thing to suggest that, once her little graze was safely bathed and dressed, we might make joyful use of the sumptuous baroque bed on which she was sitting, and the ornate mirrors all around.

She told me her name was Marina, that she was Italian, a university student, earning some money during her summer vacation — she could have been talking about waitressing. I mean, she did not name her obvious business there. But she did indirectly refer to it, I

suppose, when she said she hoped that Valetta was far
enough from Milan to avoid being spotted by anyone
from there. She said, further, that she'd only arrived in
Malta yesterday … that she didn't like the landlord of
this 'tip' (she called it) because he was too greedy. But
she couldn't get any reliable advice from the other girls
because they were jealous of her beauty and they
distrusted her as an amateur.

"But I fuck lots of guys," she said. "All the time. Only
now I tell myself I'll do it for money. And … pfft!" She
flung up her hands as if the world, which yesterday had
seemed so full of hope, was now crumbling to bits
around her.

"I'll tell them I'm English," she said. "My English is
good enough, you think?"

"Tell them you're British," I advised. "You have to
be born English but you can become British."

"My English, it's good though?"

"Better than many natives speak it. But you have an
Italian accent, naturally."

"I like you."

"I *more* than like you, Marina," I said. "See?" And I
stood up to prove it.

She giggled delightedly and reached out to touch the
bulge in my trousers, gingerly, as if she feared it might
explode — in which she was not far wrong, I may say.

"Ha!" she exclaimed. "All thees while I was thinking
how can I fuck this nice guy? Look!" And by way of
proof she lifted her skirt high and spread her thighs
wide to offer me the briefest glimpse of gleaming wet
pussy. "But," she continued, dropping her skirt again
while I carried on gawping at the image that was now
burning in my mind, "all the same while I'm telling me,

no, he's too nice for me. You will fuck me too? Why haven't you said something? Are you living in Malta? D'you know somewhere I can rent a nice room to work? I have nice rooms in" — she named the street — "but they say I cannot work there. Perhaps you have a house with a room where I could work? And then we can fuck together every night after I finish work. Free. I would love it so."

That was the point where I began to disbelieve everything she had told me. Maybe 'disbelieve' is too harsh. Let's say I began to *discount* it. She did not so much murder truth as embellish it. Perhaps she was an experienced amateuse who had just turned pro. Perhaps she'd been on the Game since she was ten. Perhaps the truth was somewhere in between. Perhaps even she could no longer tell you where. What did it matter? She was mouthwateringly delectable. She was available. She could make even the most outrageous embroidery seem like the unvarnished truth — while she was telling it. And those are the three most important qualities in any sporting girl.

I explained my situation and told her which hotel I was staying at.

"I meet you there in one hour," she said.

I looked at the bed, the mirrors, and back at her. "Why not here and now?"

She touched the tip of my nose with a delicate finger. "Naughty boy," she said. "Be patient. We have some wonderful fucking, I promise. But first I must get a new dress and go to confession. I'm already late."

"Go to confession?" I didn't disbelieve her. It sounded too absurd to be invented.

"Sure. It's where I was going when ..."

"When a priest knocked you down — and sent you straight into my arms, metaphorically speaking. Perhaps the Good Lord is trying to tell you something?"

The joke shocked her. She stood up and said primly, "One hour. Your hotel."

What choice had I?

I went back to the pavement café and sipped another coffee while I watched the girls picking up men and taking them upstairs, and I ruminated on the compulsive power of the female body over us males. In my heart of hearts there were a dozen things I'd rather be doing than whiling away an idle hour waiting for a whore to cleanse her conscience and put on a clean dress — swimming in the last of the evening sun, for instance, or reading some pulp science fiction, or sipping a light, sparkling wine while listening to chamber music, or … but why go on. I'll bet most of the men there had similar preferences, too — from playing pool to watching a fight to getting stoned. But instead, for all of us, some obsessive little imp in our minds flashed up this picture of a naked young girl, an available girl, wagging her derrière at us, parting her thighs, spreading the gentlemen's relish … and so here we are, trembling, drooling, gawping — hapless addicts of the old honeypot.

I was just about to pluck up enough courage to ask myself if I really wanted to spoil an evening with Marina when I could be happily designing a new ducting system for a group of bonded warehouses in the port when a pair of hairy male knees, vaguely familiar, blocked my disconsolate view of the pavement and a voice, more than vaguely familiar, said, "Well I'm damned, you old bugger, what are you doing here — as if I didn't know! Living the life of Riley!"

It was Rodney S, something in the City and a member of the same squash club as me in Berkeley Square. Also a member of the RNVR, which accounted for his naval officer's uniform. "Sit down," I said, pushing out a chair with one foot. "As a matter of fact, I was thinking about ducting."

"Ducting, eh?" He ran his eye over several of the girls. "Well — hollow tubular structures of *some* kind — that I can believe."

"And what are you doing here — as if I didn't know."

"Quite right, old fellow," he said, and went on to tell me of some serious ballsup the admiral had made in their naval manoeuvres on the way to Malta. They were lucky not to have lost a couple of ships in a collision, he said. "We've all been rather quiet about it," he added. "So, as a mark of gratitude, the old boy's given permission for us to bring a girl aboard this evening and stick it on his mess bill. Normally, as you know, it's a castration offence to bring a girl aboard."

"How many girls are you looking for?"

Something in my intonation made him think *I* was offering them to him — or perhaps he thought it humorous to pretend as much. "What's this?" he asked. "You in the pimping business now?"

I smiled wearily.

He sighed. "I'm only looking for one. He's not *that* generous. Nor foolhardy. So we're only allowed to bring one girl aboard."

"Poor thing! How many officers is she expected to take on?"

"Well — only two, as it turns out. There are six of us in the junior wardroom — six who are interested, that is. And four of them have said they're damned if they'll hang around while Jimmy-the-One and I roger the tail off some tart and then make do with what's left of her. Can you recommend any of these bints?" He waved a hand at the scene before us. "Or don't you go in for that sort of thing?"

If I hadn't followed his gesture, I might not have spotted her, for it was getting fairly dark by now. It was Marina, of course, looking even sexier by lamplight. There was still half an hour to go before she was due to meet me at the hotel. She was probably trying to sneak in a quick one first, or even two, for the average time around here seemed to be ten minutes.

"Marina!" I called out, just as she was about to accost a fat middle-aged tourist in a vile pair of bermuda shorts.

She glanced my way, recognized me, and, tossing her head contemptuously at the tourist, came smiling over to join me. "I knew you'd be here still," she said. "You're a moth to all these candle flames." She waved a hand vaguely toward her colleagues.

I rose, too, and met her almost halfway. "I want you to meet a friend of mine from London, a naval officer." I explained the situation briefly.

She stopped dead. "And you think I …? I mean, you'd be willing to …?" Surprise gave way to suspicion. "But why?"

"Because I want to spend the whole night with you. And I wouldn't pay you any less if we start at nine than if we start right now. So why shouldn't you earn a little extra first. Also, Rodney's my friend and I don't mind him owing me a big favour."

She chuckled. The situation intrigued her. "Only two, eh? How much should I ask?"

"My dear girl!" I protested. "You're the professional. You ask as much as you dare, surely."

After the introductions she sat down and said, "Do they serve Pernod here? I love Pernod."

After the waiter took our order she said to Rodney. "Naval officer, eh? Look!" Deftly she tweaked up the hem of her blouse and the elasticated belt of her skirt and flashed us her navel. "Navel, yes? You prefer my navel to yours?"

From his angle he could see the top of her bush, too. The poor guy hadn't a chance after that.

The waiter brought her Pernod; I had Lambrusco; Rodney had the fidgets.

"I am not one of these riff-raffs," she said. The ice clinked merrily in her glass as she waved a contemptuous hand in the direction of the other girls. "Ask your friend. I only work the best hotels. It's sixty pounds."

Rodney pretended to think this an outrageous price but he didn't fool her. "Each," she added.

Then he really did think it outrageous.

"You'll have the best fuck ever," she promised with a disarming smile.

It stirred him, but not enough.

"If you want a girl for thirty," she went on, "ask any of these. You'll surely find one who will."

He looked at them, then at her, and — as it had been with me earlier — it was no contest. "Okay," he conceded. "But nothing hurried now. Don't rush us. We want a nice long time."

"And the taxi-fare back," she added.

"I'll come and collect you," I said. "Just say when."

"About an hour and a half," Rodney said firmly, looking at her for any disagreement.

She nodded gravely.

"Come right aboard," he added to me. "Have a thank-you drink on us before you whisk Cinderella away. I'll leave word at the dock gates and with the master-at-arms."

Marina stooped and gave me a kiss, which I hardly noticed, being preoccupied with the electrifying jiggle of her breasts inside her blouse. "I am very hot stuff with you tonight because of this kindness," she whispered in a sultry tone.

And off they went in search of a cab. As I watched them recede into the night I mused on what an extraordinary world it is. An hour and a half earlier I knew nothing of Marina. Now, because she bumped into a priest and fell over, there she was, walking off with a friend of mine from London, who was going to 'roger her tail off' — in his own words — for the next forty minutes and then hand her over to another naval officer, who would do his best to roger her tail off all over again! What thoughts were passing through her mind at this prospect, I wondered? Curiosity? Little butterflies in the tummy — behind that peachy navel and above that luxuriant bush? Apathy? Tedium? Or nothing at all — just the start of another night's work? It all depended on how much of her story one believed.

And so I got my evening swim after all.

And Rodney had been as good as his word; the mere mention of his name and mine was enough to get me escorted all the way to the junior officers' wardroom. But there the smooth, satisfactory flow of the evening came to a halt.

Rodney, it seemed, was too ashamed to tell me the dire news himself. He had delegated the task to the other officer, a chap called Arthur, who worked in advertising in Leeds.

"Listen, old fellow," he said apologetically. "I'm most awfully sorry but two of the others have turned up since Marina came aboard. Word must have got round, you see. So they want a go, too. In fact, Phil is with her now and that's Kenny over there, waiting his turn. I'm bloody sorry about this but it's just one of those things."

I shrugged. "Just one of those things. Tell Rodney he can come out of hiding."

"Jolly sporting of you! Actually, he's raiding the admiral's hospitality store."

Rodney returned at that moment with a bottle of gin under one arm and some non-vintage port under the other.

"Dear fellow!" he cried — and went through the apologies and explanations all over again. "Have a drink," he concluded.

I declined, having the same opinion of alcohol as Macbeth's porter.

"It'll only be another fifty minutes," he said. "We knocked her down to fifty quid for half an hour. I must say, she's worth every penny of a hundred — only don't tell her I said so. She's absolutely fabulous. How did you find her, you lucky bugger?"

I tapped the side of my nose and winked — not trusting my voice to speak calmly.

We had all reckoned without Marina. The moment she finished with Phil (and I do mean it that way round — the poor guy looked as if he'd gone through a spin-drier — but happily, mind), she decided she wanted to eat. No matter that poor Kenny's lust had half melted him into the club armchair by then, she wanted to eat.

Actually, it was one delay I didn't mind for it meant that when we arrived at the hotel we could go straight to bed and with the food well settled in our stomachs. She winked at me, which let me hope she was thinking along the same lines.

So the unfortunate Kenny had to tie a knot in it while the duty cook rustled up one of the finest mixed grills I've ever eaten.

But there's no such thing as a free lunch; there is a price for everything. We were just digging into the ice cream when Simon and Jack — the last two of the junior officers — returned to the ship. They had both enjoyed girls ashore but from the moment they saw Marina — and remembered she was free to them by courtesy of the admiral — there was no holding them back.

Marina looked at me.

The other four looked at me.

"Who's he?" Jack asked belligerently. "Her pimp? Got other plans for her, have you, matey? Our money not good enough?"

"Shut up, you!" Marina told him. "He's the best pimp I ever had."

Either she did not fully understand the word (perhaps thinking it just meant 'introducer') — which I doubt — or it was her idea of fun.

With a weary smile at her I turned to Rodney. "Tell them, old fellow," I said.

But he now saw which way the tide was flowing. Nobody needed my permission to stick another two fellows in the queue behind Kenny. It was all down to Marina — and nobody who'd seen her that night had the slightest doubt what she would say. She'd take on the entire British fleet, the mood she was in.

"I don't know you from Adam, old boy," he said. "I also thought you were her pimp. Aren't you?" To the others he said, "Met him at a dockside café, told him our needs, and he called Marina here out of the crowd. He even advised her what to charge us."

I stared accusingly at Marina, who hung her head guiltily, ha ha. "Marina!" I said. "Tell them the truth."

But she, too, having begun the tease, now wanted to push it one step further. Taking her cue from Rodney, she delved into her bag and pulled out a fistful of sterling notes, which she piled on the table in front of me. "I haven't touched it," she said, letting a touch of fear creep into her voice. "Count it, in front of these witnesses."

I gritted my teeth and stuffed it all, uncounted, into my pocket.

Then Rodney got carried away. "So what's the fee for Simon and Jack, old man?" he asked incautiously.

"Well," I said coldly, "since they've both got their ends away already this evening, it's going to be that much harder work for Marina to fetch them off again. Isn't that right, Marina?"

Her eyes danced merrily as she nodded agreement.

"So it'll be seventy quid each for half an hour, take it or leave it." To Rodney I added, "Teach you, eh!"

"Okay," he said, crestfallen. "The joke's gone far enough. The fact is …"

"No!" Marina cried. "It's no joke. You think I'm not *worth* seventy? Look me on the eyes and tell me I'm not worth seventy."

He couldn't. All he said was, "The admiral will have a fit. And I'm the one who'll get it in the neck."

"Goes with the territory, old boy," Jack said.

"I'll pay," Simon put in.

Everyone looked at him.

"The difference, I mean. How much is the difference? What did you fellows pay — or what are you bunging down on the admiral's chitty?"

They told him.

"Okay. I'll cover the extra twenty." He grinned at Marina. "She looks worth it. I've already paid twenty-five tonight for a very indifferent screw."

Reluctantly Jack agreed to do the same. So I had another hour and a half at least to kill.

Before Marina led Kenny to his cabin — which she did quite literally, grasping him by his erection and pulling him up the corridor — she took me aside and whispered, "I be very good to you — you see. Very good."

"What's it like being a pimp?" Jack asked after she'd gone.

In for a penny … I thought. "It's not what you think," I replied. "It's not all singing hymns. I've got six girls in my string and they each expect a few hours of tender loving care from me at least twice a week. I tell you — I'm almost wrecked …"

So, what with those fantasies and several rounds of poker — at which I was lucky enough to win about twenty quid by way of compensation — the time soon passed. All the same, it was half-past ten before Marina and I sank into the back of a taxi and I gave the driver the name of my hotel.

She was as frisky as if she'd just woken from a refreshing nap. "It works!" she kept saying. "I can do it! What was that? Six men?"

"Six men."

"I can do it!"

"Did you enjoy it?"

"Sure."

"You know what I mean."

"Oh … well …" She grinned naughtily. "I forgot myself a bit — once or twice. I like Englishmen."

"You know some men hate prostitutes — even men who use them?"

She nodded glumly.

"You know why?"

She shook her head. "I saw it in that priest's eye this afternoon, when he was walking toward me."

"It's not religious."

"Why, then?"

"Because you girls lead — or *could* lead, if you wanted to — the sort of life men can only dream about. You just fucked six virile young men, eh? Four of them quite good looking and the other two not bad. And you can do the same again tomorrow — any time you want. *And the men come to you!* Now, most men would give their eye teeth to be *able* to fuck six good-looking young women, one after the other — any time they wanted."

She giggled. "Jealousy, eh?"

"No. Anger. Because you don't even enjoy it. It's just a job to you."

"*I* enjoy it," she protested.

"Sexually?"

"Oh, well, no. But I like men. I enjoy meeting, talking, sharing a laugh. I like it when they admire me. I like giving *them* pleasure."

I gave up. The gulf between her understanding and

mine on that particular point was too wide.

"Sometimes I forget myself," she confessed, taking my arm and snuggling up against me. "I hope I forget myself with you. Only …"

"Only what?" It was an ominous word.

She bit her lip apologetically. "It feels a bit … you know … down here." She pointed at her crotch.

"Sore?"

"Not sore. Tender. Just a moment."

She scrabbled in her handbag and, before I was aware of her intentions she produced a cigarette lighter and a little mirror. She flung up her skirt, spread her thighs wide, held the mirror between them, and flick-flick-flicked the lighter. I looked at the driver and saw him goggle-eyed in the rear-view mirror. When the lighter caught, he spun round and stared directly — and that was when we hit the donkey cart.

Fortunately we were doing something less than a walking pace at the time, so no one was hurt; but it still looked like a three-cognac argument.

I stuffed more than enough money in his pocket and we walked the remaining quarter-mile to the hotel. On the way she said, "You are a *very* nice man, you know."

"What's coming now?" I asked.

"You understand how a girl feels after an evening like this."

"Out with it," I said.

"I would never ask this of any other man. They are all so heartless. But you *know* I'll make it up to you tomorrow."

"You don't want to fuck any more tonight," I said woodenly.

"See!" She flung her arms about me and kissed me

passionately. "I know you'd understand. We sleep together all night — and then, tomorrow morning, oh boy!"

"That's fine," I said enthusiastically. "To be honest, I'm a little tired myself. That'd suit me very well."

I was beginning to latch on to certain aspects of her character — putting me off for an hour with a cock-and-bull story about confession ... then promising me the earth — or heaven, rather — if I'd just let her fuck a couple of naval officers first ... then insisting on dinner when she knew Kenny was desperate to get inside her ... and now this, the ultimate postponement. I had no intention of letting it happen, of course, but I wasn't going to meet her head on.

"You really don't mind?" she asked, surprised — and a little piqued at my easy acceptance.

"Of course not. What d'you think I am — a brute? I realize I've only known you for a few hours, Marina, but already you're a *person* to me — a lovely, lively, *interesting* young woman. You're not just a warm, wet hole with hair round it. I want your happiness as much as I do my own."

There was a slightly bewildered, speculative look in her eye as we enjoyed a leisurely drink in the bar. ("Nothing to hurry upstairs for now, eh?" I said.)

My resolve almost broke down when, the moment we were alone in my room, she threw off all her clothes and made for the shower. She had one of the most beautiful — and sensuous — bodies I'd ever been privileged to gaze upon. Even the thought of the six men who had been there before me that night did nothing to dampen my ardour. In fact, if anything, it increased it. I've always enjoyed poking away in another man's semen, not just because it's such a wonderful lubricant but also for the sense of shared ecstasy that clings about it, still. That's why I like brothels where they don't hurry you. I can pick a girl and then bide my time until someone else takes her upstairs, and then catch her on the stairs on her return, while her vagina is still tingling with another man's attentions, and so hasten her back to bed.

Anyway — to return to Marina.

She expected me to follow her into the shower, of course — taking every advantage of our intimacy short of the ultimate advantage. I was careful not to oblige her. And, just to rub it in, I went into the bathroom, washed all over and brushed my teeth, gave her a cheery, "See you!" and retired to bed with a book. I was naked, of course.

So was she when she joined me there.

I snapped the book shut and said, "Poor girl, you must be exhausted. Shall I just have a look at tonight's battlefield?"

She frowned.

I picked up a squeezy bottle of Intensive Care. "It's tender, you said. This might soothe it."

She saw it as yet another chance to tease me, of course, so she willingly lay on her back, drew up her knees, and spread wide her thighs.

I must say it *was* a bit of a shock. The pale, glistening labia I had glimpsed earlier that evening were now swollen and inflamed. It made me realize that — physically, at least — she had been subjected to something like a gang rape that evening. True, she had been paid for it — and paid very well by local standards — and had consented to it quite eagerly; but all that was with the heart and mind. The flesh itself — the living cells of her labia and vagina — knew nothing of that. They had endured over three solid hours of being fucked. Three and a half, in fact. No wonder they were so contused and engorged.

She was much less shocked at the sight than I was. "You should have seen their pricks when I had finished with them!" she said proudly. And she drooped the fingers of her left hand and riffled them with her right to show how flaccid they were. "Worse even than that! I beat them all. You can put some of that stuff on if you like."

I turned the lights low and dabbed four or five dollops here and there over her swollen labia and began to rub them in as gently as I could. The sight of them had so shocked me that I had abandoned any idea of seducing her that night — which had been my intended response to her teasing. But, after very few minutes, she began to moan and sigh and whisper, *"Dio!* That is *so* nice. Jee-sus! You are incredible with your fingers. Go inside. Rub me inside!"

I obliged. I massaged her everywhere except on or near her clitoris. She squirmed languorously from side to side and arched her back to put it 'accidentally' in my way, but I avoided her. Her frustration swelled into something almost palpable in the very air between us. Not that there was much air between us, mind, for, although we had started these exercises side by side, her wriggling had brought our bodies into intimate contact from torso to toe. No girl could have made her desire more obvious but, no matter what it cost me in teeth-gnashing, ball-screaming frustration, I was determined to hold out. She was the one who had said, 'No sex please, I'm overworked,' and she must be the one to say, 'Sex please, I'm overwhelmed!'

At last she said it in her own inimitable way — without a word spoken. One tiny wriggle was all it took to press her perfect posteriors into my groin. There, one small writhe was enough to get my joystick snugly nestled between her swollen labia. She pulled my hands away from down there and transferred them, smeared as they were with cream and her own natural juices, to her breasts, where I started to give her nipples all those caresses I had denied her clitoris. She meanwhile pressed my merry-maker hard into her furrow, using her fingers to complete the tunnel that was already more than half formed by her labia.

With a languid, easygoing movement I withdrew no more than a couple of millimetres — the smallest perceptible amount; then I thrust slowly in again, slightly more than I'd withdrawn. Then out again, in again, out again, in again — each time increasing the length of my stroke by the smallest degree, and always as lazily as possible. She latched on swiftly to what I was doing and began to relax, too. It wasn't so much that she abandoned herself to *my* rhythm, for the rhythm was already hers. I'd hit on it more by luck than by skill but now I'd found it, I sure as hell wasn't going to lose it! What she abandoned to me was the effort. I don't mean she lay there quite passively. Far from it. What her fingers did to the underside of my fellow while I briefly lingered at the end of each new thrust was both subtle and wicked.

Since every thrust was going slightly farther up the impromptu tunnel between her labia and fingers, my knob was getting ever-closer to the hot zone around her clitoris. I could feel the growing excitement in the movements of her fingertips. More than feel it, indeed — I could share it. How rare it is for a man and a woman to slip so quickly into such perfect harmony. Marina and I could never have done it if we had tumbled between the sheets at the beginning of our evening, immediately after I had bathed her scratches; the tensions and frustrations we were now releasing needed the intervening hours in which to grow. And when I say perfect harmony I mean a situation in which *he* is thinking more of her pleasure than his while *she* thinks more of his than hers. My knob, which is, of course, the ultimate focus of all my pleasure, was thinking only of her clitoris — indeed, drooling at the thought. And her fingers, as he drew closer and yet closer to that electrifying button of *her* pleasures, were acting only for him. It was as if her nervous system and mine had fused together — especially at that place where men and women take the greatest joy in blowing a fuse together.

And when I finally touched her there it was as if something detonated inside her. You know those newsreel shots where they demolish a high-rise building? There's a faint puff of smoke at the base and for a moment the whole thing just hangs magically on the air — and then it collapses in chaos. Well, the detonation inside her was like that magic moment when everything is just hanging there, defying every natural law. It lasted less than a second, but that was long enough for me to withdraw, change the angle of my pelvis, and push my spermspouter where it belonged, up, up, up, as far as it would go. And then she collapsed in chaos.

Frantically she did those things that only a girl can do to her own clitoris, while I rolled her nipples between my thumbs and fingers, and raked them gently with my nails ... and began my own exuberant, unstoppable rise to tumescence. Shivers racked her from head to toe. Her vagina was a cauldron, seething with a more-than-natural warmth, casting a yearning enchantment over me as my tingling spermspouter leaped to life and justified his name with a more copious outpouring than he'd managed for many a long month. Gush after gush erupted inside that spellbinding nook, bathing my knob with its sweet, sticky heat.

She was in the throes of such profound pleasures herself that I imagined she did not even notice mine. But I was wrong. Finding, to my delight, that I was still as stiff as when we'd started — that is, stiff enough to fear that it might snap right off if I tried anything too athletic — I continued to poke away as soon as the last little thrill of my orgasm had gone shivering through me.

"Unh?" she murmured.

"Mmm!" I replied.

"Ooh!" she whispered, catching her breath slightly.

"Mmm?" I asked after a few more lazy pokes.

"M-m-m-m ..." she answered dreamily, in a low murmur, heavy with passion.

We kept up that sort of highbrow conversation for the best part of an hour, which proved to be one of the happiest of my entire life — and, she later said, of hers, too. Something mystic happened between us that night. I don't know how many times we came together — in all the important senses of those two words — but the bare number hardly matters. We seemed to have burst through the ceiling of everyday sexuality and risen to some higher plane where, as soon as we finished one act, we could turn over, find some new position, and start all over again. My erection took on a life of his own — one dedicated exclusively to the service of Marina. And her vagina — no, her whole body — had acquired a similar devotion to mine.

I wonder if she ever took the plane back to Milan and went on to graduate? And even if she did, I wonder what profession she finally chose? She certainly had one she could always *fall back on.*

JO'BURG: Chayvonne and Jade

If my encounter with Marina was memorable for its unexpected intensity, the sessions I had with Chayvonne and her young cousin Jade were equally unforgettable, but for quite different reasons. It happened first in Johannesburg and, later, down on the Indian Ocean coast, back in the days of 'petty apartheid,' as they euphemistically called it. There was nothing petty about it, in fact, which is what made our encounters so memorable. Non-whites had to carry passes and they went to jail if they were caught in white areas without them. All sexual intercourse, commercial or romantic, between different races was also punishable with jail.

My particular adventure began in quite an ordinary fashion. Often when I quote for a new contract it's part of the etiquette for me to take the MD of the target company out to dinner on the first night. If he comes with his wife, or she with her husband, the conversation can be rather boring. But if he or she comes alone, it often gets around to Topic Number One, after we've exhausted all the conventionally safe ones — yes, even when the MD is a woman.

Only once in my experience has such an opening lead to my going to bed with the lady MD herself, and I would classify her as a prostitute, not because she expected direct payment but because of the tantrums she threw when I failed to give her a cutthroat quotation (cut-my-own-throat, that is). I soothed her, though. I told her she'd changed my life — which was true. I told her that before we'd met I'd never have *dreamed* of going to bed with a woman in her fifties but that she had opened my eyes to all that I'd been missing ... that the hour we'd spent together had been the best I'd enjoyed that year (well, it was February) ... and that she had doubled, if not trebled, the number of women whom I'd now consider available, assuming they were willing. All true.

The following afternoon she came to my hotel and caught me packing to leave. Fortunately I was on a full-fare ticket, because I missed all the remaining flights that day.

Anyway, that was in Denver, Colorado, where you half-expect such things. But the 'petty apartheid' incident happened a year or so later — in Jo'burg, as I said — and the MD was male. Boy, was he male! He lifted hundredweights in his office, which had a specially strengthened floor; his skin was so bronzed that, if the maître-d' hadn't known him, there might have been some doubt about admitting him; and the chunky gold medallion he wore in the vee of his deeply deep cleavage was half hidden in a mat of hair that could have concealed a whole squad of ANC guerrillas. We didn't even start on any of the conventionally safe topics.

"I'll bet you've fucked more prossies than you've had dinners in restaurants like this," he said as we sat down. (He guessed correctly, as it happened). "I know I have."

And that was the point of it, of course — not to listen to me but to have me listen to him.

Which I did, and did, and did. His surname was Flesch, which, he said, came either from the German for 'meat' or the French for 'arrow' (*Fleisch* or *flèche*, respectively). "Either way," he assured me, "I've got *one* bit of flesh that can shoot straight as an arrow to the right target every time!" I'll spare the world the rest of our conversation.

However, I got one good thing out of it — I got Chayvonne's telephone number.

Considering the source of the information, I almost didn't bother to call her. I was already convinced he had a two-inch erection and could just about manage to get his end away once a month; but his description of the girl was titillating enough to make me give her a call.

She was, he said, half Indian, half Chinese, with all the grace and beauty of both races — and their instinctive gift for pleasing men in ways that our pampered western women have long forgotten.

I asked if she was permissible within the terms of the so-called Immorality Laws; I didn't want to land myself in jail or get deported with an embarrassing note in my passport. But he just laughed and said the police were taken care of — once a week. So, after I got back to the hotel I called her.

"Hallo? Chayvonne speaking." She sounded weary

though it was only eleven o'clock. Maybe she'd just taken care of the police, I thought — which, in view of what later happened, was kind of psychic.

I told her my name and who'd recommended her to me. It didn't exactly perk up her interest. "I can't give out much on the phone," she said. "But the service I offer isn't cheap, you know."

"From what Flesch told me about you, I'd be astonished if it were."

The answer satisfied her enough to ask where I was. When I told her she said, "I can't go there. Some places they let me pass for white but not there. I'm afraid you'll have to come here." She gave me the directions.

It was only three blocks away and I was there in under ten minutes. This was before the days of ATMs and the widespread use of credit cards, so I had plenty of cash on me. Flesch had mentioned a starting price of three hundred rand, or just over a hundred and fifty quid, which was a lot for a non-white girl. But Chayvonne must have had heavy expenses, too. She was working without a permit in a white area and was selling sex to an all-white clientele.

The security at her door was impressive. There was a glass lobby where all first-time customers had to strip and show an erection. Only then did she press a buzzer that opened an electric lock and allowed the man in to her actual apartment — or studio, as she called it, for she was not allowed to live there, of course. I'm sure a secret camera photographed me in that state of arousal, for blackmail is a game both sides can play. But what a depressing atmosphere in which to enjoy the glories of sex! A man would have to be hopelessly addicted to the sport to continue with the encounter. Fortunately I was — and had not had a fix for more than a week. As I strode in, still naked, I reflected wryly that the tail was wagging the dog in more ways than one.

In one respect, at least, Flesch was no liar. Chayvonne was, indeed, exquisite. She had all the most beautiful features of both Indian and Chinese girls, perfectly blended: high Chinese cheekbones; dark, soulful, intelligent Chinese eyes; an aristocratic Indian nose; sensuous Indian lips; and a long, stately Asiatic neck. A silken Indian bodice showed her slim, flat stomach and generous hips — and it only just concealed a gorgeous pair of heavy, Indian breasts. Her legs were clad in harem pants that looked open at the crotch, though from my angle I couldn't be sure. I hoped they were. The very thought of it cranked my fellow up another notch. I gave her six hundred rand at once — and told her she was well worth it just to look at. Also I wanted all questions of money out of the way before we started.

She threw it carelessly on the hall table and led me directly to a small sitting room, with a low divan against one wall, a genuine bear-skin rug, and loads of scattered cushions, large and small. "We could fool around out here for a while?" she suggested, "Or d'you want to take me straight to bed?"

I would have preferred a lot of fooling around out here, but I detected that note of weariness in her again, so I said, "It's late. I guess you've had a long day. Let's just go straight to bed."

It stung her professionalism. "I don't mind …" she began.

I took her arm and guided her firmly among the cushions to the only other door in sight. The bed was a huge divan, also liberally scattered with cushions, all of silk. The cover, a dark red sheet, was freshly laundered. There was a bathroom beyond.

"Honestly …" she tried again.

"Listen," I assured her. "It doesn't all have to be crowded into this one time. I'm here in Jo'burg for several days — and you're going to fill an hour or two on each of them, I promise. I'll be back again tomorrow when you're rested."

There was an odd hesitation in her as she digested this news — not as if she were reluctant but as if she were wondering whether or not to tell me something. Whatever it was, she obviously decided against it.

I laid her on the divan and enjoyed a long, slow, easygoing ride — making no demands on her except just to be the beautiful, languorous, juicy young woman she couldn't help being anyway. She was too weary to fake an orgasm, or perhaps she sensed I didn't want her to. She just lay beneath me, eyes closed, smiling serenely, and responding with gentle movements while I indulged all my fantasies and desires. Her vagina felt tight and firm whenever I paused momentarily inside her, and yet it was soft and yielding to every thrust, warm and clinging to each withdrawal. When I came, she wrapped her legs around me and, lifting her tail, got me an extra inch or so deeper inside her. I spurted so hard that it hurt; but it was a pain I'd pay all over again to enjoy.

She let me soak it as long as I wanted and then opened her eyes and kissed me with genuine warmth.

"What was that for?" I asked in surprise.

"For being such a nice man, Riley. I mean it, honestly. I'm afraid that brief stay in paradise wasn't worth the money you gave me. But never mind. I think I know how to repay you better tomorrow." She grinned.

I started to tell her I was well pleased but she cut me short. "Listen," she said, "I want to tell you something. But first I have to explain my situation. This country's a powder keg, you know? God alone can tell when it's going to blow — or when the axe is going to fall on people like me. I know I'll have to get out sometime in the next year, so I'm trying to make all the money I can now and I'm salting it away abroad."

I thought this was working up to a pitch to ask me to help her smuggle the loot out — which I was quite willing to do. But no. It was more complicated than that. I told her she could get work anywhere, so why not go now. Did she have a British passport? She did. I told her I could get her some very high-class work in London, like tomorrow.

"That's the point I'm coming to," she said. "It's not just me. There's family, too. I have to be able to show I can support ... well, never mind the numbers, but quite a few people. And what am I going to say to the immigration officer? 'Look, man — I'm a high-class prostitute. Of course I can support them!' Are they going to let me in on that?"

I saw her point.

"And now there's a new complication. I have a young cousin called Jade, a pure Indian girl of sixteen. And she's in real ... Oh God, I can't go into all that now. Let's just say that for various reasons she's going to come here and share my workload. Not doubling up but taking over some of my hours and extending them. At the moment I'm here from two till midnight, which is all I can manage, six days a week."

"Yes, you sounded whacked on the phone."

"Did I? I'm sorry. That's bad. Actually, there is a reason ..."

She hesitated.

"Tell me tomorrow," I said. "If it's still important."

She smiled gratefully. I could have started all over again. "What was I saying? Oh yeah — when I started I was only doing about eight clients a day. Which is fine. But now it's crept up to double that — sometimes more. I just hate turning business away — because of needing the money, see."

"Join the club."

Another smile. Another stirring in my loins.

She continued: "A lot of the men said they'd just as soon visit me in the morning. But I can't do even more hours. So, to cut the story short, that's why Jade is starting here tomorrow morning at ten. She'll work ten till four each day and I'll take over to midnight. Which brings me at last to the favour I want to ask — but please feel free to say no." She swallowed hard and then blurted out, "Would you consent to being her first paying customer? I'll be here, too. You can have all the fun you want with both of us. But finish inside her and really make her feel she's something special. You could do that if you wanted. I really, really want her first time to be a good trip. The thing is, would you do it?"

Boy, that was a tough one! I had to think about it — long and hard. To be precise — as long as half a nanosecond. And I guess I needn't say which part of me was long and hard already.

The following morning I called up Flesch and explained the situation. He laughed and said that, since he'd got me into this dreadful mess, he'd do the decent thing and reschedule — but he wanted to hear all about it that afternoon. "And don't to anything I wouldn't do!" he concluded wittily.

I trailed Chayvonne and Jade from the moment they left the bus. She could have afforded a taxi, of course, but she was saving every penny; and a non-white, or *nie blanke,* girl on a bus marked *nie vir blankes* was less conspicuous by daylight than one with money to burn on taxis.

How did I know which bus? Easy. I'd casually asked Chayvonne what township she lived in and the hotel clerk had told me where to locate the buses that came from there. And picking out two such gorgeous females was even easier.

Jade, though only sixteen, was already as tall as her cousin; but she had the slender, slightly gawky figure of a young girl who has grown a little too fast lately. She wore a tightly wrapped sari, which cut out a lot of guesswork about her charms. Chayvonne was in coolie pants and a Mao jacket, but expensive.

As they walked they smiled frequently at each other and there was lots of reassuring, womanly laughter. Clearly, Jade was in something of a nervous state. I sauntered along, ten paces behind, my eyes glued to their sinuous movements, their trim waists, and their utterly delicious bottoms. I trembled and sweated at the mental picture of my swollen red knob nosing inquisitively in and out of the clefts that started between those curvaceous buttocks and ended in the fuzz of their Venus mounds. And then, shortly after that, both of them would be naked beneath me, quivering, I hoped, and pandering to my every desire. By the time they reached her studio I was ready to shoot myself in the thigh. I had to think feverishly of Flesch's most

erotic memories to cool me down and bring me back to
a condition where I could spin it out for an hour or two.

I gave them ten minutes to change into their working
outfits, put on make-up, perfume and powder their
bodies, pat their hair, and perform all those other litle
actions whereby women fortify themselves against the
male world — also for Chayvonne to calm her cousin
down.

But from the moment I walked in I knew the vibes
were bad. They were both wearing the flimsiest of see-
through baby-doll pyjama tops, suspender belts, open-
fork panties made of crocheted flowers, and sheer
peach-coloured silk stockings. With her small breasts
and trim waist, Jade ought to have felt like a thousand-
dollars-worth in that outfit. Well, she had a charming
smile, but she also had a lot of trouble maintaining it.
And when she wasn't smiling she had a pinched, rather
rodent-like face, with large, troubled eyes. And the
eyes remained troubled even when the smile came
back.

I ought to have backed off at once. Really, I have to
admit it was obvious to me she was in no state to have
sex with a customer. But I was so randy to enjoy her —
and there is always a tremendous kick out of knowing
you're giving a young girl the first poke of her professional career — so I stupidly ignored my misgivings.
And Chayvonne didn't help. I had copulated with
several hundred more girls than she ever had; she
ought to have paid attention to my shrugs and raised
eyebrows — all behind Jade's back, of course — but
she egged me on relentlessly. In the end it was a
combination of Oriental persistence and the intense
family devotion you get among both Indian and Chinese

peoples that forced Jade to go through with it.

I can't say it was an enjoyable experience for me, though physically she was everything a man could ask for. And as for her — the moment I'd finished she raced from the bed, straight into the bathroom, locked the door, and threw up. I felt like a geek. Chayvonne burst into tears. "What am I to do now?" she sobbed.

"Comfort *her?*" I suggested pointedly, feeling more than slightly guilty myself. "Break the door down if you have to."

She tried gentler persuasion. Jade opened the door and said, "I'll be all right. Just give me five minutes alone, eh?"

Chayvonne told her to take a long, hot soak; then she returned to me and repeated her question — what could she do now?

"Well, it's obvious what you can't do. There's no way that kid can take on clients for you."

"But she has to."

"There must be other work for her?"

"You don't understand how short time is getting. We have to make … I can't say it — it's too frightening. But we have to make one hell of a lot of money in the next six months and then vanish. Selling our sex is the only way."

I shrugged hopelessly. "But you saw her. And I *felt* her, goddammit."

"I didn't tell you everything," Chayvonne said quietly. "Her father's in jail at the moment, you see. But he's done some terrible things to her in the past, sexual things, you understand."

"Jesus!" I exclaimed angrily. "And you pushed *me* into a hornets' nest like *that!*"

"I didn't know ..." she stammered. "I never thought ... I mean — *nothing* that might happen to her here could compare with what her father did."

"But if he's in jail ...?"

"That's the point. While he was around, her brothers were too scared to try anything for themselves. But now they're starting to mess around with her, too. However, they know I have ... what shall I say — 'certain influence' with the local police, so they're also a little afraid of me. I can hold the situation maybe for six months ..."

"Let me guess — that's when her father gets out?"

"Right. So now you see the full picture, eh? She and I *have to* screw our tails off in the meanwhile. We must get all the money we can, and then vanish. Okay?"

I was very dejected when I left them. Apart from anything else, what could I tell old Flesch? In fact, I was so dejected I told him the truth — not all Jade's personal problems, of course — I just said something vague like, "It turned out that some uncle had raped her when she was just a little kid and it brought it all back."

To my utter surprise, Flesch turned up trumps. He said he had a little 'hacienda' down on the coast — a big corrugated-iron barn inside which he'd parked three mobile homes, which made it a luxury hideaway right there on the Indian Ocean shore ...

As he rabbitted on about the place, I thought he was going to suggest taking Jade down there for a long weekend and showing her how a real man could do it properly, just to rub my nose into it. But no! He was offering the place to *me* for that same purpose!

Naturally my suspicions flew sky-high. "Why not *you?*" I asked.

He coughed delicately and said his wife was going away and that he had certain standing arrangements with a 'little tottie' in the neighbourhood whenever that happened. "Besides," he said, "you'll be gone in two weeks but I'll still have my hacienda and Jade will still be in business if you manage to cure her."

Only as I was leaving — mumbling my heartfelt thanks and fingering the key to his hacienda — did he reveal the true reason for his generosity. And, in passing, he confirmed my earlier suspicions that he was all but impotent and so could not have undertaken Jade's cure himself.

"By the way," he said. "Inside the barn there's a row of latrines and privies along part of the back wall. At the end is a huge cupboard marked JANITOR, full of brushes, Elsan fluid, and stuff like that. But you'll see that the inside is much smaller than the outside. That's because the end wall is false. It's on hinges. Pull it toward you and you'll see a couple of videotape machines. You'll find lots of Ampex tapes there, some of them with quite stimulating stuff on — all recorded on the premises. Also boxes of blank tapes. If you want to pay me a little rent for the place, just tape a couple of sessions between you and the little Indian tottie, there's a good chap."

So there I had it. Flesch was an impotent voyeur who wanted to be paid in kind! (I should add — or maybe it's already clear — that this was before the days of home-video — though Betamax was a name one saw in some magazines and a few stinking rich people like Hugh Heffner of *Playboy* had cameras using that system — and the incentive to use them, I guess. But the idea of videoing oneself or others on the job wasn't generally

around. It's important to remember that — in view of
what later happened.)

I went back to Chayvonne, who, after some opposi-
tion, agreed to let me try to straighten Jade out, but
only because she was so desperate. Also she saw the
force of my two main arguments: first, that I'd had a lot
more women than she had; and secondly, that if Jade
couldn't make it with the man who, unintentionally,
upset her so much, then making it with someone else
wasn't going to prove anything. It had to be with me if
she was to feel as confident as she needed to feel in
order to take on all comers (so to speak).

We could have gone on a long time, arguing back
and forth, if Jade hadn't stepped into the room and
said, quietly, "I'll do it — and he's right. It has to be
with him."

I chartered a plane to Durban, then rented a car, and
Jade and I were alone among the dunes and seagulls by
four.

From the outside the place was more or less as
Flesch had described it — either a large barn or a small
aircraft hangar. It had huge storm shutters over unglazed
window-openings facing the sea; these would let down
to form serving tables when he held big beach parties
there. We opened them for air and to let in what light
was left that day, for there is little twilight in those
latitudes. Inside, the floor was bare concrete with rush
matting. Bean bags, cushions, an infinite variety of
chairs — chosen more for their sexual possibilities
than for comfort — were scattered casually about.
Also sofas, divans, chaises longues, and a strange
contraption that was obviously a love seat — a piece of
furniture on which a girl's body can be arranged in a

variety of lascivious positions and enjoyed in a whole number of ways by one or more men — or other girls. The bedrooms, bathrooms, kitchen, etc. were in three large, luxurious mobile homes parked inside the barn and raised on concrete blocks. I looked for the video cameras but they were well concealed, except for a couple of Betamax cameras lying on one of the beds.

The first thing we did was take a swim in the ocean; then we had a little barbecue — which she called a *braai;* then we talked. We'd already talked a lot, of course — about everything and anything as long as it had no connection with the downy little gap between her legs. But we got there at last.

I told her that no matter what Chayvonne might have said, no matter what sense of family loyalty she might feel, if she thought she really could not go through with this thing — then "please, please say so now. You won't offend me and you'll come to no harm and we'll get in a lot of swimming and still have a good time."

"Why would you do that?" she asked.

"Because I like women every bit as much as I like sex. Sometimes I like women more than sex. This could be one of those times. Just don't feel pressured, that's all. There is no bargain between us that you may feel you have to honour."

There was between me and Flesch, of course, but what the hell?

"But what else would I do to earn so much money?" she asked. "You know I must earn money?"

"Let's worry about that after. There must be something. I'm sure I could find you domestic work in England."

"I can type," she said hopefully.

"Even better. The main thing is — you don't *have* to do this. There is another tunnel with another light at the end of it."

She gave it a lot of thought; it was no hasty, off-the-top decision she made. "I love Chayvonne," she said simply. "I owe her so much. I'll go through with it."

She started to unbutton her blouse, but I reached out and stopped her. "We've a long way to go before we start that," I told her.

Her relief was unflattering but understandable. All that first evening we sat and drank wine, nice and slowly, never enough to get her tipsy, never so little that her conversation dried up. I got her to tell me everything she thought she knew about sex.

Her answers were horrifying; she knew several hundred more things than a girl of sixteen has any business knowing, even if it *is* her business. And all of them were vile. I truly think there is a place for castration in any civilized penal code — but don't get me started. Our conversation ended on a suitably farcical note, anyway. She saw how angry I was and so, to cool me down, she began saying it hadn't been so bad, and she was getting over it, and anyway, if she could just get over this initial fear and revulsion, everything would be fine.

Then she said something I ought to have paid more attention to. She reached out and touched my hand, saying, "Only I don't think simple niceness is going to work, man."

"What, then?" I asked. I was already dismissing it as the misguided thoughts of a confused young girl.

"I don't know," she replied. "A shock of some kind? Fight fire with fire?"

"And end up with every feeling nerve you possess being burned out!"

I really ought to have listened but, instead, we went to bed and I held her as if she were a baby of mine — one of the trillion-trillion I've spent in women's bellies and never seen. Her long confession had exhausted her. But it had also relieved a lot of her tension. And (or so I comforted myself) to be held by a man who, for the moment, wanted nothing of her sex, was an additional solace, too. Anyway, she fell asleep pretty quickly.

My anger had passed when I awoke. In its place was a sense of black despair. How, having heard that awful story, could I entertain the slightest hope that I might give this child even the most rudimentary understanding of the mutual pleasures a man and a woman can find in each other's bodies?

Jade was up and about, naked as Eve, humming to herself and cooking a four-stack of waffles each, laced, as the menus all say, with maple syrup. What a fabulous body! God, if only I could pull it off!

For black despair read dark gray.

But I still wondered what I was trying to do — and whom I was trying to kid. I was no psychiatrist. I knew there were religious techniques for changing people's whole outlook in a blinding flash of revelation, but they turn drunks into saints and whores into angels. All those psychic reversals — they involve some great whammo of a shock. I remembered vaguely that she had hinted at something of that sort the previous night. But what was I to do? Sneak up on her with two bare wires and a magneto? Or rape her?

Still, I had promised to try, so I reasoned it out with

her as far as I could. And I told her, too, to gain her best cooperation. "As I see it, kid," I said, "the first thing to do is forget me, forget what I might want, forget what *any* man might want — just wipe us off the slate. And then we can concentrate on you. Let's work on the way you feel about yourself. How you think about your body, especially your own sexual feelings. Whatever they are — good or bad, and in your case, entirely bad, I'd guess — you've got to find a place to hide them inside yourself before you can work professionally. But — here's the tough bit — you've got to know what the pleasure of sex *is*. You've got to know what it sounds like and feels like to a man when a woman has her jollies underneath him — or on top, or wherever. You've got to be able to deliver that — six, eight, ten times a day."

"Also to know what the pleasure feels like for a man?" she suggested.

I cleared my throat modestly. "Well, I think I can definitely help you there — but not yet. Let's talk some more. Talk till you're sick of it. Till you're fit to scream. Talk it right out of your system."

There went a couple of hours. Sometimes we sat inside, sometimes we walked up and down the sand. Mostly I let her do the talking — to get all that degradation out of her. But then I thought I ought to be topping up the emptiness it left behind with something more positive. I tried telling her how beautiful she was, but that was wrong. Much too premature. I suddenly became a threat again, because men tell women how beautiful they are for only one reason.

We went back indoors and, taking a chance, I ran some of the videos. They were good. Flesch had money

and these were the best that stuff can buy. And, thank
God, he wasn't into SM or stuff with animals or children.
A couple of hours of people looking happy about sex,
and especially of women in transports of ultimate
pleasure, had some slight effect on Jade, I think. I took
every chance to relate it to her. One of the girls was
also Indian, about eighteen. I kept saying things like,
"Oh, this girl is good! Just look at that!" You couldn't
freeze frame in those days — at least, I didn't know
how to — but you could run the tape back and play it
again.

Of course, I didn't just concentrate on the Indian.
Any girl with a back like Jade's, or hips like Jade's, or
breasts or thighs like Jade's came in for especial praise.
Then, for most of the afternoon, we forgot about sex
entirely and just swam or lay in the sun. Well … she
forgot about sex, maybe. I was getting as horny as I'd
ever been.

After supper I had a brainwave. "Why don't I take a
camera," I said, "and make *it* look at you the way a man
would? You take off your clothes in a sexy way — like
you saw some of those girls doing — and I'll turn the
lens into a man's eye. I'll make it *adore* you, I promise!"

She could never have done it if I had asked her to
undress for me. The camera made all the difference.
Instead of relating personally to *me* she was performing
impersonally to *it*. As she turned and swayed before
me, I zoomed in and out on every sexy bit of her as she
laid it bare — her calves and thighs, her slim young
arms, her baby breasts and nipples — which she caressed
most lasciviously — her willowy waist, her trim belly,
her tight, pale bottom, and her downy mound of Venus
— which was where I intended to finish the recording.

But, quite unasked, she sank into an armchair, threw one thigh over its side and spread herself wide for one glorious final shot of her parted labia and the sweet little crinkle-edged hole between them. No man ever adored a girl's holey-of-holeys as lasciviously as my camera lens did then.

The playback held her enthralled. She watched it three times. The second time I saw something that made me sit up: when she caressed her breasts for the camera, her nipples swelled and hardened! I hadn't noticed it during the filming at all. I said nothing until the third run-through. When I pointed it out, she bit her lip and blushed. I kissed her softly and told her she really was beautiful.

That night I said to her, "Now this is all we're going to do." And I knelt over her and lowered my lips to her nipples and suckled them firm again. I let my aching, bone-hard tool just bang about over her belly, bush, and thighs — wherever it would, sort of casual and accidental.

I stopped before her breathing got too disordered. But there it was — the first tiny but truly sexual pleasure she had ever experienced. I had a wet dream that night, which I often do after several days of abstinence, and usually on the night before I know I'm going to go out and pick up a girl. They say it's the gene's way of perpetuating itself: sweeping out tired, stale, week-old semen and making sure she gets only the fresh-made, lively stuff.

I played with her breasts again in the morning, this time with my fingers — lying behind her and pinching and folding her nipples gently. Her pleasure seemed sharper, so I took a risk. I took a vibrator from one of the drawers, warmed it up, and got her to apply it to herself while I went back to pleasuring her breasts.

She got so close to an orgasm it was like electricity — in fact, she thought it was some kind of leakage of current from the vibrator. It took her quite a time to calm down. Then we tried again. This time she was more ready for it, and sighed and moaned with the pleasure, but still she couldn't come fully to a climax.

I remembered myself at fourteen, masturbating for hours at a time and having more orgasms than I could count before dropping off into an exhausted sleep. I tried to see if it was the same with her. We stayed the whole morning in bed and she kept getting so close — and then falling off again. If I hadn't swept out all my tired old semen during the night, I'd never have been able to stay out of her. The odd thing was she'd never had an orgasm in her life and yet she knew, or her body knew, she was within a whisker of getting there. The tension became unbearable.

At last I felt the time was ready. I thought the touch of real hard flesh might help her. But the moment I got near — just pressing gently with my knob against the back end of her cleft — she went into a spasm of fear that killed everything.

It mortified her, of course. She truly did want to try and conquer it. But I backed right off and said we'd stay there for as long as it took.

Over the next two days we tried everything — getting her drunk, long hot baths, sensual massage, more porn videos … And time and again we came so close to success; but always at the last moment her old fears and revulsions ducked up and killed it.

In the end I admitted defeat. The orgasm was the

key to it. Instinctively I knew that if she could achieve it, I won't say we'd be home and wet but we'd be in there with a chance of solving the rest of her problem. But, seemingly, it was not to be.

"Maybe back in Jo'burg …?" she suggested.

"Maybe," I replied. "Yes … sure. Change of scene. Home territory."

We couldn't look each other in the eye.

We tidied up the place and packed. I was just taking a final look round, standing at the door, when Jade — who had already gone out to the car — came running back in with a look of abject terror on her face.

"It's the police," she said.

I didn't even check. "Get in there and hide under one of the beds," I told her.

It was a police car, all right. I didn't like the slow confidence with which it came nosing down the sandy lane to our barn. Nor the deadly gentleness with which it bounced to a halt. Nor the way those two great cliffs of young white manhood got lazily out — Hunk and Hulk, I'll call them. Nor the dreamy, knowing smiles on their faces. Nor the truncheons that hung at their waists. Nor the way they adjusted their crotches as they strolled toward me at the door. In fact, I didn't like one single thing about them.

"Where is she, man?" Hulk asked.

"There must be some mistake. I'm alone here."

My English accent creased them up. "Ay'm aleouwn heah!" they mocked, taking off their caps and bowing to each other. Then Hunk turned to me and his smile vanished. "She was seen, jong. You were both seen. Now you may not understand our morality laws, but it makes no difference. It's jail for her and it's jail for you." He picked up my arm and handed it to Hulk. "Cuff him to something."

Hulk smiled apologetically at me. "Hold it a mo," he called after his brother guardian of morality. "I think we're being a little harsh here." He looked solicitously at me. "I suppose you haven't even heard of our morality laws."

I assured him I hadn't.

"You see," he said to the other. "It's not his fault. I think maybe we can work something out, eh?"

I took what I thought was my cue. "You've obviously come quite far out of your way on this wild goose chase. If I can … make it up to you in some way, perhaps?"

Hunk abandoned his search and came back to me. "Of course you can make it up, jong. Just tell her to come out from where she's hiding. Then we'll have a good look at her. Then we'll tell you how to make it up — in cash or" — he sniffed — "in kind."

"Or both." Hulk grinned.

Jade stepped from the video studio and said quietly, "It's all right. I'll give them what they want."

"No!" I shouted. "Stay there." Frantically I turned to the two men. "It's not what you think. She's had bad syphilis. I've been curing her."

Jade joined us, smiling serenely. "It's not true," she said quietly, and with far more conviction than I had been able to show. "He's only trying to shield me." She said to me, with even more conviction, "Honestly, man — I'll be all right." She smiled at both of them. "Which of you first?"

Hulk unholstered his truncheon and held it at the base; the crudely phallic implications made them smile.

They gripped it with increasing parody of a masturbatory climax and orgasm until Hunk's hand capped the top. Hulk masturbated it two or three times from the base and said, "Good luck, jong. Don't be *soft* on her, now."

Hunk grabbed Jade by the elbow and started pulling her toward one of the bedrooms. She smiled back sweetly over her shoulder. "Why don't you both come along? Unless, of course, one of you is ashamed of his prick in front of the other?"

This was a Jade I'd never seen before — the Jade I'd spent three days searching for.

It took me all of ten seconds to understand her perverse-seeming invitation; I only twigged when I saw that she had led them into the room with the hidden, *remote-controlled* video camera. It wouldn't do Jade much good — that is, it wouldn't get her out of being raped by these two thugs — but it would give Flesch something to drool over, and some evidence he could hold against them if they ever called again while he was entertaining *nie blanke* girls out there. Suddenly I felt very proud of Jade.

I mooched slowly around, getting ever nearer the recording studio. As soon as I was close enough I whipped in, set it to record, switched the monitor line to the TV set outside, and took the remote control for the camera out there with me. If they looked out to check on me, they'd think I was just watching some old soap.

By the time I was settled she had almost finished her striptease. Hunk and Hulk stood staring at that delightful pubescent body with some very threatening-looking bulges in their pants. Cool as a cucumber she went over to them, knelt before them, and undid their flies. The two *things* that sprang out frightened me — Lord knows what they did to her. A lot of big, hunky men don't have tackle to match, but these two did. Like a little pro she took Hunk's great rod straight into her mouth. It was not something we had done, of course, but she'd seen it on the videos. And, thanks to her father, it wasn't her first time, anyway. Hulk got excited just watching. He began holding that massive tool in his right hand, just like a truncheon, and whacking it down into the palm of his left. When she went to suck him, he thought it exquisite to knock her about the face with it, slapping her on the cheeks and nose and forehead. She just said "Mmmmm!" and closed her eyes and let him do it.

"Come on!" Hunk said gruffly. "She's got me randy, man. Fuck all this play acting."

He pulled her to the bed and almost threw her down on it. She gave out the most convincing sigh of pleasure I'd ever heard from her — just like the girls in the porn videos. So there it was again — she knew she was being taped, so she was performing to camera. Why didn't I think of it before!

Hunk leaped on her, forced her legs wide apart with his great rugger-player's knees, and, without checking to see whether she was lubricated or not, rammed himself in to the hilt.

"O-o-o-o-h!" Jade gave out a great cry of delight. "That is so ... fantastic, man!" she told him.

He grunted, lifted her slender little body up to him, and rammed her brutally for a minute or so — she faking orgasm after orgasm for him, also just like in the videos. Then he collapsed and lay flat on her for the finish.

Meanwhile Hulk had been tossing himself off —
skommelling, as they call it there — very slowly, standing
almost over them. She opened her eyes and saw him at
it.

She gave him a seraphic smile and, without a word,
manoeuvred Hunk into a side-by-side position with
her. "You'll love it this way," she promised him
seductively — pointing meanwhile to her now-available
backside for Hulk's benefit.

He dropped onto the bed, spooned himself up to
her, and went straight into her bumhole. Hunk's eyes
came wide open with shock. Hulk roared with laughter.
Too late to stop himself, Hunk came. And the mighty
throbbing and jetting of that great engine must, in turn,
have pushed Hulk over the brink. I watched them in
their spasms, their pelvic thrusts ramming them deep
into her — and all the while she gave out gasp after
gasp of ecstasy, and thrashed around on their double
impalement of her.

There was no finesse in them. Two minutes later
they were dressed. A minute after that, with ironic
salutes at me, they left.

For a moment I was too sick to go to her; I have
never been so ashamed of the entire male sex as at that
moment. On the video she was lying absolutely still,
staring at the ceiling.

When I stood at her door she turned her head to me
and smiled. "Have they gone?"

The acceleration of their motor answered her. She
gave out a rebel yell, straight out of a Hollywood
Western, and lay there kicking the mattress with a sort
of palsied shivering of her legs, which she held rigid
and well apart. Her smile almost split her face in half.

"You managed it," I said, crossing the room to be at her side. "You were superb."

"Superb!" As she echoed the word she stopped kicking and just lay there with her eyes closed, smiling seraphically. "Superb."

Great slugs of semen were weeping between her labia. I took a handful of tissues and began wiping her there.

"Mmmmm!" she said again, reaching up for more pressure from my hand.

"There's no need to go on now." I laughed. "You've even convinced me. Lift up and I'll wipe the other hole."

"Why?" she asked with a lazy grin.

I stared again at the mouth of her vagina, where more and yet more semen was oozing out. "You mean … *both of them?*"

"Mmmm!" she sighed. "You'd better call Chayvonne back and tell her we cracked it at last. And, listen, man — poor, good, patient man — would two more fantastic days and nights here be long enough for you to work off your frustration? Not to mention me paying off my debt to you?"

HAMBURG: Gisela, Mutti, and Romy

I always avoided girls-in-windows until I saw Gisela. Maybe the whole idea of putting a semi-naked girl in a shop window, like any other bit of merchandise, was a shade too honest for me. The slight deception, or element of fantasy, involved in meeting a girl in her own 'house' — either her own solo workplace or the salon of a regular sporting house — was more to my taste. But Gisela, as I say, was different. For a start, she had her back to the window.

I was walking down Herbertstraße in St.-Pauli, Hamburg's world-famous red-light district, looking at the girls in the windows and working up an appetite for a more private purchase in the Eros Centre (motto: *Sex with a heart* — although the German version, *Sex mit Herz,* must make a lot of foreigners think that the car-rental business is something other in Germany). And there, among the simpering, lacquered-smile faces of the girls in all the other windows, was this coldly contemptuous back.

I stopped and stared.

It wasn't even a particularly naked back. She was wearing an only slightly see-through negligée of black tulle, through which once could just about glimpse her rather trim figure. The thin, dark line of her bra strap was visible only when she moved; she was either wearing skin-coloured panties or none at all. Her trim waist swelled out to invitingly generous hips and her long, blonde hair straggled halfway down her back in a loosely tied hank. She appeared to be sitting at a table, writing.

The German equivalent of a Mills & Boon romance, perhaps? Or a thoroughly Germanic treatise on 'The Socio-Sexual-Economic Nexus in St.-Pauli'? I had to know.

I knocked at her window. She glanced briefly over her shoulder, long enough for me to register that she was quite pretty and that she was wearing John Lennon-style glasses. So it was probably the sociological thesis. She called out something I didn't catch and pointed toward her door, which was of the stable-door type, like most of them in that street. In summer, the girls open the top halves and lean out so as to establish more immediate intimacy with the passing *Herrschaft*.

But this young lady did not seem interested in establishing any kind of intimacy with me. When I opened the upper half and poked my head in, she said, in German, "Come right in and close it behind you. Give me just one more moment, please." And she went on reading and jotting down marginal notes for a full minute more. The beating of my heart and Mozart's Haffner Serenade on the radio were the only sounds to be heard.

She knew what she was doing, of course — to my hormones and my libido, I mean. The front seams of her negligée spilled sideways over her arms, covering nothing of her body from the front. Her bra was the merest lacy frame all around her naked breasts, which were large and jiggly. Her nipples were large, too, also bright pink and burnished. And she wasn't wearing skin-coloured panties, either — so that when she sat, as she did then, with her left leg up on a footstool and her thighs wide open, I had a clear view of her open pussy between two legs of the table; her pale inner labia shimmered invitingly out of the dense curls of her luxuriant auburn bush.

"Good morning," I said in English.

"Sorry about this," she replied, also in English. "I'm very rude, I know, but it's a critical point in the argument."

"No argument from me," I assured her and sat down in a chair to enjoy the view afforded by her open negligée and thighs.

She smiled but continued with her remorseless jotting of notes. "There!" she said as she finished the last of them with a flourish and laid down her pencil. She took a good look at me for the first time and, by some subtle body language, managed to convey that she was happy with what she saw. "English," she said. "I'm Gisela, by the way."

I nodded and said, "Riley."

"In Hamburg on business?"

"Yesterday I was, and again tomorrow I will be. But today … ah!"

"All day?" She glanced at her clock and saw it was half-past ten.

"Well," I admitted, "I didn't exactly intend to start this early but when I saw you sitting there — turning your back on the passing manscape — I thought, 'Wow — there's a girl with confidence!' So, here I am."

"For how long? How much time d'you want with me? Come back later, if you prefer, only I must leave here at one-forty-five. I have lectures this afternoon."

"You're a student, then?"

"Yeah. But I'll be back here between four and six. What I mean is you don't *must* fuck me now. Give me thirty marks deposit and I'll keep twenty minutes open for you at four."

It was all very well for her so say I didn't *must* fuck her there and then; she had no idea what desires she had awakened in me. I couldn't have postponed for half an hour. But I was intrigued at the thought that she'd accept a deposit, just like that.

"What if I just take a chance you'll be available?" I asked.

"You can do that, of course, but I'm very popular during those two hours."

I grinned. "And what if I can't wait at all — which, let me say, is much nearer the truth! What would half an hour cost me now?"

I fully believed that thirty marks for twenty minutes was only a deposit; the currency then was three marks to the pound, and a girl as pretty and as voluptuous as Gisela could charge a lot more than that.

And I was right. "Half an hour is ninety marks," she said. "It's easy. Three marks a minute. Twenty minutes — sixty marks. Okay?"

"Okay." I gave her ninety marks. She closed the shutter and the room was transformed into a small pink parlour.

The Mozart finished and they announced a couple of pieces by Beethoven, a piano sonata followed by one of the late quartets. "I want to record the quartet," she warned me, slipping a blank casette into her machine; I raced out of my clothes meanwhile. "Now!" she added as she came back to me, "I give you plenty of nice sucks then you give me one good nice fuck. Is that fine?"

'Fine' is the weakest of all the words I'd have used to describe the following half-hour. She led me to the wash basin in the corner and put five extra degrees of stiffness into my fellow just by the skill with which she soaped him.

"You go with many prostituteds, I think?" she asked.

"Prostitutes. Yes. It's interesting that your word for a prostitute is 'a prostitut*ed*' — *eine Prostituerte*. The

English word suggests that the girl made the choice. But the German word suggests that she *has been prostituted* — that someone else made the choice for her."

"It's often the truth."

"You think the German is more honest?"

"Yes. I am not 'a prostitute.' The English sounds wrong to me. I am 'a prostituted.' At this moment I am being prostituted. Someone else *has* made the choice for me — you have! I am being prostituted by you." She pulled an ironic face. "You see! I'm not a very good prostitute or I would never argue these points with you. If my mother could hear me, she'd kill me."

I thought it an odd remark but I let it pass. In any case, conversation was suddenly difficult because she took a small towel off a large stack and wrapped it affectionately around my erection and began squeezing it dry.

"But isn't it the truth?" she went on. "You made the choice here, not me."

"You chose to accept the money. I don't suppose you absolutely *had* to."

"That's true," she conceded. "Also, I'm actually looking forward to it with you, so I suppose I *did* make a choice in a way."

She waggled my bone and, holding the knob gently between thumb and all four fingertips, led me back to her bed. "Also," I managed to say, "you chose what we'd do — the half-and-half."

"Half-and-half!" She hit her forehead the way people do when they remember something they'd forgotten. "I *knew* there was an English word for it. Suck-'n-fuck is so inelegant, no? Would you rather do something else? I can do anything you want, even anal."

"No. Half-and-half is fine. I'd have been too shy to ask for it myself."

I lay down and spread my thighs as I said this. She settled between them and was just about to start playing with me when my words sank in. "Shy?" she asked. "You?"

I was enjoying the sight of her pretty, gamine face just inches beyond the stiff, fleshy rod of my erection — to say nothing of the grip of her fingers around its base. She waggled it disapprovingly as she accused me. "It's true," I told her. "Some girls I can't relate to — no matter how good looking or willing or experienced. They're just … girls-who-are-there-to-be-used. Truly sex-objects. But you I can relate to. Okay, it's nothing profound, but it's there. You're a real person, not a sex-object. You were from the moment I saw you. So that's why I'd have been too shy to ask for it."

"You're a fool, then." She winked at me. "Just for that I'll make it extra-extra good. Then you'll see what your shyness would have cost you, and next time you'll not be so foolish, perhaps."

Her tongue went out — a hot, wet, gleaming, pink blob of muscular softness — and ran the full length of my erection, right up the most sensitive line to its tingling, throbbing crown. In some curious way it was a pleasure even more rewarding than a straightforward orgasm, because it flowed into every part of me. My arms and legs felt as if fizzy water were flowing through their veins, while my body was filled with the most voluptuous sensations of warmth and relaxation. From that very first lick I knew that, no matter if my entire day came to an end in thirty minutes' time — the day I had set aside to the gods Eros and Pan — I would still count it one of the best of my whole life.

She was the best suckstress since Gazelle, in Bangkok. She had the most amazing instinct for knowing how near I was to coming prematurely and backing off just enough to keep me on the edge of that precipice. In fact, in one way she was even better than Gazelle, for Gisela's method of cooling me off was quite literally that. She opened her lips a fraction of an inch all around my tool and, holding it gently but firmly between her teeth, breathed in sharply, so that cold air rushed in all around, chilling it right down. And oh! The indescribable warmth as her lips closed around my flesh again and her tongue began its rasping caress and her throat its loving squeeze!

Then, of course, the answer came to me. I'd change now to twenty minutes of hot lips, sinuous tongue, and gripping throat, leave the remaining thirty marks as a deposit, and come back at half-past five that evening for a second go — the second part of a day-long half-and-half (for, of course, she would hardly ever be out of my mind over the intervening hours).

I was just about to suggest this when the sonata finished. She leaped up to start her recording but, to her annoyance, the announcer came in to warn of severe traffic congestion on some nearby *Autobahn*. Six kilometres of tailback! he said. What happy times they were! Nowadays such a tailback would be classed as 'flowing freely.'

To fill the time I said, "Who's here between two and four o'clock?"

"My mother. Didn't I say that?"

I swallowed my shock as best I could. "You told me

she'd kill you if she could hear you saying those things."

"Ah. Of course I pictured her to be here already, eavesdropping on us."

"Was this her room before ... I mean ..." I was trying to ask if she'd been on the Game a long time, of course.

Gisela laughed. "No! I've been doing this about a year now. I shared the room with one of the regular girls who could use those hours for visiting men in their homes or offices. That's all she does now. So, when she said the arrangement would have to end, I rented the room full time and got my mother to join me. Five weeks ago. I do from twelve-thirty to two and four to six every day and all day Saturday, plus Wednesday mornings like this morning — thirty hours a week. And my mother does the rest — eighteen hours."

"And the evenings?"

"Another part-timer — Romy. She's a ... how d'you say — ersatz teacher?"

"Supply teacher?"

"Okay. She's a supply teacher by day and ..."

"An ersatz lover from six to ... midnight?"

"She finishes earlier if trade is slack, later if it's booming. Also from two o'clock on Sundays."

So, of course, when I knew who'd be lying on her back on this same bed between two and four that afternoon, I also knew I'd not be able to resist a visit at that time. So it was back to half-and-half for now — or, I was delighted to see, more like quarter-and-three-quarters.

She pressed the button and the quartet began. "Now," she said, "you can have fun inside me."

I sprang from the bed. Her eyes went wide. "Let's start standing up," I suggested.

"Ah, good. I like many different positions, too."

I made the mistake of bending her forward over her chair to start with. I spent a pleasurable and self-absorbed minute down on my knees behind her, kissing her two meaty labia and exploring between them with my tongue … then another equally heedless minute in the standing position, slowly rubbing my knob up and down the warm, hairy furrow that pouted so invitingly toward me, picking up her juices in preparation for a smooth inward thrust. The moment came at last when I could no longer stay outside her. In I slipped. In, in, and evermore slowly in, relishing every fresh millimetre of her firm, smooth vagina and that luscious warmth, which is somehow both liquid and yet firmly solid. She let out a happy sigh and I closed my eyes, concentrating all my attention on the feverish, exquisitely thrilled flesh at the crown of that questing ramrod.

Some movement of hers distracted me and I opened my eyes to find her making yet another marginal note in the book she had been reading earlier. Ah me!

I slipped my hands beneath her and cupped the large, soft globes of her breasts, letting her nipples protrude between my fingers, which I then squeezed and relaxed in time to the slow poking I had meanwhile begun. She gave out a little sigh, well rehearsed, and let her pencil drop. From then on she was a hundred-percent pro, dedicated to offering her body for my pleasure alone.

There was no pretence that she was turning on, too; but, on the other hand, she gave every *other* sign of enjoying her work; she seemed proud of being so good at it and she seemed equally happy at my enjoyment. As I thrust, she arched her back a little more, offering me an even deeper penetration; when I withdrew she bent her back slightly the other way, increasing the friction between the sensitive underside of my knob and the more corrugated portion of her vagina.

She reached one hand between her open thighs and caressed my balls, until I had so say, "Careful!"

Then she stood upright, leaning back into me and holding my hands more tightly to her breasts. She put her own hands behind my head and pulled my lips tight against her ears. On impulse I licked behind her ears with the very tip of my tongue. She shivered and caught her breath — something more than a professional response, I felt. I sucked her lobe. She swept the hair away to give me a free run, murmuring, "Ja! Ja!"

When I put my tongue into the shell-like whorls of her ear itself, she heaved a huge sigh, pulled herself off my tool, spun round, grabbed it and impaled herself again, and, sweeping the hair off her other ear, clung tight to me, flattening her big, soft breasts against my chest. "Fuck you!" she whispered tenderly. "And fuck me, too!"

I got the feeling she was torn between letting herself go and pulling herself together. Most probably I was supposed to think that, of course; it was her professional skill at work on me. On the other hand, I know at least one sporting girl who, once we had become friends, admitted to me that she had an orgasm with just about every client. "Not a big one, of course," she said: "Two seconds long at most, often less than one second. And I like to get it over with early, so I can concentrate on the guy and giving *him* a good time. Often I give him a little preliminary display with my vibrator and I try to get it over and done with then, before he gets into me."

Perhaps Gisela was one of that same kind. She certainly gave a good impression of a girl trying to enjoy a secret orgasm by simulating a lesser degree of pleasure. Or perhaps, being a student of psychology and sociology, she'd worked it out that, since every punter knows that sporting girls fake their orgasms, the really clever ones would also fake an attempt to conceal a genuine one!

People think sex with sporting girls is simple and straightforward: You pay, and then it's wham, bam, thank you, ma'am! All I can say is that it's rarely been like that with me. As soon as there's the slightest bit of *human* contact there, you glimpse the usual mishmash of human contradictions and muddle-headedness. What am I saying? That they're people, too? Big surprise!

Anyway, there was Gisela, who couldn't get enough of my tongue in her ear, lifting one leg right around me, clutching me tight, shivering like an aspen in the breeze. "Can I?" she asked, lifting her other foot tentatively off the ground. "How's your back? Say no if you have any doubt."

I assured her it was okay and she lifted the other leg around me, twining it ankle-to-ankle with the one that was already there. At the same time she let out such a huge sigh of pleasure that I knew we were back on the familiar territory of the ersatz lover and her equally ersatz joy.

There were more little squeals as I waddled over to the bed and fell upon it, with her beneath me.

"Whoo!" she gasped, linking her hands behind her head as if to say, 'Put yours anywhere you like now.' She kissed me on the cheek. "I think I know what you'd like now," she said in a low, suggestive tone. "Just to lie on top of me and poke me slowly for the next" — she checked the clock — "fourteen minutes."

"Would I?" I asked dubiously.

"Just try it a time or two and you'll see."

I did. And I did, too — like it, I mean. At the end of each of my thrusts she did something with her muscles down there that made her vagina squeeze me almost as hard as her throat had done earlier. When I gasped at the pleasure of it she giggled. "Am I right?"

"Or is this just a dream?" I whispered. "God, I'd love to have dreams like this!"

"I can't do it for every man," she said.

"Does it hurt? Don't do it if ..."

"No, it's just very tiring, that's all. But if it's appreciated, I don't mind going on until ..."

"You keep it up till I come and I'll give you an extra thirty marks."

After that I poked away in ecstatic silence, enjoying every microsecond of each and every thrust. As I got nearer and nearer my crisis I lifted my torso off hers so as to increase the depth of each penetration still further. She chose the moment well to take my nipples between her fingers and begin tweaking them gently and raking them with the tips of her fingernails. Darts of fire and ice shot throughout my body and, almost before I knew it, I was spouting huge gushers of seed deep into her belly. She meanwhile increased the intensity of each spurt and the duration of the orgasm as a whole by giving me those incredible squeezes in perfect timing. She must have been wearing a cap because my sticky didn't vanish into her as it usually did when (as was common in those post-Pill, pre-Aids days) I rode a girl bareback; instead it formed a hot, hydraulic cushion around my knob, which was doubly thrilling. Finally it came dribbling out of her, making little lip-smacking, bubble-bursting noises as I continued to poke in and out.

I stayed stiff and would, in the normal course of things, have offered her ninety for another half-hour.

But then I remembered her mother and decided to keep it for her.

Women can often be sexually roused by situations, as opposed to anything physical that may be going on. One sporting girl — Dawn, she called herself — told me of a night when she visited a man in his hotel room and realized, the moment she set eyes on him, that he was a world-famous conductor. Indeed, she'd sat in the audience for one of his concerts that very afternoon. She would have enjoyed a talk about music but the man was very formal and distant with her. "Just lie on your back with your legs slightly open, please," he said. "I miss my wife so I'll keep my eyes closed and try to pretend you're her. Please don't move or make any sound or fake an orgasm or anything like that." It'd be hard to imagine anything more physically off-turning than that! Dawn herself agreed when I said as much. "But," she went on, "I just lay there thinking I was doing this thing with one of the most famous people in the entire world, and then I just came and came and came! How d'you like that — one of the few customers I wouldn't have to fake it for, and he practically forbids me to *breathe!* I tell you, that was the hardest fuck of my entire life."

I found myself remembering Dawn as I walked back down the Herbertstraße at ten past three that afternoon, because I, too, found myself getting mightily turned on by the very situation. Well, it could hardly be by anything physical, since I hadn't so much as clapped eyes on 'Mutti' yet. *I'm going to shag the mother of the girl I shagged five hours ago,* I kept telling myself. *And in the very same room, too.* There was also something exciting in the thought that neither of them knew it.

I did once, in my student days, spend a weekend at a girlfriend's home and, after a bit of house-crawling in the small hours, enjoyed an hour on the old fork with her. When I left her room to return to my own bed, absolutely shagged out — or so I thought — I found her mother waiting for me with a face like a thunderstorm. She beckoned me to follow her to her room (she was a widow) and I followed with my heart in my boots, thinking I was certainly for the chop. But as soon as she closed the door behind her, she slipped off her dressing gown and threw herself, stark naked, all over me. The daughter was sweet and hot and giggly but the mother was like a ride in whipped cream. The daughter found us, dead to the world, when she brought her mother breakfast in bed the following morning; she went straight back to college but I stayed for the full weekend — the first of many, in fact. So perhaps ancient memories were fuelling my excitement that afternoon in Hamburg.

The shutter opened as I drew near and a huge bearded man, a sailor by the cut of him, came out, hitching his trousers and breathing a deep sigh of satisfaction. Seeing that I intended to follow him in there he made a circle of his thumb and index finger and wagged it at me twice — the universal gesture of excellence. I nodded my thanks and knocked on the door he had just closed.

Mutti began speaking — in German, of course — even as she was opening the door to me. "Whoo! Let me get my breath back, young man. Did you see the size of him?" Her eyes dwelled, with a certain wistful affection, I thought, on the back of the departing bear. "Norwegian," she said as she closed the door again.

"He told me you were the best."

She smiled. "So I am." She held out her hand. "Annika."

"Riley," I said — but I continued to think of her only as Mutti. She was shorter than Gisela and more auburn than blonde. She was also plump, but with a firm, Germanic plumpness, quite different from the Anglo-Saxon puffiness so common in England and America. Her skin was finely textured, with a waxen shine on it, like a baby's. She was wearing the same show-everything bra her daughter had worn that morning, the very same one, I think; and why not, since her breasts were as nearly identical as made no difference. She also wore the same negligée. Unlike Gisela, however, she wore black silk knickers with lacy frills around the bottoms. Unlike Gisela, too, she had little English — just words like 'jigajig, suck, fuck, good time, …' and various parts of the body. So she offered half an hour of suck and fuck for ninety marks and I accepted. If Gisela was telling the truth when she said Mutti had been on the Game for only a few weeks, the woman was showing a remarkably cool, professional temperament. Just how professional she had become I was about to discover.

She took me over to the washbasin and gave me a lathering as thorough and as exciting as Gisela's had been. "I like big pricks," she said in German, keeping it simple. "Some men … huh!" She held her finger and thumb two inches apart. "You like Hamburg?"

Fortunately my German is up to trivial conversations; at a push I could even give an opinion of a book or movie. "Munich may be grander," I replied, "but Hamburg is wonderfully cosmopolitan."

"We have culture, too. Is that nice? You like that, eh? I can see." She rubbed her thumb gently back and forth across my fellow, just underneath the knob. "Feel my breasts if you want. I enjoy that."

I shivered. "Your breasts are very beautiful." They were, too — a delight to fondle.

"We have beautiful walks, too," she went on. "You should go out along the Elbchaussée. There are villas there to take your breath away — like palaces, some of them. It's nice to fuck me between my breasts. We can try that later."

I trembled, gulped, swallowed ... maybe I said something intelligible, too.

"I think you're ready for some real fun," she said, wrapping my erection in one of those little towels. The stack was quite a bit smaller by now; each missing towel represented twenty or more minutes of bliss for some lucky man.

She made a circle of her thumb and middle finger, locking it around the column of my prick, just below the knob — by which grip she led me over to the bed. "Also good fish restaurants," she said. "You should surely try the Fischereihafen. There's a good view of the fish harbour there."

"I'll remember that," I murmured as I lay down and spread my thighs.

"But this is my favourite meal," she said as she whipped the towel off my erection and gazed at it hungrily. "We got it nice and dry. Now we get it nice and wet again! Ah me — such is life, *mein Liebchen!"*

She kissed it, and went on kissing it while her lips slowly opened and her tongue stole out and began licking in small, secret circles inside that continuing kiss. Wider and wider her lips parted, though never breaking contact with my flesh, until at last the whole of my knob was engulfed inside her mouth, where her ever-vigorous tongue was still hard at work. I closed my eyes, lay right back, and let out a sigh of huge satisfaction.

She had the same trick as her daughter — breaking off every so often and opening her mouth to breath in cold air, which felt like an icy blast as it flowed over my hot, wet knob. Unlike her daughter, however, she took these moments as an opportunity to continue our conversation — or *her* conversation, rather, for I was incapable of anything but surrender to her considerable erotic skill.

"There's also good seafood at Bavariablick, here in the St.-Pauli brewery, but it's not cheap." Then back went her mouth and my mind blew a fuse as wave after wave of wanton, voluptuous sensations passed right through me.

Shc gave me much more head than her daughter had done, but I was past noticing the passage of time — until she lifted her head with a sudden jolt, cried "Damn!" and sprang from the bed. "Missed three minutes," she added as she stabbed the record button on her video player. Then, with an apologetic smile at me, she added, *"Black Forest Clinic.* I never miss it."

A soap opera, I presumed. "Doesn't time fly when you're having fun," I said.

"Yes!" She flung herself on her back beside me. "Now we fuck."

I reached for her knickers but she said, "No — soon — but first up here, remember?" And she took a swipe at an open jar of cold cream, which she rubbed lasciviously between her breasts — and all over my erection when I laid it on her breastbone. It wasn't something I'd done too often; more out of curiosity than any lecherous desire. But when she put her hands to the sides of her breasts and pushed them tight together, I have to admit that curiosity found its satisfaction at once — leaving lechery to crave for that same happy condition.

For the sheer number of thrills-per-thrust it beat even Gisela's muscular vagina by a good margin. Every woman I'd poked between the breasts in the past had simply pressed them tight together and left me to forge my own tunnel each thrust. But Mutti varied the pressure continually and made her chest rise and fall so that the sensation was never the same twice. More even than that — she bent her head toward her chest and reached for my knob with her flickering tongue and her gleaming teeth.

How she didn't break her neck I'll never know, but, of course, it encouraged me to poke as far as I could so that my knob vanished into her hot, succulent mouth with each new thrust — and stayed there just long enough for her tongue, and increasingly her teeth, to do the most amazing things to it.

In fact, they were so amazing that I lost the running of myself entirely and, at last, just kept it there while she skilfully built me up to one almighty orgasm in her mouth. The moment she felt it coming she pulled me to her and took my knob deep down into her throat, where she gulped and gulped and gulped, at first on nothing, then on gushers so copious and fierce that the pleasure of it and the pain of it combined to drive me to the very edge of consciousness.

"That was good, eh?" she said, pushing me out of her and smacking her lips when the last petty tremor had died in me.

"Fantastic," I sighed.

I looked at the clock, to learn that twenty-nine of my thirty minutes had gone.

"You must try our Hamburg specialities, too," she went on as I got dressed again. *"Bohnen, Birnen, und Speck* — very good." She smacked her lips. *"Und Eisbein und Sauerkraut mit Erbsenpurée* — my God!" She buckled at the knees at the very words, which mean pig's trotters with sauerkraut and pease pudding. Well, it takes all sorts.

Only when I reached the door did I realize she hadn't even taken her knickers off for me!

Outisde I saw Gisela coming toward me, to relieve her mother for the four-to-six shift. Her stride was jaunty and she called out greetings to girls, and men, on either side. She did not look my way, however, until she was within five paces; then she burst out laughing. "No!" she cried. "Did you really?"

I nodded and pulled a face that, I hoped, said, 'What an experience!'

"Did you go all the way?" she asked.

"After a fashion — your mother's fashion, not mine. Does she ever take her knickers off?"

"Not often!" She threw back her head and laughed uproariously. Then she asked if I was complaining?

I had to admit that I was absolutely not complaining. She asked, "I suppose you'll try and make it with

Romy tonight? Three in a row, eh, you naughty boy!"

I said I thought not, but already a little imp was urging me to give it a try at least, just for the hell of it.

"You have an English phrase for three in a row?" she asked.

"A hat trick," I said. "Actually, it's doubly appropriate in this case because a prostitute's pussy used to be known as her 'hat' — because it was *often felt* and hats were also quite often felt. Made of felt, that is."

She took out her notebook and wrote that down.

I had intended walking down to the bank of the Elbe and strolling back to my hotel in the city centre but I had such an ache in my balls that I had to find somewhere to sit for at least half an hour, maybe more. There was a little café almost opposite Gisela's workroom, a place where shy men went in order to sip coffee and schnapps, watch the scene, and work up enough courage to knock on one or other gates of heaven. I went there and picked a window seat, thinking it might be interesting to see what Gisela had meant by 'popular' between four and six. I soon discovered that it meant six men in two hours!

I still have the page from my Filofax where I jotted down the times. Her shutter opened at 16:02; closed at 16:03 (young student, jeans, long hair); opened 16:18; closed 16:18 (the guy was waiting outside — looked like a building labourer in his mid-twenties); opened 16:45; closed 16:52 (a seaman in his forties); opened 17:15; closed 17:16 (he was waiting, too — a middle-aged businessman); opened 17:35; closed 17:38 (a young tourist, looked American, in his twenties). The shutter stayed closed after he came out at two minutes to six. Romy arrived at six on the dot and opened for business five minutes later.

Free of balls-ache at last, I strolled across to have a closer look. She was petite, about five-foot-six with an elfin face and long raven-black hair, worn loose. She wore a red leotard that showed every curve of her slim, young body. In fact, it had holes around her breasts that let them poke out; she wore a translucent bra whose edges were inside the leotard, so you had to look twice to see that they weren't miracles of modern surgery; the uplift was straight out of my favourite fantasies. The whole crotch was similarly absent, as was the large circle that should have been covering her derrière. Concealment in that region was provided by a pair of frilly scarlet knickers with a purple heart (detachable, I'm sure) over the target for tonight.

From the moment I saw her I knew it was no contest. That *was* my target for tonight. If Gisela had been the clean, wholesome young student, Romy was the scarlet lady herself, the incarnation of sin and all degenerate practices.

I sauntered down to the banks of the Elbe and started strolling back tward the centre. On the way I passed the Fischereihafen restaurant that Mutti had spoken of so warmly, between licks. *Why not?* I thought and gave it a try. Her word proved as good as every other use of her tongue had been that afternoon. I had no more than half a bottle of wine. I took a taxi back to the hotel and slept the meal off for a couple of hours. It was just eleven o'clock when I taxied back to Herbert-straße and the session I had promised myself with Romy.

It looked as if she hadn't moved since I'd seen her last; over her shoulder, though, I saw that the pile of towels was down to just one or two, so her night had probably been as busy as Gisela's evening. If that were literally true, it would mean she'd done fifteen men since I'd last seen her. My spirit fell; she'd have nothing left for me. I should have returned earlier. Perhaps I should go away and return tomorrow?

The fact that I was looking for excuses ought to have warned me, but that competitive male *thing* wouldn't let me off the hook — even though here I was competing with no one but myself, my pride, my lust. I rapped at her door. She opened the top half and engulfed me in the reek of cheap perfume and stale semen — the gluepot stink of debauchery. I've smelled it in brothels and vaginas the world over but I hadn't noticed it there that morning. I made to open the bottom half of the door and go in but she put her foot against it.

"First we agree terms," she said. "Ten minutes of straight sex in one position is forty marks; four positions, fifty marks. Twenty minutes, a hundred marks. Fifteen minutes oral is sixty-five marks. *Soixante-neuf* is ninety. Anal is also ninety. Dominance is negotiable. I don't do SM." She smothered a yawn.

"D'you take everything off?" I asked.

She shook her head. "Only this." She tugged at the purple heart. "It's enough. Ten extra for the knickers. Ten more for the bra. And fifteen for the leotard."

"So half an hour, naked, will cost me a hundred and eighty-five?"

"Bravo, Einstein!" She only half-smothered the next yawn. "My advice — take ten minutes with just this off" — this time she pulled off the purple heart; which was on Velcro, gave me a quick peep at the portals of heaven, and slapped it back on again. "If you want more, pay for it, and we'll continue from there."

She knew I was hooked; I had 'trick eyes,' as a hooker once told me. She knew she didn't have to put out to get me. I disliked her for that. In fact, I disliked her for just about everything except her superb body, her fabulous breasts, her gamine prettiness, and a sultry aura of sexuality that just seemed to hang around her no matter how hard she tried to stifle it. I gave her forty marks and got undressed.

She stood watching me, arms folded, radiating disapproval though she stopped short of tut-tutting at everything I did. She didn't like the way I folded my trousers so she picked them up and folded them again; she grabbed my shirt as I was about to put it down and showed me a wine stain on the sleeve. "You should take more care of your clothes," she said. "They last much longer. Why haven't you got an erection yet?" She grabbed my fellow and gave him a couple of unfeeling squeezes.

Unfeeling on her part, that is; *I* felt them all right. They were brutal. The half stiffness vanished as it fell limp and flaccid once more.

"Dear God!" she exclaimed scornfully. "That's all I needed."

"Has it been a particularly trying night?" I asked.

She bristled. "I don't need sympathy from people like you, thanks very much. Come on — I'll wash it anyway."

She did all the right things with the warm water, the soap, her nimble little fingers but, once again, my fellow's response was no more than half-hearted.

"Have you been drinking?" she asked as she wrapped it in one of the last towels on the stack. She put her nose close to my lips and sniffed, apparently without confirming this new thesis. "Is it always like this."

"It went fine at the dress rehearsal this morning and the matinée this afternoon," I joked — unwisely.

"Well, I can't do anything with *that*," she said, ignoring my reply. "Give me another sixty-five marks and I'll try sucking a bit of life into it."

"But you said it was sixty-five for fifteen minutes of oral."

She shrugged. "Take it or leave it. I'm not a charity, you know."

I gave her sixty-five and lay on the bed with my thighs spread for the third time that day. But there all similarity ended. Her sniffer went back into action as she poised over my crotch. "At least you took a bath before you came here," she said grudgingly. "Some men are pigs."

She was as skilled with her tongue and lips — and teeth — as both Gisela and her Mutti had been, but, in a way, that was the root (sorry!) of my problem. Those two scrumptious females had slaked so much of my lust that little was left for poor Romy. I felt awful — angry with myself and sorry for her. At last, after valiant efforts on her part, she produced something like a tolerable erection out of that flaccid bit of hosepipe down there.

But my heart failed to lift to a corresponding degree. From the look of grim satisfaction on her face I guessed she imagined she'd got me there at last. But I knew it was a purely mechanical phenomenon — like a piss-proud stiffness in the morning; there was no erotic feeling behind it at all. I lay there in misery, waiting for the disaster to befall.

It did not take long.

"Now!" she said dourly and leaped up to squat with her fork spread invitingly wide over my deceptively rampant tool.

I watched as in a slow-motion movie sequence — and a slow motion of a cartoon, at that. You know how pliable and rubbery cartoon characters are? Then you get the picture. For all that she was a part-time prostitute, Romy was professional enough to be able to juice up her vagina and pussy at a moment's notice. So the big, pink, bearded clam that now descended toward me with pinpoint — or prickpoint — aim gleamed invitingly wet and gave out messages of the welcoming succulence and warmth that lay within.

"Please! Please!" I shouted into the empty silences of my mind, hoping against hope.

But Eros and Pan must have been busy somewhere else along the Herbertstraße at that hour. Mister Softee cringed at the first touch of those adorable, frilly labia. When his half-firm knob was lodged at the very entrance to paradise, he crumpled altogether — a little button of pink jelly on top of a still-stiff shaft.

Not for long, though. She must have sensed his collapse and so she made one desperate stab to get what stiffness remained inside her. Down she plunged — squelch!

And it worked! I was inside her at last! Oh, the thrilling warmth of that welcome! Gisela was forgotten. Mutti, too. Romy's was the only vagina in the world and I was inside it for my — and her — very first time!

Well, it did happen like that, I swear it. I know it only lasted a second or two, but the impulse was there. Announcements of my fellow's death were premature. However, when she lifted her bottom for another triumphant engulfing, what fell out of her was a shrivelled little slug, pink and moist and steaming.

"Shite!" she yelled, fixing me with a malicious stare.

A shower of her spittle spattered my chest and face and I was too afraid to wipe it away, in case she took it as criticism. "Sorry," I said miserably.

"I should think so, too. Don't you like me? Aren't I sexy? You haven't even touched my breasts."

"I didn't like to ask how much each touch would cost."

She treated that remark with silent contempt and leaned forward, resting on all fours with her breasts swinging invitingly over me like two ripe melons. They looked sexy enough through the gauze but the feel of them was all wrong. The gauze wrinkled harshly. I'd have had more fun, or cheaper fun, anyway, groping a blow-up doll in underwear.

She could feel my lack of enthusiasm. And I knew what she was going to suggest even as she drew breath to speak.

"Yeah — I'll give you ten more marks," I said. And did.

It was certainly better. She had breasts that make men's eyes pop out. If she taught teenagers by day, I'll bet half the class didn't hear a word she said — and no prizes for guessing *which* half. I played with them happily until I almost forgot that this wasn't really the whole point of the exercise. And she, too, was silent for a change, except for a bit of professional heavy breathing and the occasional murmured 'Mmm!' that didn't fool me a bit.

Or was I fooling myself? There was a tension in her that had been absent earlier. She held her breath from time to time and there was an odd gleam in her eye, a compound of her former annoyance and a new disbelief. And her nipples definitely swelled and grew firmer.

That was when she pulled herself away. "Enough of that," she snapped. "You don't get round me that way."

Her chest rose and fell. Her anger now had an edge of fear, even panic — not fear of me but of herself, of something in herself. She just wanted me gone.

"I think you're wasting your time," she said petulantly. "You'd better get dressed and go."

"Do I get any money back?"

She laughed harshly. "That'll be the day!"

A kind of recklessness overcame me then. I didn't care whether or not I got an erection but I wasn't going to be whipped out of her classroom like a naughty schoolboy. I still had the power, the potency, of money.

I put another ten marks on the bedside table. "I want you to take your knickers right off next," I said. Then another twenty. "Followed, *when I say,* by your leotard. I want you naked for sex in a several positions." I put down another fifty for that. "Take it or leave it."

She licked her lips nervously and eyed the pile of notes. Avarice fought with darker, less identifiable doubts buried deep inside her. "And if you still don't get stiff?" she asked, as if she half expected me to take it out on her.

"That'll be my problem," I told her.

"Okay." It was still not whole-hearted; she took only ten marks and pulled the strings that secured her knickers.

Why *couldn't* I get an erection?

Well, of course, the answer is too obvious to state.

And yet there before me stood one of the most voluptuous young females I'd ever not enjoyed, wearing a wantonly seductive leotard, tailored to permit unrestricted access to all her most delightful parts … and all I could waggle at her were a few inches of pop-star's rubber hose.

For the next twenty minutes we tried everything, but it was the saga of Susie in Perth all over again. Actually, if Susie had tried only half the things poor Romy tried on me, she'd have been lofted on a gusher of sperm like a whalespout. But not a flicker of interest did Romy arouse down there on the ground floor.

She grew angrier and angrier at my wasting her time.

I got angry, too. *Her* time? Who paid for it, for fuck's sake! Or even for no-fuck's sake.

There was just a flicker of interest when we settled to some *soixante-neuf* for she had one of the neatest, prettiest, most eatable pussies I'd ever buried my face in. And she worked on that flicker until she turned it into a flame.

At last! I told myself for this time there was a genuine, if slight, feeling of arousal behind it, too.

"Now!" she exclaimed again, springing from the bed this time and bending herself forward over the back of the chair, legs splayed and derrière pouting oh-so-invitingly at me. She was completely naked by now.

It should have worked, too. It really should have worked. The sight of a girl in that utterly inviting and trusting position has always had the most powerful erotic effect on me, and on my fellow. But even as I rammed him into her for the second time that night I felt him shrivel as before and, on my third desperate thrust, he dropped out of her and hung as limp as he'd ever been. I was utterly mortified, of course.

She flipped. It was just too much for her to bear, after all her hard work.

"You bastard!" she yelled, turning round and giving me a stinging slap across the face. "You shit-face! You arsehole! You cunt-butter-slime! ..." Insults I'd never heard poured unhindered from her throat while she flailed at me with her fists, slapping and punching me wherever she could. When she hit my elbows and it hurt her more than me, she got madder than ever. And lashed out even more blindly.

I was so taken aback, and so preoccupied in defending myself, that I didn't notice I had meanwhile developed the mother and father of all erections. Only when it started hitting *her* did either of us notice. She stopped at once and stared at it.

I stared at it, too.

For a moment it was as if *it* was a third party who had crept in between us while we had been so busy fighting.

"My God!" she said in a half whisper.

"Now!" I grabbed her gleefully.

"No!" She wriggled in my grasp. "You've had your chance. Time's up."

"And it's not the only thing!" My grip was relentless and fierce and, for all her struggling, I was far stronger than her — strong enough to turn her round and bend her over the chair again and whack my excellent erection hard into her.

Third time lucky! It not only stayed stiff this time, it even seemed to swell some more as she continued to shout insults at me and to wriggle and squirm in my unrelenting grip. In fact, it stretched the skin so tight I feared it might burst, like a sausage in hot fat. But the feeling was so joyous, the sense of potency so vast, that I would have gone on ramming away no matter what disaster befell us. A force-ten earthquake would not have deterred me now.

As I poked and poked, with each thrust repaying me all my earlier frustrations, she fell silent and ceased her delightful wriggling. *That won't work either, bonny lass!* I thought savagely, for I was still consumed with anger at her assault. *Playing doggo is just playing into my hands.*

But she wasn't playing doggo at all, as became clear a moment or so later. She gave out a sigh of pleasure and struggled to rise from the position in which I held her pinned.

But that wasn't going to work either. Having played the whore so badly earlier, she wasn't going to be allowed to play the game properly now.

She whimpered, she pleaded, she began to wriggle and squirm again, this time in genuine, or genuine-seeming, rapture, so that eventually, out of sheer exhaustion — for I could feel my orgasm coming on pretty soon — I relaxed my grip.

Effortlessly she rose up, lifting her arms behind my neck and pulling my face to hers, reaching her lips hungrily for mine. She knew my hands would go at once to fondle her uplifted breasts ... that my fingers would start to caress and squeeze her swollen nipples. It suddenly dawned on me that something in her, too, might have been turned on by the unleashing of her anger — that this was no sporting girl's pretence but the genuine thing. And in that moment I came. Deep inside her I felt my ramrod swelling and twitching and kicking, almost as if the skin truly were rupturing from the impossible tension. There was little left to shoot, of course, but whatever bit of the male nervous system it is that determines the length and intensity of an orgasm, it didn't know that, so it went on pumping and pumping my emptiness into her belly with all the vigour of a week-long abstinence.

And she meanwhile was going gently berserk, impaled upon me there — gasping for breath, kissing and biting my face, grabbing up painful handfuls of my hair and pulling me harder and harder to her.

When we had both calmed down a bit she felt I was still stiff inside her, so that she had to do half a cartwheel to get off me. She leaped on the bed with as much eagerness as — and a lot more joy than — she had earlier leaped off it to bend over the chair. "Come on," she said softly, opening her legs and pointing, rather unnecessarily, at that darling little slit of a hole nestling snugly between her labia.

As in a trance I went to her, knelt over her, positioned myself for the first jab. She closed her eyes, stretched her neck, spread her legs wider still, grabbed my fellow, and manoeuvred his knob to exactly the right position, changed her grip, and slipped him in like a vibrator.

"I have no more cash left," I warned her wickedly.

"Shut up!" She dug her nails into my back and pulled me hard against her. "Just do it. Do it! Oh my God — do it, do it … do it!"

Half an hour later, exhausted, she said, "I haven't had an orgasm for two years. I'd forgotten what it felt like. Can you go again?"

I remembered the way it had been in Bangkok, on my second visit there, when I went for the record — my own, personal, all-time best. The phenomenon of second sexual wind. "I probably could," I admitted.

"But not here," she said. "Can we go to your hotel? Where are you staying?"

I told her. "But I'll have to charge you for it," I added. "Thirty-five marks."

She looked at me as if I'd slapped her — thrown her generosity back in her face.

"For the taxi," I explained. "I gave you my last *Pfennig.*"

She laughed, and punched me playfully on the shoulder.

"Careful," I said. "You know what effect that has on me!"

We both looked down at my erection, which was now in a state of permanent priapism.

"I think I'll have to find the secret of making it all soft again," she said happily.

"And you will," I told her. "I'm sure of that. You may have to make several attempts, but I'm sure you'll find it before dawn."

Interlewo

There are about three billion human males in the world, of whom, say, one billion are too young, too old, too sick, or too gay to have sex with women - leaving two billion active heterosexuals. Let's say they average 2.5 fucks a week.

That's 5 billion fucks a week, overall.

Or 714,285,700 a day.

Or 29,761,900 an hour

Or 496,000 a minute

Or 8266 every second.

If the average orgasm lasts 20 seconds, then 165,344 men are climaxing inside a woman, somewhere in the world, at this very moment.

If the average fuck lasts 12 minutes, then 5,952,000 men are fucking a woman, somewhere in the world, at this very moment.

If we broaden the field to include all kinds of male orgasm, ranging from the 14-year-old boy, trying to keep his tossing-off down to 8 a day, to the octogenarian struggling to reach 8 per year, we can assume 2.5 billion males, each averaging 1.5 orgasms a day.

Or a grand total of 3,750 million orgasms a day.

Or 156,250,000 an hour.

Or 2,604,200 a minute.

Or 43,400 every second.

Following the same logic as above, 868,000 males are enjoying an orgasm at any particular moment, somewhere in the world.

And 52,084,000 are actively working their way toward one.

Broadening our scope still further to merely fantasizing about sex — which is something the average man does every 15 minutes of the waking day (each mini-fantasy lasting about 10 seconds), then we have 10 minutes 40 seconds of mini-fantasy per male per day. Add in two longer non-masturbatory fantasies of about ten minutes duration each and we have half an hour of passive sexual thought per male per day.

The figures therefore work out as follows:

At this very moment —

* Nearly six million men are fucking a woman somewhere in the world ...

* More than 50 million males are actively engaging in some kind of sex ...

* And another 50-odd million are thinking about it quite seriously ...

... every second of your day and night.

And, come to think of it, since six of the world's twenty-four time zones are pretty well empty, give or take a few Siberians, Polynesians, New Zealanders, and Tristan da Cuñans, you may increase all those figures by 25 percent.

So at this precise moment more than 200,000 men are jetting their juice inside a woman; and with every tick of the second hand, 10,000 more men join them with that first stupendous, mind-blowing spurt ...

How many of those men are getting their end away with prostitutes?

Well, estimates vary but the more cautious of them agree that there are at least 20 million prostitutes in the world and that they average four clients a day each. The average fuck with a professional (I am surprised to learn, but the research seems reliable) lasts only six minutes; clever girls! So, at this particular moment, something over 330,000 men are screwing a prostitute; of them, something like 925 are just beginning to enjoy an orgasm and a further 18,500 are enjoying or finishing one.

In short, more than ten percent of the world's screwing is commercial.

Think about it. Especially if you're one of those people who'd like to legislate commercial sex out of existence.

If you aren't, then think about it, too — though I guess you'll mainly wonder, *Who the hell is getting my share?*

BEIRUT: Aimée, Jolie, and Genevieve

For the best part of a decade an 'air-conditioned apartment' in Beirut meant one with a wall or two blown out by shellfire. When the hostilities ended, people like me had a field day. I don't know how I discovered Solly's, a rather run-down café-cum-brothel practically on the beach to the west of the city. I've seen old newsreels, going right back to the days of the League of Nations Mandate, and it was there then, looking just as ramshackle, too. The café section was built lean-to an even more ancient fort from the days of the Sultan, which, in turn had replaced one from Saracen days. The Sultan's fort was of the kind you see in every movie about the French Foreign Legion, but on a smaller scale. There a modern legion of men laid daily siege to three valiant young ladies who were proof against all assaults except a bombardment of dollars, pounds, deutschmarks, or any other tradeable currency.

The outer walls of this brothel-fortress formed a square of about forty feet; they boasted no windows, not even musket slits, which had been filled in long ago. And there was no other entrance than through the café, for Solly — the original Solly — had built his establishment slap-bang over the main gate. That was in the days of the Mandate, before World War II. *That* Solly had been a Jew; he had died back in the fifties. The Solly I met was fifth or sixth in line and was, in fact, an Armenian — a morose man with a droopy moustache and lower eyelids that hung clear of his eyeballs like a bloodhound's. Every now and then they filled with water, which he blinked and sniffed away. Just from the way he wiped the bar counter, slow and morose, you knew his life was full of woes; but what they were I never learned, for he shared them with none. He spent most of his life in the company of those three gorgeous young ladies, who would have brightened my darkest day.

I didn't finish describing the old fort or barracks. It had a ten rooms arranged about a central open court-yard — four each side and two facing the opening where the gate had been. The four corner rooms were small and were used mainly as stores for the café; the remaining six measured about twelve by fourteen, though each had one corner cut off to allow a passage-way through to the adjacent corner room. One of the Sollys had built a dividing wall down the middle of the courtyard, separating the three rooms on the left — where he and his family lived — from the three on the right, where Aimée, Jolie, and Genevieve worked.

Actually, they worked in the café, too, serving the clientèle, but if trade was slack they sat on high stools by the bar, drinking endless Pepsis, thumbing through old magazines left behind by the Americans, and tormenting the world of sex-starved men with their display of three of the most gorgeous derrières you could ever hope to see within four yards of one another.

Solly picked them — "Hand-picked them," he told me. Then, with a twisted grin, "Well, more than my hands are involved, actually." He made sure the customers' choice was always between a blonde, a brunette, and a redhead; Aimée was the blonde, Jolie the brunette, and Genevieve the redhead.

I toyed briefly with the notion of repeating my triumphs in Bangkok and Hamburg by going for all three in the same day — a blonde morning, a brunette afternoon, and a redhead night. But, as the man said, 'What d'you do for an encore?' — and I had at least another five days in Beirut. So I plumped for a more sensible blonde Monday, brunette Wednesday, and a redhead Friday. That, as it happened, was also the order of precedence among the girls, for Aimée, at thirty, was the oldest and most experienced, while Genevieve, at eighteen, was the youngest and the newest recruit to the game.

There were other girls, part-timers who stood in for the three regulars, but I caught only fleeting glimpses of them. In any case, my eye had been on those three ever since I walked into Solly's and saw those three tempting bottoms perched on their stools; and when I say 'my eye' I don't mean either of the ones in my head — I mean the one in that tyrant who hangs around between my legs and hoists himself up for a peep (and then some) at anything vaguely humanoid with two X-chromosomes.

Now I remember how I discovered Solly's!

The girls had this delightful habit of going for a quick dip in the sea after pleasuring a customer. That was during the day, of course, when trade was light and the sun was shining. So there I was, midmorning on the hotel balcony, scanning the beach through powerful binoculars thoughtfully provided by the management, looking, of course, for bathing beauties. There were a satisfying number, even at that hour, but one in particular caught my attention — a curvaceous, well-fleshed blonde whose generous breasts leaped out of her bikini top even before she hit the water. She wasn't over-eager to fit them back, either. And when she was in the water, and those two big, fruity bosoms floated like pale jellyfish in front of her, she made a few wriggling motions and then held her bikini bottom high over her head in a smiling, triumphant flourish. She made this gesture to someone above her, at the top of the beach. I tracked the glasses that way and that was when I saw Solly's for the first time. SOLLY'S BEACH CAFE, was painted on the side, and, below it the legend: OPEN PAST MIDNIGHT in French, German, English, and (I presume) in Arabic script. In front of it stood three men, cheering her in response to the bikini-waving bit. I saw them but, of course, could not hear them over that distance.

On the subject of responses, there was an immediate one from my tyrant down there — a twitch of interest, an electric frisson, an increase of about an inch in length, a swelling of the girth, a slightly more horizontal angle of dangle. I tracked back to the blonde, who was now making an exaggerated mime of cleansing her pussy beneath the waves. Once her point was made she stepped back into the bikini. It was all decorously done under the water and yet it was unambiguously lecherous in her every movement.

The tyrant was now horizontal and thrusting at my

zip, not painfully but with more than minor discomfort. I
knew that I was alone in the room (or so I then supposed
— but more of that later) and that my nearest horizontal
neighbour was half a mile away, so I took the tyrant out
to give him air and freedom.

When I got my sights on the blonde again she was
walking up the beach in a manner at once lascivious
and yet graceful. I mean, with a figure like that she
could have done an imitation of the crudest 1930s
Hollywood vamp. My tool got so stiff and vertical, just
watching her from all that distance away, that it almost
tucked itself back into my flies.

When the sweep of my binoculars brought the men
back into view I saw that one of them was now holding
a big bath towel at the ready to wrap her in — which he
did the moment she came within reach. He turned like
a matador, she slipped an arm around his waist, and
they strolled back into the café. The two remaining
men rearranged their erections inside their trousers.

I looked down at my own and said, "Did you see
that!"

His crimson face stared up at me and he beat the air
in time to my pounding heart.

"I wonder what that place could *possibly* be?" I
continued. "Don't you think we ought to stroll up there
and investigate?"

His nodding head beat more lively at the thought.

I raised the glasses for a further look and saw that
one of the remaining men now held the — or a — bath
towel draped over his arm. At that moment a tall,
svelte brunette with admirably long legs came out of
the café and walked past him. She wiped his cheek with
that gesture they use in all the movies set around the

Mediterranean, where bar girls say yes without the need for subtitles. She was wearing a blue sharkskin one-piece with good engineering support for her breasts, which needed it as much as the blonde's had done. Middle Easterners, as I already knew, like their women to be on the curvaceous side, with breasts like pillows and thighs and bottoms all puffed up with the promise of pneumatic bliss.

The tyrant's beat took on an edge of impatience down there.

The brunette went in only waist deep before she slipped out of her costume and performed a much less demonstrative washing of her fork, taking no notice of her admiring audience, who must have had the most thrilling view of her naked breasts dipping in and out of the waves. Unfortunately for her, this display meant she had to turn her back on those waves, one of which — the legendary seventh — bowled her over from behind. In the tumbling melée of foam and limbs that followed I saw a flash of parted thighs and the black delta of Venus between them before she scrabbled for her costume and, sleek as a crocodile (except that I never saw a croc with such an alluring pair of buttocks), slid back into deeeeper waters to put it back on. Then she actually ran up the beach to the waiting customer with the towel — that adorable, leggy, wiggly, swaying trot that extremely feminine females can't help making. He picked up her momentum and they practically raced indoors.

"The mystery thickens," I told the tyrant. "We simply have to go there at once and discover what on earth is going on at Solly's Beach Café."

I was so excited as I tucked him away again —

promising him it would not be for long — that I failed to notice my bed had been made while I had been otherwise occupied, not to say utterly absorbed, out there on the balcony. But, as I promised, I'll get to that later.

When I'm working flat out I go into a sort of workaholic stupor, during which I can forget entirely about sex — even that old, familiar outing with Madame Palme and her five fat daughters. When I emerge at the far end of such a phase, I can't *believe* how long it's been, not just since my last orgasm but since my last erotic fantasy of any kind. That's what the tyrant was trying to tell me up there on the balcony, as a matter of fact, for it had been at least ten days of unwitting abstinence.

So I trudged along that half-mile of sand in something of a *sex*oholic stupor, weak at the knees, hollow in the gut, with my heartbeat all over the place, and my prick varying from twenty to two hundred percent of a full erection.

When I was halfway there, a party of six men left the café, including the three I'd seen standing outside. They strolled slowly toward me and, as they drew near, began giving me knowing grins and winks.

"The blonde is the best," called one, in French. "Ask for Aimée."

"Rubbish!" cried another. "Pick the brunette — Jolie!" There was some indelicate pun on *la plus jolie* ... something or other, which I didn't catch.

"Ignore them," a third advised. "The young redhead's the one. *Elle est du tonnerre!* She's called Genevieve."

I thanked them and passed on. Each of the three who didn't offer me advice backed one of those who did; so it was fairly obvious that Aimée, Jolie, and Genevieve had each had her tail tickled at least twice already that morning. The very thought of it notched my lust up to screaming point.

The entire outing almost came to an embarrassing finale the moment I stepped across the café threshold and saw those three delicious, delightful, delectable derrières hanging over three tall bar stools, right opposite the door. Aimée, the blonde, was wearing a skin-tight one-piece dress of knitted powder-blue cotton yarn; Jolie, the brunette, was in a tight black miniskirt and a red silk blouse; and Genevieve, the teenage redhead, wore short, designer-torn jeans and a knitted cotton boob-tube.

I was the only customer there. Three pairs of eyes surveyed me coolly in the mirror above the head of the current Solly. I'm sure he weighed me up, too, but I wasn't aware of him until he pointed to a table to my left, just inside the door. Aimée slipped down off her stool and came over with a menu. I suddenly realized that the hollow feeling inside me was at least partly explained by the fact that I'd rushed out without my breakfast.

"D'you speak English?" I asked.

Most of that hollow feeling, though, was caused by the size and beauty of her breasts and her ripe, voluptuous femininty, especially at such close quarters.

"Maybe," she replied. " I understand English. You understand French?"

"Better than I speak it."

"It's the same with me and English. I speak you French. You speak me English. Okay?"

"Okay. One question, though — do I have to wait

until after you've had your next swim?"

She laughed. "No! You want a little loving now? You want me or Jolie or Genevieve?"

"You," I told her. "But first I must eat."

"Okay," she said. "It's more fun to wait a bit and think about it."

I ordered coffee, yoghurt, pitta bread and honey. Beirut honey is the best I know. She brought me the coffee and yoghurt at once but as she turned to go back to the bar a tall, well-built Italian entered and gave her bottom a playful slap. "Come on," he said. "I'm ready to explode with it."

Well, I knew how he felt.

Aimée glanced inquiringly over her shoulder at me. I shrugged and released her from any obligation she might feel to me. She took his hand and led him through the curtains at the back, giving me my first glimpse of the courtyard beyond. As she went she held her other hand behind her back, secretly showing me four fingers and her thumb. The man exchanged some badinage with the other two girls as he passed — too rapid for me to catch. He was about forty, with a little toothbrush moustache and wavy, iron-grey hair, and, I guessed, extremely proud of his trim figure and springy step.

Solly brought me the hot pitta bread and honey. "You got that, did you?" he asked after introducing himself. "She'll only be five minutes, truly."

"How can you be so sure?"

"He's a regular — a phenomenon. Whoo!" He blew gently on his fingertips and waggled his hand. "Every Monday, half-past ten, he comes here and has Aimée first, then Genevieve, then Jolie. Five minutes each. Then he comes back at three and has them again —

Genevieve, then Jolie, then Aimée — twenty minutes each. And he comes back yet again at nine and has them *again* …"

"Let me guess," I said. "Jolie, then Genevieve, then Aimée?"

"You got it — one hour each! Then — or so he says — he can forget sex for the next six days."

Even as he spoke Aimée returned, wearing her bikini again. She threw me a wink — and the towel — as she passed. "Won't be long," she said.

Jolie, meanwhile, rose and went out into the courtyard. Genevieve came over to my table with the coffeepot but I said I'd have a refill after partying with Aimée. I almost changed my mind then and there because she was, to *my* taste, much the sexiest of the three, with her sharp, pretty features, her lean, alluring shoulders, her firm young breasts, her willowy waist swelling to an ample pair of hips and tapering again down her long, slender thighs. When she turned and walked away, her brief jeans showed as much of her moons as jeans usually show of the average building-site labourer's; hers were infinitely more seductive, of course. But the more I saw of her charms, the more inclined I felt to save her up until the end of the week — to leave Beirut in a blaze of carnal glory.

I was licking the last of the honey off my fingertips when Aimée stepped like Venus from the waves (give or take a bikini). She made such a show of her walk toward me that I had forgotten even Genevieve by the time I wrapped the towel around her. I began to pat her dry at once but she giggled and said,"No — inside, you naughty, impatient boy!"

"How many times a day do you go for a swim?" I

asked as we crossed the café to the curtain at the back.

"Ha ha!" She wagged a finger at me as if to say that would be telling. "It's not every time," she replied. "Just to give us a little rest — and our poor *concons* — when it's busy."

As we went through the curtain I saw the Italian come out from the middle room, to my right — which I correctly assumed to be Jolie's room. With a cheery wave to us, he walked up the courtyard to the room next door — Genevieve's, obviously.

Aimée confirmed it by poking her head back through the curtain and calling out, *"Vivi! Tu peut le lui rendre tout chaud!"* — which usually means 'you can take your revenge' but literally means 'you can give it him good and hot!' I'll bet she did, too!

But by then I was once again oblivious to Genevieve, being fully occupied in drying Aimée's ample and well-proportioned charms.

"D'you want long time or short?" she asked. "I can offer most pleasures but not fantasy or bondage or sm — or not here, anyway. But that leaves ..."

I interrupted to ask what she meant by 'not here.' She explained that Solly's closed on Friday evenings and reopened on Sunday. She could offer special services at home then (but not to tell Solly). "Here it's just for *soixante-neuf* — you know *soixante-neuf?*"

I grinned. "I know it — and love it, but ..."

"Also *cunnilingue*, And I'm a wonderful *fellatrice*. Also ..." She mimed wanking with a salacious grin. "And many positions ... standing, sitting ... ah!" She waved her hands at the impossibility of describing them all — and grinned again to suggest that doing them was much more fun, anyway.

"How much for one hour?" I managed to ask at last. *"Hein?"*

"One hour. I come twice — once very quickly, then, the second time, nice and easy. How much?"

"No *soixante-neuf?* No *cunnilingue?* No …"

"Everything. One hour … everything. How much?"

"Whew!" She fanned her face, eyed my clothes (designer labels?), my watch (a genuine Philippe Patek?), my teeth (gold crowns?), my shoes (handmade leather or Corfam?) … she would have made the perfect Harley Street receptionist. She certainly had me pegged to a T because when she named a sum that translated to a hundred and twenty pounds, she hit on the very maximum to which I was prepared to go. It was also just about double what any local would have paid. So when I suggested ninety would be more appropriate, she accepted it happily and held out her hand.

After she had my money she became a different animal — confident, skittish, playful. We were now on her territory. She took my head between her hands, kissed me briefly on the lips and then lovingly, lingeringly, all over the rest of my face. "Long time no jigajig?" she asked me in English. "You come pretty damn quick first time?"

"Pretty damn quick," I agreed.

Back in French she asked me if I'd prefer to wash my own cock, in case of accidents?

I washed in a bowl in the corner. Only the coolness of the water prevented me from brimming over. She, meanwhile, took my shirt off from behind and then, when I was naked but for my sandals, she bent down and inspected me closely for disease.

Satisfied I was clean, she backed against the wall, opened her legs slightly, and said, "Here is good."

Her vagina had a wide, soft mouth but soon narrowed to a gratifyingly narrow tube. I went up inside her very slowly, fearing that a sudden thrust would bring everything to an end at once, and I was determined to enjoy at least a minute of her cooperation. I started withdrawing for another slow, measured thrust but she pulled me tight to her and murmured, *"Non, chéri — comme çi."* And she lifted my arms gently above my head and patted them as if to say, 'Stay there!'

And then she raked her fingernails lightly all down the undersides of my upraised arms, down, down, down to my nipples, which she then began to torment with lazy circular movements and gentle pinchings. Also suckling them with her lips and fondling them with her tongue. And the sensations this spread through me were sweet beyond description and exciting beyond measure. She spun out the start of my orgasm by at least five minutes and when it finally hit me, the throbbing at the tip of my prick was, in a curious way, the least exciting part. The whole of my body was consumed with a tingling, throbbing sensation that burned without heat and passed through me in ripples rather than the usual crashing waves. And it persisted, too, long after the last feeble squirt from my now sated tyrant. I glowed from head to foot.

I was still more than semi-stiff, so that she had to do a little gymnastic leap to get off me.

"Now I can wash you, yes?" she asked. "It's safe?"

"After what you've just done," I replied, gazing at her through heavy-lidded eyes, "you can do *anything.*"

"Leave it all to me," she said. "I'll do everything —

and I guarantee to make it last fifty minutes, okay?"

Was I going to argue?

I lay back on the bed and melted as her marshmallow mouth closed around my washed and fully revived erection. Cascades of her fine, blonde hair fell on my belly and thighs, adding a tormenting tickle to the tingle of her tongue, teeth, and throat. She sucked greedily. She swallowed like a drowning woman. She bit and chewed as daintily as any tigress with a cub in her teeth. She brought me slowly to the brink of another orgasm and then, with a skill born of years at the man-pleasuring game, stopped and breathed sharply in, letting the sudden chill of the air take me back down by several degrees. Gisela's trick in Hamburg.

I would have been sweating by now, even had we been at the North Pole. In late-summer Beirut, with the humidity already climbing, I was perspiring enough to lubricate the whole-body massage she now began to give me. For a while she just lay upon me, breathing deeply but otherwise still, as if gathering her forces for something special. It gave me the chance to 'sample' her, bit by bit, if I can put it that way. I explored each part of her motionless body with an equally inert part of my own. My shoulders examined her hands — without moving. My cheek perused her cheek. My chest, bony and wet, checked out the big, soft cushions of her breasts. Her belly lay mutely upon mine, I felt its every inch. And it was the same with our thighs and the lower parts of our legs — and, of course, *there,* at the centre of all bliss, where our contact was hottest and wettest of all.

And all these feminine delights I felt *simultaneously,* which is something I could never have done with my hands. My heart began to race. I felt hers beating strongly, too. After a while, when she breathed in, she could not suppress a little shiver. I thought at once of young Venus in Bangkok, who never climaxed with a client inside her but always tried to have her jollies when giving him whole-body massage; I wondered if Aimée had acquired the same easy habit.

Foolishly I moved my head to look at her expression, by which I showed I had noticed her tiny display of feeling. She at once faked a petty ecstasy, to cover it up. But that only confirmed to me that there was something she wanted to cover up in the first place. I stretched out stiff and closed my eyes, trying to suggest that I was going to abandon myself to my own sensations and lose all interest in hers.

And why didn't I do just that? What is it in a man that so desperately *needs* to hear a woman moan and sob and catch her breath, to feel her writhe and twitch, in an ecstasy she owes to him? Especially when the woman is a whore who cannot possibly be expected to respond to every client like that — indeed, most whores would say, to *any* client like that. A whore in Birmingham once told me that in ten very busy years only one punter had ever told her she needn't bother to fake an orgasm for him; others have told me they've never been asked not to bother. It seems we are so uncertain of our own skill that we need such 'proofs' of it every step of the way.

So I paid little attention to the rather commonplace sighs and gasps that Aimée poured into my left ear as she began to wriggle up and down and side-to-side upon me. Instead I concentrated on her heartbeat, which was powerful and rapid, and upon the much smaller flutters and hesitations that shivered her breathing in between the fake ecstasies.

The fakes, I noticed, tended to come when she wriggled her body upward along mine, bringing her breasts within suckling distance of my lips. As my mouth closed around her big pearly nipples you'd have thought the pleasure I was giving her was racking her whole body apart. From this I surmised that — with a client, at least — her breasts were no longer erogenous zones. A punter could do what he liked with them and he might as well be scratching the back of his own head.

By contrast, the tiny tremors and the little quiverings of breath tended to occur when our two sexes were closest together — most especially when her clitoris was oh-so-casually pressed against the root of my fellow. I guessed that at such moments she would be most abandoned to the sensations in her own body and least aware of any subtle movements I might make.

And subtle I was, too. Even I was hardly aware of the extra pressure I exerted so minutely when the pressure of her Venus mound was firmest against me. But one does not need to be aware of something in order to feel it — as Aimée soon proved by the increasing disorder of her breathing at just those moments. At the same time her fake ecstasies grew increasingly lacklustre, in the same proportion.

She lifted her head and glanced at me, checking to see if I was aware of her responses — the real ones, I mean. I was aware of her movement but paid it no heed, giving her the impression I was utterly abandoned to my own sensations. I'm sure she smiled to herself as she settled her head back on my shoulder and threw herself into her massage with even greater abandon — a smug little smile of satisfaction that she could risk a little more open display of her pleasure without giving the game away.

Actually, I think that once a genuine passion takes hold of a woman it robs her of all self-awareness. I've enjoyed sex with girlfriends whose cries have put on lights in houses across the streets but who, when we talked about it afterward, have denied uttering more than the most modest whimper. Aimée was not quite so abandoned as that, of course, but I'm sure that if we'd videoed our happy hour together, she'd have been surprised at the degree to which she abandoned her professional caution to her genuine sensations.

And yet she was a professional, for all that. A girlfriend having her jollies will indulge each thrill to its utmost little spark and she'll end up in a state of exhaustion, happy and well deserved. But Aimée, so to speak, licked the cream off the top and threw the rest away. After three or four uncontrolled spasms of delight she passed seamlessly from an understated but genuine orgasm to one that, by contrast, was almost comically over the top. And in that way she was able to mask her breathlessness and pull herself together — salvaging her pride by assuring herself that I had noticed nothing.

And why not? If she saw the chance of five minutes' quiet pleasure in an hour of hard, repetitively boring labour, why not steal it when no one's looking? I'd do the same.

I think it had a more profound effect on me than it did on her. I was so touched that she had condescended to take this small but genuine pleasure with me that I did not go on to do what I often try when I have a sporting girl at the end of my tool and thirty or forty minutes of indulgence still ahead of us — that is, to do all I can to turn her fake ecstasy into one that is genuine.

Again, I don't know why I like to play such a childish game. My success rate is hardly brilliant. To claim five percent would be boasting. And it hardly increases my own pleasure — as I proved in the thirty-odd minutes during which Aimée and I took turns to lead and follow each other in the ancient four-legged frolic. And when I came at last — bang on the fifty-minute mark as she had promised — it was in a way I had never previously experienced.

She was lying on her belly with a couple of pillows under her fork, lifting her derrière up into my groin, and I was as deeply into her as I could possibly go. Now normally in that position I'd have been thrusting away like a piledriver on overdrive, pinching my buttocks bloodless with each new jab. Instead my buttocks were all puckered up and bloodless, all right, but it was with the effort of keeping me deep inside her there while she, lying equally still, did the most amazing things with her vagina. She must have been flexing and rippling every muscle in her entire pelvic region to achieve some of those wonderful effects.

She continued milking me like that all through my orgasm so that the spasms merged and I seemed to spend into her in one continuous stream — the remainder of my ten days' worth of high-octane lust.

But the trouble with enjoying an hour of superb, gourmet sex in mid-morning — especially after so long a period of abstinence — is the same as with a good, gourmet Chinese meal: Within a couple of hours you're ready for more. The same is true of Chinese girls.

Actually, the same is true of *all* girls, so what am I going
on about? It was certainly true of Aimée, Jolie, and
Genevieve on that particular day. My prick, which
snoozed contendedly until lunch had come and gone,
began to stir by midafternoon, reminding me of that
long, shameful abstinence. By the time I was sipping
my evening aperitif, it was in a hot rage down there,
threatening once again to burst my flies, just as it had
done on the balcony that morning.

My brain fell into a depressing cycle: I would decide
to go back to Solly's after dinner and take an hour of
horizontal refreshment with her; I'd break out in a
sweat at the very thought of it, my belly would go
hollow, my knees would start to tremble. Then my
puritan half would ask, 'Where's your self-control,
man? If you give in now, you'll give in tomorrow, too,
and Wednesday, and Thursday … You'll be a wreck by
Friday, utterly incapable of giving young Genevieve
the attention she deserves.' But then again, my lecher
half would almost swoon at the prospect. 'What a fate,
man!' it would exclaim. 'Lead me to it!'

I resolved the problem in the way that any well-
brought-up English public-school man would have
resolved it: I ate a leisurely dinner and went up to my
room, intending to take a long, cold shower and retire
to bed with *Black Bodies and Black Holes — Funda-
mentals in Thermodynamic Heat Transfers,* which is my
favourite reading in moments of crisis.

I had the shower, all right. A good, long, cold one.
But it did nothing to quell my lust. I gritted my teeth as I
dried myself and shouted down the lecher-voice, which
was up to its former urgings in my skull. The room was
in darkness when I returned, though I could have

sworn I had left the bedside light on its low setting. I put my hand to the switch, only to discover that it was, indeed, already on. I was just reaching for the light bulb when four gentle fingers and a thumb closed softly around my erection and a quietly husky female voice murmured, "Don't."

What does one say in such a situation? One certainly doesn't say, 'Have you seen the book I was reading?' but I my actual words were almost as daft. "Pardon me," I said, "but who are you?"

She chuckled as she replied: "I saw you this morning, out there on the balcony, while I made up your bed." She gave my erection an encouraging squeeze. "I saw this fellow, too."

In those circumstances my next words were also pretty stupid: "You're the chambermaid," I said.

"Not between now and midnight. D'you want to have jigajig or not?" She let go of me and lifted the sheets invitingly.

It may seem odd when you remember how horny I was feeling even before this surprising turn of events, but I think any man, no matter how lecherous, would hesitate just a little when a girl he'd never seen before — and who is, even now, just a dark smudge on a pale pillow in an unlighted bedroom — offered herself to him so directly. What tipped the balance for me was the hot, female fragrance that her lifting of the sheets wafted up to my nostrils.

Most sporting girls are so scrupulous in their hygiene that they have no body odour at all. Even the juices around their pussies are washed away so frequently that the fresh juicing-up they do for a new client's benefit is clear and odourless. Now I don't mean to imply that this delightful young chambermaid reeked like a mountain goat. Indeed, I'm sure she'd taken a shower after work that day. But there lingered about her that glorious perfume of a real, live, man-loving girl, a fragrance instantly stimulating to any red-blooded, woman-loving man but one that is almost impossible to pin down in words. It is part-vixen, part-cinnamon, part-shellfish, part— Never mind its parts. We all know which parts of *her* it comes from and why it knocks us out.

The moment it filled my nostrils, not to say my entire head, I was on the old, familiar hook. I hadn't been going with sporting girls for so long that I'd forgotten what a real female smells like but it's a bouquet whose overwhelming power is impossible to remember between times. I collapsed at the knees and fell in beside her, a slave to whatever she desired.

As I began a leisurely exploration of her unknown body she said, "Did you go to Solly's at all today?"

Her breasts were a small, firm handful with nipples already swollen and slightly moist. I combined a vague *Unh-hnh* with a token clearing of my throat.

"Which one did you have? I'll bet anything you like it wasn't Genevieve."

"Why d'you say that?" Her whole body was feverish and trembling. She was prick-teasing herself as much as me with all this chatter.

"Never mind. I'll tell you about Genevieve later. I'll bet you had Aimée."

"Right." My hand strayed down over her belly.

She lifted her Venus mound invitingly into my path. "How much did you pay her?" she asked.

I paused. "D'you want me to pay you?"

"No." The Venus mound rose higher. Her voice was quivering. "I'm just curious."

I spread my fingers in a vee and slid them down into her fork, one each side of her labia. She craved their gentle pressure on her clitoris and gave a low moan, wriggling a little to make that contact. "You can give me a little gift after," she said weakly. *"Une bonne bouche."*

Literally, of course, that means 'a beautiful mouth.' And *bonne* also means 'chambermaid.' And so, since we were speaking in French at the time, I made an elaborate pun on 'mouth, lips, beautiful, gift' and 'maid' — all while I slid down the bed and rolled between her thighs, ending with my head poised meaningfully over her fork.

"Oh ... oui!" she whispered and spread her legs wide. At the same time she slipped a pillow beneath her derrière and reached for my head to pull me into her spread. My eyes were still not accustomed to the dark but enough light spilled upward from the hotel forecourt to show the black triangle of her delta against the paler dark of her belly; so at least I knew she was a fair- or olive-skinned brunette.

The provocative scent of her sex was now in my very blood. I hesitated while I sniffed it in, wanting more and yet more of its precious balm to my randified spirit. She let out a little whimper of complaint and hoisted her fork up higher still, clutching at her thighs to spread them even wider; the sinews cracked as her *bonne bouche* strained for the touch of mine. And now, too, the dark gash of her crevice resolved itself into the familiar () of her outer labia and the frilly confusion of the fleshy oyster they usually guarded. I could not resist the urge to insert the tip of my nose in between them and slide it smoothly up and down the furrow.

It was still cold from the shower. She let out a yelp of surprise and then thrust herself at me, just at the moment when I was at the portals of paradise. So in went my nose, drowning in her juices. And out went my tongue, to lick those that had already seeped out to invite me in. Oh, what a feast was there my cuntrymen! I don't go in for much cunnilingus with sporting girls because, as I say, of their over-scrupulous (though understandable) attention to sexual hygiene. But with Anona (as I shall disguise her here — the feminine of 'Anon'), a girl who was clean and wholesome in the ordinary way, I made up for many past disappointments.

At first she jiggled with excitement, trying to move her pussy counter to the slow licks and sharp jabs of my questing tongue but then, as the full pleasure of it began to flood her veins, she relaxed and turned mentally inward, concentrating upon herself and her own satisfaction. The orgasms began soon after that.

I don't think any previous lover had gone at her down there for such a long, uninterrupted feast — it was almost half an hour. And nor (though I say so myself) had they been quite so responsive to her needs as they changed from moment to moment. When she wanted a hot, soft tongue pressed flat against her clitoris, making those tiny involuntary movements no tongue can avoid (look at your own in the mirror if you think you can hold it absolutely still), mine was there. And when that wave of pleasures subsided and she didn't know what she wanted next, there was that same tongue, now hard and prehensile, waggling and twisting away inside her vagina, as deep as it could go. And so a new storm of rapture would seize and shake her.

At last, when my tongue was aching with fatigue and felt ready to drop out at its root, she gripped me by the hair and gently drew me off her and up, up, up until our faces were level. I thought she wanted me to kiss her and was a little surprised at it; most girls don't like the taste of their own pussies, even at a time like that. But before I could make even the most tentative offer of my lips she flipped over beneath me and thrust her derrière provocatively up into my groin. At the same time she groped for my left hand, which she then conveyed round her to be planted firmly on her breasts. Her other hand fished for my right, which she drew down over her belly where, by way of encouragement, she started its fingertips grazing gently among the moist forest of her Venus delta.

Her attitude and actions were so like those of a man who has bought the time and willingness of a sporting girl that I almost blurted out some joke about *her* paying *me* a little *bonne bouche* when the time came. But she was already away, dancing aloft on new waves of orgasms, which it was my pleasure to assist for as long as possible.

Pleasure, yes, but — I have to say — it was also, in some curious way, a kind of duty, too. Unlike the effect of a Chinese meal, my frolics with Aimée that morning, though they had left me with an appetite for more, meant I was now in no danger of a hasty or unintentional spermspouting of my own. I could both give Anona the pleasure she craved and take my own in large but measured portions — and still have room to stand back a little, to marvel, and to wonder.

And what I mainly wondered about was why this

particular act of pleasure with her was different from any other. Something in her attitude to me gave it a subtly different tinge from anything I had experienced before. And yet it was not so utterly unfamiliar that I saw it at once. It was only when she grabbed both my hands and swapped them over that I managed to put my finger on it (so to speak). Like most men, I suppose, I've often wondered if there are sporting houses where women can go and choose toyboys, just as we can go and pick our sporting girls — and, more particularly, could I take a holiday job in such a place for a week or two? And where such musings lead, sexual fantasies are sure to follow; so I have often … well, sometimes … fancied myself already employed in such a house, which, in turn, has led me to ponder the thoughts and attitudes of the women who might make use of such a facility. And, of course, they (my fantasy punters) thought and behaved exactly as Anona was behaving now. I was a warm, snuggly, tireless, willing, infinitely compliant human sex-machine, conjured into temporary existence for her exclusive pleasure.

"You are *good,*" she whispered as she lay there panting between one round of orgasms and the next. "You know why?"

"Yes," I said.

"I bet you don't."

"Because I can do everything *you* want."

She giggled. "You are going to be very annoying to Genevieve."

"Why? You keep mentioning her."

"I'll tell you later. Now I want to lie on top of you, face to face. Can you lie still and leave everything to me?"

"God, it's *hours* since I last did that," I told her.

"Pig!" She laughed and punched my shoulder as we turned over and she settled on top.

Well, I tell you — Aimée may have been several years in her trade but she could have learned a thing or two from young Anona that night, even though the dear girl was doing everything for her own pleasure and only incidentally mine. I got so caught up in it that I can no longer recall any detail of what followed. I only know that it went on for another hour, that there was hardly anything we *didn't* do, and that the guests in the adjoining rooms, on either side as well as above and below, must have gone mad with envy of us. But eventually I came, all in one great, liberating, exhausting, limb-stretching rush. My balls, having emptied themselves so copiously into Aimée that morning, had little left to offer, but they scraped up every last drop they could muster, which exertions left them aching like fury.

I think I fell briefly asleep; if not, my travelling clock jumped five minutes in the twinkling of an eye. It showed 23:45 and I recalled that she had said something Cinderella-like about having to be out by midnight. "Can you stay all night?" I whispered.

"No," she said.

"I'll pay whatever you like," I went on rashly.

"It's not money. It's … me."

"Don't tell me you didn't enjoy it!"

She kissed me passionately. "It was the best since … I don't know. A long time."

"Well then."

"The answer's still no. I'll tell you this before you give me my *bonne bouche* — so you won't say I took it under false pretences. If I'm not in my own bed in the staff annexe by quarter past midnight, I'll be sacked."

"Tomorrow night then?"

"Tomorrow night I'll be spending these hours with the American in two-oh-eight, the one with the frizzy gray hair."

"You've arranged it already?"

"No, he doesn't know it yet."

I laughed feebly and sat up on one elbow. "Then how can you …?"

"I have sex with a different man every night. Just one. And always end before midnight. I *never* do it with the same man twice, no matter how good he was. I'm sorry."

"But how … I mean …"

"I don't wish to discuss it. That's the way I am. I don't have to explain myself to … anyone."

"No, no — of course not."

I know a dead horse when I smell it; I certainly wasn't going to flog this one any more. "Tell me about Genevieve," I went on. "How d'you know her?"

"My brother is married to her sister. But I know about her from the men I go to bed with here, men who have suffered her Friday-night orgies. Shall I tell you? I think I just have time."

"Maybe you'd better."

"She's twisted. One man told me she's insane. She hates men. She quite likes sex but she hates men. Most of all she hates the fact that they're necessary. She tried to be a lesbian but she says it's useless. She must have men."

"She's in the right trade, then!"

"Not according to her. Ten minutes … twenty minutes

… what good is that to her. She just gets frustrated, especially as she has to do what *they* want. So any man who goes to Solly's and boasts about his stamina is fair game to her. She makes eyes at him and suggests he spends all Friday night with her. You know they close for the sabbath at six on Friday evenings? Anyway, she suggests they come to her place for a meal and hours and *hours* of you-know-what. But when they get there she finds some reason to go out to an expensive restaurant instead and then when they get home she puts them through such sexual … what can one call it?"

"Gymnastics?"

"Perfect! She demands more than any man can give a woman. Of course she takes her full pleasure of them first. Everything's lovey-dovey to begin with. But when they flag … you know?" She held up a limp finger. "Watch out! She's Lilith, Jezebel, and Salome all in one!" Then she chuckled again. "I've had to spend *hours* undoing the damage she's tried to do." She kissed me warmly and rose to dress. "I can shower in my own quarters. Are you going to give me a *bonne bouche?* You don't have to."

I gave her as much as I'd given Aimée that same morning. She had the grace to blush.

The following night I managed to read several soothing chapters of *Black Holes and Black Bodies*. So by Wednesday evening, when I strode into Solly's to sample a kebab or two — and whatever else was going — I felt as full of steam as a young yard bull. The kebabs were fine and so were the stuffed vine leaves, the rice, and the things like mini shredded wheats drooling in honey and nuts — not to mention the succession of sweet, muddy coffees that finally washed

it all down. But Jolie looked more and more *jolie* to me
with every new mouthful. All the same, I was in no
hurry, and so the meal, in the usual Middle Eastern
fashion, spun itself out over a couple of hours or more.

No one took Jolie back into the fort during all that
time. Aimée had two men, one for more than thirty
minutes, and Genevieve had four, all quickies. She
positively radiated discontent; perhaps that was why.
Her body cried out, 'Enjoy, enjoy!' but her spirit said,
'Keep off the grass!' Ten minutes is enough in such
circumstances.

Anyway, when I said to Jolie, "You've been standing
up, waiting on tables, for a long time this evening,
chérie. Wouldn't you like to go and lie down somewhere?" she grinned, took my hand gratefully, and led
me to her room at the end of the yard.

I often wonder what passes through a sporting girl's
mind at such a time. I know what *I'm* thinking: Here's
this svelte, slender brunette whom I hardly know ...
we've barely exchanged a dozen words ... and in less
than a minute from now she'll give me as much freedom
of her body as I care to pay for ... and she'll permit me
to do the most intimate things of which men and women
are capable ... and what will her breasts feel like? ...
and will her vagina be big and warm and loose or small,
firm, and juicy? ... and will she just lie there like butcher's
meat or will she wriggle beneath me like an eel? And so
on.

But I'd bet an elephant's fanny to a gnat's prick that
she isn't thinking any such thing. It'd be 'Did I take the
Pill this morning?' or 'Would I look good in that blue
shantung?' or 'Bermuda next winter?' The nearest to a
sexual thought would be a worry about the size of my

erection — the fear that it might be uncomfortably large!

I wanted to blurt out that she isn't to worry. No one has ever complained that mine is too big. Of course, every sporting girl will tell you yours is one of the biggest they've ever had up them, but I've pressed them to the truth and been told that mine is, in the words of one witty girl, 'about as average as they come.'

"And long may they keep on coming," I quipped back merrily.

"Long and short, stout and slender … I can take them all in my stride," she quipped back. They love to get the last word.

"I think I'd like a nice long time with you, Jolie," I told her. "An hour, say? How much would that set me back?"

"It depends what you want to do," she replied.

"Nothing strenuous. Nothing athletic. Nothing unnatural. Nothing degrading to you. Just an hour of tender, loving sex between a man and a woman in several relaxing positions."

And that was exactly what we did. Nothing much to talk about. Nothing I especially remember. She had a beautiful, rather sanitized body with large, firm breasts, big, brown nipples, and a surprisingly small yet deliciously yielding vagina — all of which I enjoyed and exploited to the limit of the ninety pounds she wanted for the favour.

When we returned to the courtyard of the old fort she said, "If you'd like to relax a little more and, you know, just be alone under the stars, you could stroll around the battlements up there. Only on this side, of course." She pointed to the steps that had once led many a sentry up to a bleary-eyed watch.

I was feeling pretty bleary-eyed myself — but in a comfortable, contented sort of way — as I followed their ghostly footsteps. But my lassitude deserted me the moment I arrived at the top, for the view was one of the most splendid I have ever seen, at night, anyway. Stars I had never noticed in our damp, polluted English air — nor in most of the cities to which my work took me, either — were there above me in their myriads. And seeming so close that I was tempted to reach up and pluck them. An eerie phosphorescence was upon the sea, too, leaving a milky trail behind each little white horse that broke upon the sands.

But I was not left to enjoy my solo communion with nature for long.

"During the war," a woman's voice said behind me, "we used to pray for the phosphorescence nights like this — nights when the Israeli commandos did not dare to come ashore in their little rubber boats."

It was Genevieve, of course. Perhaps she had an arrangement with the other two to send any man who showed a little stamina up here for her to seduce.

"I can understand why they'd choose to come ashore just here," I replied. "What sort of welcome did you girls give them?"

She laughed and took my arm. "You strike me as a man with a great deal of stamina," she said bluntly.

I sighed. "If you're desperate, *chérie,* I'll do what I can, but I couldn't promise you more than an hour. Your friend Jolie was *very* good to me."

"Not now!" She tutted and shook my arm as if to say, 'Silly boy!'

"Oh!" I hope I sounded both disappointed and

intrigued. I leaned close to sniff her perfume.

"Friday night," she said. "You know we close at six on Friday evenings?"

"For the sabbath?"

"It's a tradition from the original Solly, the Jew. The present Solly is a Druse but he's also superstitious — doesn't like changing old traditions. Bad luck, he says."

"It sounds like good luck for me, though — if that's what you're suggesting. The firm I'm advising here is Jewish, so I'm free on Saturday, too."

"Would you like to spend all Friday night with me then?" she asked. "Not here but at my place. I have some very exciting ... well, you'll see them yourself if you say yes."

"And what does saying yes cost — to be practical for a moment?"

"Three hundred."

"Dollars." I did not make it a question.

She hesitated before she said, "All right." I'm sure she had meant pounds but the temptation I offered her, with my calm, cocksure attitude, was too great for her to risk a refusal from me.

To tighten the screw I said, "I'll make that pounds sterling if you'll go the full twenty-four hours with me — all Saturday, too. And you'll let me have sex with you as many times as I want?"

She clutched at my arm and swallowed audibly. This was going beyond her dreams: the chance to exhaust and humiliate a man for a full twenty-four hours!

In for a penny, in for a pound, I thought. "Only I warn you, it'll be hard work on your part, keeping a sexual old glutton like me satisfied."

She was shivering at my side. I could hear it in her

voice. "How many times?" She almost croaked the question.

"You won't get much sleep by night nor any rest by day."

"Yes, but how many times?"

"It's not a question of *times,*" I explained. "I once had ten different girls in a single day in Bangkok …"

"Ten!"

"A dozen? I don't know. It got very boring. I just kept going so as to win the bet. I'll never do that again. I've since learned a bit more self-control."

"Hm!" she grunted angrily.

"I can now make a single fuck last all night … then sleep for two or three hours … then make a second one last all day." I crossed the fingers of my free hand and prayed this latter boast would prove true. No, actually, I prayed that she would be so sated by our all-night exertions that she wouldn't mind whether or not I carried out my second promise. After my experience with Chantal and Vanita in Mexico City, I was fairly confident of fulfilling the first one.

"Three hundred pounds sterling, then," she said.

By now my eyes had grown accustomed to the dark. A waning moon rose to help me and by its light I saw that she really was one of the most … I can't say beautiful but certainly most sexually alluring young women I'd ever seen. Her eyes said, "Come to bed!" Their jovial sparkle promised unnamable delights to any who took up that invitation. Her lips hung slack and voluptuous; just to see them was to imagine them closing firmly round your tool. Her breasts trembled softly as she moved yet it was they — firm, high, and proud — that held up the flimsy boob tube that covered them, not the other way about. But before I could lower my gaze to assess her nether charms, I heard my voice saying, "I'll give you twenty-five for a stand-up quickie here and now."

She licked those wanton lips, uncertain as to how serious I was.

Thank heavens the old tyrant had heard my offer and was already hoisting himself up for a quick shufti. I had to bend and rearrange him. She saw it, of course, and, when I straightened, she slipped a disbelieving hand inside my trouser band and felt him rushing up to meet her. Disbelief turned to shock, but of a delighted rather than a horrified kind.

"Okay," she said cautiously. "Where?" She looked all about. "We're not supposed to, you know. Except in our workrooms."

I didn't believe that. She was angling for danger money. "What does Solly *think* you're doing up here with me?" I asked.

She grinned and pushed it no further.

"If you lean back against this castellation ...?" I suggested.

It raked back at about ten degrees from the vertical — perfect for me and not too strenuous for her, I hoped. Not if I really could make it a quickie, anyway.

She dropped her shorts with the speed of a meteor and lifted the boob tube up to rest across the tops of those perfect breasts. She stood there a moment in the moonlight, letting me admire the bits of her that were naked — her slender waist, her generous hips, her curvaceous thighs, and her concave belly, which descended into the sparsest little bush, in which the swollen folds of her furrow were the most prominent feature. "You, too," she said. "It's much nicer naked."

Then she laughed because she realized she had spoken to me as if to a young kid on his first time. I took it in that spirit, too. "The things I'm learning!" I said breathlessly.

Actually, the breathlessness wasn't put on. Her nakedness excited me and I was as hot and hard for her as if I hadn't had a woman for a week. What followed was quick and primitive. I don't believe in psychic phenomena and stuff like that but I do believe there is *some* kind of weird communication directly between male and female sex organs. When I'm naked and standing close to a naked woman with her legs braced apart, her pussy juiced up, her hips tilted forward, straining to welcome me in, there's a tingle and a warmth in my erection — in all that region of my body — that just can't be explained in any other way. From then on I'm lost. I'm on a kind of sexual autopilot. Mentally I'm standing a little apart, almost as if I'm watching myself.

What I saw that night was perhaps a reincarnation — or rein*carnal*ization — of a scene that must have been enacted a score of times down the centuries when that building was a genuine military fort. I was a Roman-Saracen-Crusader-Ottoman-Legionnaire sentry on watch — a lucky sentry who had somehow smuggled his bit of fluff up there on the battlements, for something to do between the orderly officer's rounds. And did I *do* her! In my mind's eye I could see my buttocks tightening and curling as I rammed myself into that warm, squelchy, receptive softness between me and the unyielding stone of the rampart.

And that weird communication I spoke of must have

worked between prick and pussy, too, for Genevieve, sensing that this wasn't going to take long, flung herself into the spirit of the occasion with abandon. She bit my shoulders and neck to the point of real pain. She dug tigress-talons into the taut muscles of my back. And when she sensed I was rising to my climax she lifted first one leg then both around me, as if she would engulf the whole of me inside her. It was all done inside three minutes.

She kissed me briefly on the lips as we disengaged. "Friday," she whispered.

"And Saturday, too!" I replied.

Thursday and Friday I worked hard at my contract and tried not to think of Solly's and Genevieve and all the other twenty million sporting girls around the world. Hard work — as I'm sure most of those same girls would confirm — is a sovereign way to keep one's mind off sex!

It was hardest around midnight because, on both Wednesday and Thursday at around that hour, I chanced to run across Anona on her way back to her own bed, having just left her lover-of-choice for that evening. Not that I was stalking the corridors for a glimpse of her, mind. I was on my way back from the bar, where I liked to spend the last twenty minutes of the day sipping a relaxing nightcap. On the first occasion, she saw me, too — winked, fanned her face, whispered *whew!*, rubbed her pussy tenderly, and sashayed past me, swinging her hips in jovial provocation. On the second occasion she had already passed the lift when I emerged and she did not glance back to see who had got out. Her normal walk was even more provocative than the one she had favoured me with the previous night. Her bottom might have wriggled less obviously but my imagination ran riot as to the lust those gorgeous curves had provoked in tonight's playmate, and the wanton games they had played to indulge it.

Lying solo in my bed, trying to do nothing that would make my boasts to Genevieve more difficult to honour, I thought how easy it must be for a girl who was as hooked on sexual pleasure as any man. And as catholic in her taste, too.

To jump ahead in my story by a few days — since I'm on the subject of Anona — I had an illuminating conversation with her when she came to make my bed on the last day. I was *not* peering through binoculars at Solly's; nor was I unintentionally showing her the target for tonight. In fact (to anticipate the other part of my story, too), after Genevieve it was several days before I was able to get even the feeblest erection; so it was definitely a time for talking rather than doing.

I said to Anona: "Can I ask you a question?"

"The answer is still no," she replied.

"Not that. I was wondering if men ever turned you down?"

"Lots," she said. "About one in five."

She called that 'lots'! Who would believe a man who claimed that one in five women turned him down in corresponding circumstances! But I believed her, even when she said, "But then half of them seek me out later and say they've changed their minds."

"And do you go with them then?"

"Never. Why should I? I like a man who looks at me and says yes at once. There are no complications then."

"What do *you* get out of it Anona? Apart from little *bonnes bouches?*"

She stuck her tongue out at that. "Sex," she said. "With no complications."

"Exactly. Look, if you met a man who had sex with women every night, or as often as he could get it, would you be asking *him* these questions?"

"I guess not."

"Well then!"

And that was that. Every hotel should have one.

But, to return to Genevieve and my impulsive promises to her ...

As the Friday afternoon wore on I began to feel all sorts of phantom pains and vague illnesses, which, with luck, might develop into something serious enough to let me bow out with honour intact. But the cocksure tyrant down below would have none of it; hack off my arms and legs and *he'd* still carry out the bargain — that was his attitude.

I was going to rely on a snort of the white stuff, of course — for the second time in my life. Having accidentally discovered its unusual effect on me with Chantal that time, I was not going to overlook such a valuable ally. But would it still work? It was a couple of years since that happy discovery. Maybe it had just been a lucky combination of its stimulant effect and my psychological condition at the time. I didn't move in drug-taking circles so I had no close male friend with whom to compare notes. Anyway, the cocktail of my rising lust, mixed and shaken with all these uncertainties, had reduced me to a quivering jelly by the time I turned up at Genevieve's house, which was in the expensive Al Wadi section of the city.

And that was the first surprise, for the place was a miniature palace — grand even for that salubrious

quarter of Beirut. However, I was soon to discover that
she rented no more than half of the first floor. Even so,
it was quite a pad for a girl who served customers, and
was served by them, at Solly's. It belonged to a million-
aire who had fallen on hard times during the troubles. I
also think he had drilled holes through the walls and
ceilings of Genevieve's apartment but, of course, I
wasn't able to prove it. I don't see why else he would
have tolerated her antics under his roof.

Anyway, there I stood at an arched entrance, cut
through a four-foot-thick wall and barred by an elaborate wrought-iron gate. I pulled the bell chain and,
while the jangling died, I peered through the curlicues
into a garden filled with lush, exotic plants of every
kind. Somewhere out of sight a fountain splashed.
Moments later a peacock strutted up the path toward
me, resenting the haste of whoever was coming along
behind him. It was Genevieve, of course — but not she
of the cotton boob tube and the torn short jeans. She
could have stepped straight out of *Vogue*. No starlet
being swept in to the Oscar ceremonies on the arm of
some fat old movie mogul could have dressed in a
more expensively revealing gown. It was as light as
woven air and it left no man in doubt as to what beauties
it so inadequately covered.

"I know I promised to cook for you," she said gaily,
"but I've had such a tiring, frustrating day at Solly's, I
thought we'd eat out instead. You have your credit
cards?"

Of course I was dressed for easy undressing, not for
what I was sure was going to be the most expensive
joint in Beirut. They'd have shown her to the number-
one table and sent me to eat in the scullery. So we had

to go back to my hotel while I changed.

She lounged on my bed, contriving to hitch her skirt in such a way as to show me she was naked underneath — no stockings, no panties, no girdle. Did I say 'show'? I mean 'confirm.'

"Did you fuck *her* in this bed?" she asked.

"Who?" I responded.

"You know who." She mentioned Anona's real name. "My cousin."

Someone was a little hazy in her grasp of relationships. So far my money was on Anona.

"I'll bet you did. I'll bet she told you a pack of lies about me — how I set out to humiliate men and so on."

"Do you?"

"Only if they ask for it."

"Ah — you mean bondage freaks, dominance, and all that sort of stuff."

"No!" She was scornful. "Men who promise grand opera and can't even sing a nursery rhyme."

"Oh, *them,*" I said. Suddenly there was a great hollow in my guts — and I didn't think food was going to fill it.

Something had happened to her between Wednesday night and now. When we parted then she had been subdued, not in a crestfallen way but more sort of thoughtful — as if she was prepared to give me the benefit of the doubt. Now she could not wait to carry the assault into my camp and put me down before I'd even got up.

Even more of my money was going on Anona in the truthfulness stakes. Also, I realized, Genevieve was as nervous about tonight as I was. I wondered if that was true of every Friday's assignation, or had I touched some especially raw nerve within her?

I was right about the restaurant. She took me — in every sense of the words — to the Old Serai, the best in all Lebanon. I realized I was going to have to pull in my horns for a week or ten after leaving this city — although, if I managed to fulfil my boast, horns and horniness in general were not going to pose a very urgent problem for some time after.

Genevieve wanted to talk about sex, to shock people on nearby tables if they tried to eavesdrop, but, in a highly feminine way, she wanted me to say the actual words, to make it seem like my choice of topic, not hers. Instead I chose to talk about the ancient history of Beirut and how it showed in the present condition of the city.

She did not give up easily. I would remark on how a succession of occupiers — Phoenicians, Romans, Syrians, Turks, Venetians … and so on — had each tried to remake the city according to their own ideas and, instead of enriching it, had left it utterly non-descript.

"I wonder if it's the same with people?" she mused. "Prostitutes, for instance. You could say that a succession of occupiers each try to remake the prostitute according to their own ideas. Would you say they leave her utterly nondescript?"

"I'm told they certainly enrich her," I replied. "The city is named after Berytus, a daughter of the emperor Augustus. But Caligula renamed it Antoniniana."

"Names are funny things," she said. "Prostitutes never tell clients their real names. Why is that, d'you think?"

"Laurence Olivier says he'd be tongue-tied if he had to go on stage and act the life story of Laurence Olivier in an improvised play. But call him 'Henry the Fifth' and a whole army could not dent his confidence. The rot really set in, here in Beirut, when the Druse prince Fakhreddin stared building in the Venetian style ..." And so on.

Whatever I said, she tried to twist our talk back to sex, prostitution, and such — which I then had to parry back into history, culture, and such. It became a game, and, in the way of games with opposing players, it had the curious effect of drawing us together.

Even now I dare not recall what that meal cost me.

On our way back to her place, she made the taxi stop at the end of the boulevard, with about two hundred yards still to go. She took my arm and held me back to a slow pace. "Listen," she said, "I'm going to tell you the truth now."

"Could be dangerous."

"Could be difficult. I don't have much practice."

"So are you sure it's wise?"

"No, but here goes anyway: I release you from your promise to me, or boast, or threat, or whatever it was. You don't have to, you know, *perform* all night."

Half of me almost fainted with relief — the half from my navel up. The rest of me mutinied in dumb, scarlet anger. "Why?" I asked, caught in the crossfire.

"We could just have an ordinary night of ... you know."

"Sex?" I suggested.

"Don't be crude," she said.

My navel-down half was growing weary of all these words. "D'you think I can't carry out my promise?" I asked — while my upper half screamed in my skull, 'Are you mad? Don't you realize that this gorgeous creature is making you the best offer of the year!'

"I'm afraid," she replied.

"That I can't or that I can?"

"Both. If you can't, that would be one kind of disappointment. If you can, well, it would be ..."

"The end of the road?" I suggested.

I don't know where that insight came from but it touched a nerve in her. She clutched me tightly and said, "How did you know?"

"I don't," I replied nervously. "I don't really understand anything. I wish you'd explain."

She sighed deeply, was silent a long while, and then said, "You mean the *real* truth." She gulped. "The real truth is that Friday night is *my* night. My night for sex. I can't have sex the way those animals down at Solly's do. The men, I mean. It's so mechanical."

"It's a good thing," I pointed out. "Otherwise you'd be exhausted."

"That'd be better than being frustrated — which is what I am now. In a way I wish I *could* have sex so simply. Sometimes I feel myself turning on with a man and I think, 'Yes! Yes! Let it go!' Then I look into their eyes — their glazed-over, piggy little eyes — and I just want to throw up. So on Friday nights I pick a man who I think has stamina and ... well, you know the rest."

"And none of them has ever measured up?"

"For an hour, yes. Or two. Or three."

"Or five, or six?" I suggested.

"Yes," she conceded. "Even five or six."

It was my turn to gulp. "And that's not long enough?"

"I know!" she cried angrily. "I'm being utterly unreasonable. Three hours should be plenty. But I want ... I want ..."

"The moon?"

"I want to *burn* it out of me for ever. I want to blow every fuse in my body — every sex-fuse, if there are such things. I want to be freed of the burden of sex for ever after. Don't *you* want that? Think of all the things you could do with your life if you didn't have to go chasing after cunt so often! Surely you can't *really* enjoy it all that much? I've known men burst into tears after sex. I'm sure it's at the waste of time and money and spirit."

"I've never done that. For me the rest of my life is just filling in the time between having girls. It's all I really live for."

"Yes," she sighed. "You are different, you see. I knew it the moment you walked into the café last Monday. I could feel that *difference* all around you like an aura. D'you believe in such phenomena? I don't. And yet it happened with you. I knew you'd be my Man Friday this week. And I knew that by Saturday morning I'd either be ecstatic or suicidal — to know that my wishes had at last been granted."

She stopped and turned to face me, staring up into my eyes. Her own were restless with emotion. "Will I bless you or curse you then?"

I shrugged. I had never wanted a woman so much in all my life as I wanted her then — not just her sex but the whole of her. She had peeled her soul raw and I wanted that, too. And somehow I realized that she was really asking me to make up her mind for her. She had put her dilemma in such rational terms, as if a little dose of psychotherapy would resolve it for her. But underneath it all she was really saying — with her eyes and the whole stance of her body rather than through her lips: 'Either you turn on your heels now and never see me again or you take this momentous decision for me — lift me up, sweep me on ... do everything you promised last Wednesday.'

No prizes for guessing which part of me leaped into the breach, as it were. "It is already too late," I said.

Precisely what I meant I cannot now say. I hadn't taken my snort by then, so it couldn't have been that. But she understood, or chose to behave as if she did.

We had reached the arched gateway by then. She opened it and drew me through into the dark of the garden. There was an old wistaria, fat and gnarled, growing up the wall immediately to the left and, as the gate clanged to behind us she drew me onto the soft earth of the shrub bed. "Now!" she said urgently, leaning back against the wall and fitting her bottom into a dip in the wistaria trunk. It must have supported that delectable flesh on many a previous Friday night. Her dress was already up above her waist and her hands were urgently helping mine with my flies. The intense pressure of my swollen tool only made it harder. The even more swollen knob of it was already thrusting out above the waistband in its impatience to be at her, so I had to undo the hooks and belt as well. She whimpered with frustration at the few extra seconds' delay.

Once it was out and free there was no finesse in what we did — and there was no doubt as to who was in charge, either. She might have forced the initial decision upon me but the reins were now firmly back in her hands. And with those hands she grabbed my erection at its root, forced it downward to the point of pain, scooped it into her fork, and fitted the knob of it at the threshold of heaven's gates. Male reflexes did the rest.

She let out a cry of joy that pierced the night.

A light went on in one of the downstairs rooms, flooding the garden and freezing us in our guilt. Reason might have told us that no one standing in that brightly lighted room, staring out into the (to them) dimly illuminated garden, could possibly see us in the leaf-dappled shadows of the wistaria. But guilt assured us that the whole world could see us, clear as day.

"Did I sound like a peacock?" she asked.

"No," I told her. "In any case, they don't call after sunset."

"Let's go inside," she said, wriggling to get off me.

"I am inside," I pointed out. I was still stiff, too, and ready to go on.

"We'll start again," she said, managing to squirm herself off me at last.

The titillating reek of hot vaginal juice rose around me, transforming her from whore to girl. It was a key moment in the events of that night. I rebuttoned my flies as I followed her toward the house, and then my hand, still obedient to my earlier plan, went to my inner pocket, checking that the all-night powder was still safely there. Then an inner voice said, 'You don't need it, man.'

The words were somehow tied in with her translation from whore to girl.

It went on to remind me of a weekend I had spent with Shirley (I'll call her) — my very first girlfriend, or the first one with whom I spent a whole night in bed. A night and a day and then another night, in fact. All we did that weekend was eat seven bowls of cornflakes, washed down with four pints of coffee, smoke three packets of fags, and have sex sixteen times. Or sixty times if you counted *her* orgasms; sixteen was my tally.

'You can do it again,' the voice concluded.

'I was sixteen then,' I objected. 'I could wank four orgasms off in twelve minutes then.'

'Okay, but that was forty hours with Shirley. For-*ty*. This Genevieve will be happy with four-*teen*. So of course you can do it! And you don't need that powder. Honestly — trust me.'

The argument ended in farce anyway because, the moment we were indoors, Genevieve herself took a packet of the familiar white powder from a little basket beside her aquarium, which also held the ants' eggs and other goodies for its inhabitants. (What sizzling scenes those big bright eyes must have observed!)

"One for you, too?" she asked, scraping a naked razor blade across a glass-topped table so as to true up a line for herself.

"Not for me, thanks," I said, gazing around the room.

"You should try some. It does for sex what a cupful of sugar does for coffee." She rolled a twenty-dollar bill and snorted it, half up each nostril. "Ah!" she sighed ecstatically as the high hit her. "Are you sure?" Her hands were poised to replace the sachet in the basket.

"It does *that* to me," I lied, making my longest finger droop.

"Eek!" She pretended to panic and carried the dangerous substance out to the kitchen.

If I had expected to pass the night in the studio of a high-class courtesan, I would have been disappointed by the tasteful modern apartment in which I now stood. It could have featured in any recent issue of

Modern Interiors and Gardens.

"What does turn you on then?" she asked as she returned.

I reached my arms out toward her.

Such a simple, loving gesture got beneath her bright armour; she had no ready response to it. She stared at me, a little confused, half smiling, reassessing me with a curious gaze. Then she remembered to breathe again.

I went to her instead, reaching my hand over her shoulder to dim the lights. Then I took her in my arms and offered my lips to hers. Before they met, however, I murmured, "I'm not going to pay you a penny for tonight. And you understand why, don't you." It wasn't a question.

I took her smile for acceptance, especially when she said, "Tonight — *and* tomorrow."

"I'll hold you to that."

"Hold me to anything!" She pressed her lips to mine and I remembered the feeling of being in love. I don't mean I had fallen in love with her but our relationship had shifted far enough away from that between whore and punter for me to discover ancient echoes in that simple kiss. I guess it was the same with her, not only from the fervour with which she threw herself into our … well, yes, I can now call it lovemaking, but also from her lack of objection to my warning about pay.

It's hard to nail the difference between lovemaking and sex with a sporting girl. After all, a penis engorged with lusty blood is just that; and a vagina all juiced up to receive it is not altered because a few bits of coloured paper have earlier changed hands. And the physical movement of the one inside the other is identical, as is the climax of at least the male partner to the act. The real differences are all in our minds — and therefore, to be sure, in our behaviour, too.

At the simplest level — and speaking, as I must, entirely from the male point of view — sex with a sporting girl is the superior form. When you, the paying customer, tire of one position you simply put your partner in another and carry on ... and on to the next ... and on to the next. At no point will you hear the slightest murmur of complaint, unless you choose something outrageous or not contracted for when the coloured paper changed hands. Lovemaking cannot be so one-sided, except where the *other* side gets his or her jollies out of being so dominated, ordered around, and generally ignored. But such cases are rare and serve only to remind us not to make absolute rules where *any* kind of human activity is concerned. A man who has sex with his girlfriend exactly as he would with a sporting girl will pretty soon be told where he gets off. Probably quite literally, too.

So in lovemaking a man cannot simply abandon himself to his own selfish satisfaction. Abandonment there is, but it comes right at the end when, by his sensitivity to *her* needs — and hers to his — the pair of them have arrived safely at the very threshold of that unstoppable rise into the seventh heaven of a mutual orgasm.

The intriguing thing that night was to see how easily both Genevieve and I managed to make that transition. It ought not to have happened. I, who had enjoyed a hundred sessions with sporting girls for every one I'd had with a genuine lover, should have lost all sensitivity and become incapable of recognizing, let alone respond-ing to, the subtle signals of her needs. And she, who could not remember the last time she had opened her legs to a man without being paid in one way or another, should have so thoroughly repressed her own disappointed response to an unwanted change of pace or position that she could not signal it to me, subtly or otherwise, found instead that the smallest little sigh or pleading whimper was enough to whip me back into line.

It gives the lie to those moralists who claim that commercial sex ruins people for the genuine article. It does not — any more than the fast food we gulp down in a hurry ruins our ability to enjoy a gourmet meal at our leisure.

So, all I can report of that night with Genevieve is that we genuinely made love — passionately, ardently, urgently, wantonly, slowly, deliberately, languorously, lasciviously, tenderly, roughly — and that, as I had told her in a moment of unintended clairvoyance, the actual *number* of times didn't really matter. We made love and we slept, and made love again and slept again, and so on until dawn gave us rest. And all that time we simply stayed side by side in bed — or one on top and one beneath. There were no heroic sexual gymnastics over the backs of chairs or straddled across sofas and chaises longues.

"When do you start humiliating me?" I risked asking her as the sun climbed over the horizon and the peacock started his strangely human cry.

For a reply she buried her face against my chest and began to weep softly. When it had run its course she said, through a bunged-up throat and nose, "What am I going to do next? I've wasted a whole year of my life."

I realized then how old I was growing. A year seemed

a long time to her! I had forgotten such a period in my own life. "I think you should go to Paris, or Hamburg, or Rome — any civilized old city that understands these things — and let some darling rich man take very good care of you."

She considered this in silence awhile and then asked, "But what about a work permit and things like that?"

"You won't need one," I assured her.

"Why not?"

"Because it won't be *work* for you now, will it! From now on it won't be work at all."

KENYA: Shara and Gemelle

Kenya almost touches the equator. It also averages several thousand feet above sea level. The resulting extremes of heat and cold mean good business for engineers like me. So far I may have given the impression that I just breeze into a city, wave a magic thermo-dynamic wand, solve everybody's heating or cooling or air-conditioning problems, and breeze out again. Oh, life should be so simple! Of course there are myriads of local bye-laws and building regulations and inspection routines and stuff like that, which I could not possibly be expected to know about in each and every country. So the first thing I do is team up with a local man in my line and hire him to take care of all that legal and procedural side. The science and technology, of course, is universal, and that's my side of things. If I haven't mentioned any of my local partners so far, it's because the only business I mix with my pleasure is the kind done by the world's oldest profession.

Roux, my local partner in Nairobi, had no such scruples. The first thing he said to me was, "You can't come to Kenya, jong, without spending a weekend at Surfer's Paradise."

Roux was a renegade South African who had got mixed up in ANC politics in his youth — when the ANC was still subversive — and had fled to Kenya. There he had dropped out of South African politics and, after trying his hand at a number of trades, he had become an expert in construction regs and bribery, which was how he and I teamed up. Despite his Huguenot name he was as black as they come. When he spoke like an Afrikaaner, it was to tease.

"I don't go a bundle on surfing, actually," I replied. "There's only one sport I cultivate." I demonstrated it with a vaginal left hand and a penile right.

He cackled and said, "Then its Surfer's Paradise for you, man. Or for *us,* rather."

He explained. Surfer's Paradise was a sex-holiday camp down on the Indian Ocean. Kenya had several such establishments in the days before AIDS. The innocent name had fooled the authorities long enough for the place to generate enough income to pay the bribes to ensure that officialdom continued to remain (officially) fooled by it. There were even a few circular, African-type grass huts — rondaavels, they call them — reserved for genuine surfers. For the rest there were seven magnificently endowed young black men, who could make out equally well with male or female partners, six black teenagers for those who liked 'em young, and ten or so full-grown black females in their twenties. It was an easy-going, African sort of place. Old men whose own performing days were over could go there to watch and remember. Old women could take 'full seminal service' if they wished, or simply be massaged in all the right places by strong, gentle black hands. Couples could go there and use the facilities to make their own intimate videos of themselves at play. Or they could co-opt one or more of the sex workers to spice up their romps a bit. Anything went as long as it didn't damage the merchandise or endanger life.

"I'll book us both on a Friday-evening flight to the coast," he said.

But in the event our work caused us to miss the flight and so we went down overnight by train, arriving at SP just after ten on the Saturday morning.

Anything less like a traditional holiday camp would be hard to imagine. It was a random collection of rondaavels scattered among the sand dunes that fringed the Indian Ocean coast. Some were clustered in groups, others were alone in little sandy hollows; none was more than a quarter of a mile from the water and most were much closer than that. We each paid five hundred pounds up front, in return for which we could have all the sex we wanted, up to midnight on Sunday, with any of the girls who happened to be available (or men, if that happened to be our bag).

We picked a divided rondaavel — half for Roux, half for me — about half a mile from the main building. It had a wide verandah looking out over the ocean, which was about a hundred yards away at high tide. Leading off it were two bedrooms, each with its own shower, bidet, and lavatory. The outer walls were actually of brick, clad in rushes and grass to give it a traditional look. So was the inner, dividing wall, but only up to about seven feet, though I did not discover that until later; above seven feet it was the traditional wall of sapling wood, rushes, and grass. The building stood in a small hollow in the dunes, close to but isolated from several identical neighbours.

Roux chose it and I wondered why he was so delighted to find it vacant, but a moment later his enthusiasm was explained. As soon as we had dumped our overnight bags he took out a pair of binoculars and trained them on the ocean. A lascivious grin spread over his countenance. "We're in luck, jong," he said to me. "The totties are at play."

He passed me the glasses and I saw what was obviously the half-dozen black teenagers, naked as Eve, disporting themselves in the surf. Whoever picked them had a grasp of what most delights the male eye. They stood in water halfway up their long, slender thighs and let the rushing white surf bowl them over and carry them up the beach, where they would leap to their feet and, springing over the foam of the next incoming wave, rush back to catch the one after that — on whose tumbling, tossing, restless back they would repeat the whole process.

You can imagine what delightful little frozen snapshots those six tall, slender, naked young black girls, with their budding breasts and their half-girlish, half-womanly bottoms, made against the dazzling white of the foam. But that was as nothing compared with the erotic spectacle they provided when, playtime over, they came back up the beach to their dormitory. At least, it was *called* their dormitory, though how often any of them actually slept there was a good question. And now I understood why Roux had been so insistent on choosing this particular rondaavel, for it was right next door to the one for the 'totties.'

I offered him back his glasses but he said, "No, no, man. I've seen it before. You just watch!"

When I put them again to my eyes I saw that, instead of just walking back up the beach the girls were playing leapfrog all the way. As soon as a girl saw she was now last in the line she straightened up and vaulted the five girls bent double ahead of her; so at any given moment there were two, perhaps three, girls doing the splits in the air and the remainder bent double with their swelling little breasts swinging beneath them. I almost forgot how to breathe as I watched their sport, gloating in a rapture of lust for their gorgeous young bodies.

"Come on, jong," Roux said. "The best is yet to come!" And he led a small charge to the top of the dune that separated our path to the sea from the one the girls would be taking. We arrived just as they drew level with us — at which point they became aware of us up there on the skyline and so made their show even more provocative.

And what provocation!

For now the bent-over girls had their bottoms facing us. They braced their legs wider apart, which showed off their pussies to perfection — pearly pink clefts screaming out against the glossy ebony of their skins. And the wider-braced legs forced the vaulters to spread their thighs even wider, and there, too, each little tottie flashed us a most wanton display of her secret places one, two, three, four, five times in a row. There was one in particular caught my eye. Her outer labia were chocolate-hued, thick and meaty, but the inner ones were like triangles of tattered pink lace. With the help of the glasses — and my own fertile imagination, I'm sure — I thought I could see each tiny anatomical detail as perfectly as if she were spread and supine a few inches from my drooling lips and goggling eyes. It was an imaginary conjunction that I intended to make real as soon as possible.

"You pick a tottie," Roux said, "and I'll pick a girl that's full and ripe, and we'll swap over after an hour, okay? Or would you like the other way round?"

"Tottie first," I gasped, eyes still glued to that one particular teenager.

"Somehow, man, I thought you'd say that." He laughed and gave the bulge behind my flies a jovial squeeze. "Save some for Gemelle. She's worth it."

The totties reached their dormitory rondaavel and I handed the glasses back to him. The girl who had taken my fancy stopped at the threshold, turned, and looked back toward us — the only one to do so.

"Seen anything you'd like?" Roux asked.

I pointed her out. He raised the glasses and said, "Shara. She's good. I was going to suggest her anyway."

He waved. She waved back. He beckoned her to come to our rondaavel. She skipped indoors and almost immediately reappeared, putting on her costume as she trotted to join us. I say 'costume' but all it comprised was a small oblong woven of coloured beads, about six inches by five, hanging by the finest of chains around her slender waist so as to dangle in front of her Venus delta.

"D'you know them all?" I asked.

"In the most biblical sense of the word, man!" he

replied. "Why d'you think I'm so poor — and yet so happy?" As we drew near her he lowered his voice and said, "Shara is sixteen. She's only been working here a month. She was very shy and awkward that first weekend but I should think she's pretty experienced by now." He raised his voice and spoke to her in Swahili — probably telling her of the swapping arrangement he and I had agreed on. He certainly told her she was going with me first because she turned to me with the most dazzling smile and held out her arms.

Instead of falling into her embrace I scooped her up and carried her across the threshold like a bride. She giggled, "You Tarzan, me Jane!"

Actually, her command of English was genuinely at that sort of level, so we didn't have much of a conversation. I told her my name and she said, "I wash you first," pointing toward the shower stall.

I thought she intended to shower with me, which I didn't want just then. I wanted to lick her ebony skin in all sorts of intimate places and with the tang of the ocean still upon it.

My merest hesitation was enough to let her guess it, of course, and she said, "This. Only this," as, with a mischievous grin, she tapped my erection where it was struggling to burst out of my shorts.

She unbuckled my belt with an expert flick of her long, nimble fingers and yanked my pants and boxer shorts down as if she could not wait to see what was coming her way. When she saw its hot, red head, all swollen and urgent-looking around the dark dot of the spermspouter eye, she gasped and looked up at me as if to say she'd never imagined anything so magnificent could possibly exist.

The curious thing is, you know it's all an act and yet you're flattered and you let yourself fall for it. I did, anyway. Or half-and-half. I grinned as if I believed her and chucked her under her sharp little chin as if to say 'Oh yeah!'

She grinned back in a kind of complicity and my stomach fell away inside me; I could hardly wait for those gorgeous thick lips and those stunning white teeth to get to work on me where they'd give most joy. But then, when she slipped her cool fingers around the ardent, throbbing column of my tool and led me gently toward the washbasin, I looked down at her provocative young derrière, jiggling ahead of me, and couldn't wait to feel that part of her quivering in my groin, too. She glanced back over her shoulder, saw how utterly she had me enslaved by now, and I think her grin took on a tinge of smug superiority.

She plonked me firmly on the bidet and, kneeling before me, squeezed a blob of liquid soap into the palm of her left hand; it looked so like semen that I almost gave her a second helping of the real thing. When she turned on the water and started washing my balls and all around my bumhole, I put my hand round my knob to show her not to go at that with her soft, lecherous caresses.

She understood and, when she had finished washing the rest, she squeezed another spurt of the semenlike soap onto the palm of my hand. She watched with something close to fascination as I completed that most delicate part of the operation, as if she wanted to learn how to wash a man there — a man like me on the very edge of a premature disaster — without bringing on the unwanted crisis. When I had finished she looked up at me and nodded solemnly, as if to say, 'Now I know.' She had a lovely little triangular face with the smoothest, most unblemished skin you could imagine. Her head was slightly conical toward the back, at the top, and her hair was a mass of tiny, frizzy whorls.

By now she realized that whatever we did together, I was going to come pretty quickly. She also made it clear that she wasn't going to play the passive part; she wasn't going to let me put her in this position or that, where she would stand or kneel or lie just so while I did what I wished with her. She had an agenda of her own.

I shucked off my sandals as we went back toward the bed and was taking off my only remaining garment, my teeshirt, when she pushed me back, forcing me to sit on the bed. Then, as I flung the teeshirt aside, she tugged at me behind my knees, pulling me forward until just my buttocks rested on the edge of the mattress. All this while those sublime lips danced enticingly only inches from my erection, which, if it could have spoken, would have shrieked for her to close that gap and kiss them, regardless of the risk of a sticky soaking. In fact, I was so sure she was intending to go down on me that I parted my thighs wide to invite her between them. At the same time I reached my hands toward her swelling breasts.

But she brushed them firmly aside, pushed my knees together again, and sprang to her feet, spinning around so that the backs of her knees rested firmly against the caps of mine. Her jaunty young buttocks danced enticingly before my delighted eyes. My hands rose again to touch them and this time she permitted the intimacy, indeed welcomed it with a sigh and the first of a series of slow, lascivious wriggles that sometimes frustrated my caresses, sometimes crowned them.

What a glorious thing it was to run my feverish hands over the perfect, jet-black skin that formed those two beautiful curves, which radiated all the exciting come-on of her girlish youth and all the encouraging delight of her sexually mature womanhood. The thin line of the silver chain around her waist complimented it perfectly and helped to define sexy contours that the darkness of her skin concealed. And, if I dipped my head an inch or two, I could just see a pinpoint of light between the tops of her thighs and the pussy whose distant flash had so excited me out there.

After a while her breathing became disordered, punctuated with sharp little intakes of breath and wordless whispers or barely voiced cries. She put her hands on her hips, with her long, spidery fingers splayed downward, moulding themselves to the swelling curves there. At the same time she parted her legs slightly, enough to place her knees either side of mine. Now, in dark silhouette in the very apex of her fork, I could begin to make out the thrilling whorls and complexities of her sex. I parted my knees to make hers part wider still and, for a brief moment got an electrifying glimpse of the feast that awaited me; but she was determined to ration her favours along her own schedule and firmly clamped them together again between hers. I should not have wished to be a disobedient horse with her on my back. Those slender, birdlike thighs were all muscle and they packed a squeeze that promised indescribable delights to come — or a punishing crush to any living thing between them that did not perform to her desire.

My caressing of her delectable young bottom — and now of her waist and thighs, too — was clearly much to her desire and she let me roam freely there while she gave every sign of her own mounting excitement. My tyrant down there approved of these delays, too, as he throbbed in excited sympathy with her amorous gyrations.

I did not believe her passion to be genuine, of course, but her simulation was most convincing. I was rather surprised, however, to see little patches of sweat glistening here and there all the way up her back. I blew a cooling breeze at them and she hunched her back toward me, inviting more.

When she had cooled down a bit she arched her back again and shuffled a tantalizing little step nearer still. Once again I dared to part my thighs, to widen her spread, and this time she allowed it, but only an inch or two, spreading her own thighs a little wider in consequence.

Now, by ducking my head, I could see the whole of her pussy in silhouette — the full, succulent outer lips, and the soft pink triangles of the inner ones, hanging in tremulous folds between them. She bent forward, folding them outward and bringing them even closer to my impatient gaze. Their dark outlines gained some colour as the softly diffused interior lighting touched them — not the shocking pink they had flashed out there in the equatorial sun but the smoky coral of a damask rose by twilight.

She slipped a hand between the ever-widening fork of her thighs and, placing her index and long fingers, one on each inner lip, spread them wide to reveal the pinched and puckered vestibule to paradise, already wet with invitation. My knob, too, was wet at its very tip, gleaming with that straw-coloured serum that always oozes out when the moment of penetration is near, as if to say that it could show willing as vividly as any girl.

I gazed in quivering fascination at those two pinned-down labia, which now, being stretched, looked like two spinnakers from racing yachts at full speed before the wind. I licked a thumb and stuck half an inch of it into the even tighter eye of her bumhole, where I made it wiggle and tremble as fast as I could. The long muscles each side of her vestibule, running up toward her clitoris, went into spasm and then relaxed, making her hole seem to goggle in astonishment; the gasp she let out only added to the illusion.

She staggered back another inch or two, spreading her thighs yet wider to straddle mine, which I now spread wider still. And with each little extra parting of her thighs, her fork came progressively lower, so that although we had started out with six vertical inches and twenty horizontal ones separating her sex and mine, the difference was now less than two in each direction. I fancied I could already feel the ardent heat of hers, in which case she could certainly feel the impetuous fever of mine.

What a moment of exquisite torment that was! Half of me wanted to prolong this tantalizing, teasing proximity, fluttering my fingers over the smooth round-ness of her buttocks, running a gentle knuckle up and down in the wetness of her crack … inserting it a dainty quarter-inch into her hole … raking my fingernails with the lightest imaginable touch down the backs of her arms … watching how she shivered and squirmed at each caress and how the little beads of sweat broke out again all up and down her back. The other half wanted to grip her by the waist and pull her back and down on me in one fierce, spermspouting stab that would shut my universe down for a small eternity.

In the end it was she who chose the moment. She backed toward me and lowered her tail to the point where our sexes touched — no, *kissed*. True lovers' lips never kissed so tenderly nor with as much fervour as our organs did that day. The moment I felt the moist heat of her juiced-up crevice clench itself around the tip of my knob I gripped the column at its base and waggled it swiftly, urgently up and down, picking up enough juice to guarantee the smoothest, easiest plunge.

But as it was she who had started this sequence so, too, she chose its moment of consummation. After my knob had traversed the full length of her groove a half-dozen times or so, she gauged the moment to perfection and collapsed downward upon me at the perfect moment for a perfect entry.

For a moment I was too stunned to do anything. The hot, liquid clutch of that tight, firm, young vagina around my swollen cracksman was just so stupendous I wanted to sit there and luxuriate in it for ever. And Shara, with that amazing permissiveness she had already shown to my unspoken needs, just sat there, shivering deliciously all over, letting me enjoy it. Only when my hands stole around her body, one to seek out her clitoris, the other to fondle her breasts, did she jump into life again.

She scrabbled desperately with her bare feet, their toughened soles slipping on the tiled floor, as she struggled to make me lie down on my back. As soon as I became aware that was what she desired, I stretched myself out fully and pulled her backward on top of me. She settled there with a great sigh and, groping for my hands, found them and lifted them up to cover her breasts. Her large nipples were now so swollen and taut that they felt like mini-breasts in themselves. I gave them a tender little squeeze, at which she shuddered and collapsed upon me utterly.

She was magnificently responsive to any caress I gave her there. Nor would she let me fondle her anywhere else. When my right hand tried to steal down over her taut, sunken belly, she cried "No!" and pulled it back to where it had been. Within a few moments her nipples began to exude a fine film of moisture, making them feel smoother and tighter than ever. "Yes!" she moaned, rocking her head from side to side against mine.

I licked behind her ear and she reached it toward my tongue for more, crying out, "Oh yes!" once again.

I touched her cheek with the tip of my tongue and at last she turned her lips to mine, her soft, thick, salty lips, which I kissed with passion.

Her eyes were closed and she did not open them. Instead she stiffened — every muscle in her lithe young body. Her heels braced themselves outside mine on the floor. Her buttocks tightened hard as steel. The muscles of her back swelled and trembled. Her shoulder-blades pressed my chest as if she had magically doubled her weight. I watched her face with astonishment as she opened her mouth wide, inhaled deeply, and then held her breath … and held her breath … and went on holding her breath.

I could not swear that any part of her actually moved and yet I felt the tiniest tremors as they shivered through her body and all four limbs. It dawned on me then that she was truly having an orgasm. And in that same moment mine let go as well — not a great, body-shattering affair (they never are when they sneak up on you like that, are they) but one that radiated a grand, melting sort of warmth all through me. Nor did it knock me out, mentally, nor leave me weak in every limb. Even at the time, with the juice still spouting, I remember thinking, *Good! That will leave plenty for a second go!*

And so it proved.

I let her have her jollies as long as she wanted, which was a good few minutes more. It was a curious reversal of the usual roles, especially between people who had hardly exchaged a dozen words as yet. I, the paying customer, became the detatched, cooperative partner while she, the hired one, abandoned herself to her pleasure, heedless of me except insofar as I augmented it for her!

Now that she had arrived on her plateau she no longer thrashed her head from side to side, nor cried out, "Yes, yes!" as she had earlier. Instead she lay, rigid in every muscle, panting in shallow breaths, and shivering deeply every ten seconds or so as each new wave of orgasm took her.

At last, thinking this could very well go on for ever, I once again took her nipples between my fingers but this time, instead of caressing them or scratching them lightly from the outer margin of the aureole to the innermost bud of the nipple, I pressed them lightly and then tried to furl them over, into themselves. Of course they were stretched too tautly for that but the further stretching brought on by my attempts was all the erotic stimulus she needed to brim herself over from her sequence of enjoyable but containable orgasms to one that gripped her and shook her and left her gasping. It did not last long, not after what she'd already experienced, but it finished the session for both of us.

I wanted to flip her over on the bed and start at once on the next, for I was still as stiff as a rod and ready for a nice, long, relaxing poke, with me on top and in control. But she, recovering her poise remarkably swiftly, sprang from the bed and raced to the bidet, where she washed out every last dribble of what, only moments earlier, she had been so happy to accept.

I followed her there, still pretty stiff and ready for more. I wanted her to see it in case she had any idea of leaving. She grinned and clapped her hands when she saw it, yielding me her place on the bidet. Then she squatted in front of me and gave me the thorough — and thoroughly voluptuous — washing she had not dared risk earlier.

"I like it," she said, soaping all round my knob with skill.

"So I noticed," I replied.

She giggled but I don't think she understood. "Shara is naughty," she said.

I reached forward and rubbed my knuckles gently up and down her nipples. 'Shara is very, very good," I told her.

She pushed my tool down, painfully, for it now felt stiff enough to snap at the root, and washed away the soap. "You give Shara good big tip?" she asked.

"We'll see."

"But Shara is good?"

"If Shara is good *again,* yes — big tip." I leaned back on the seat and thrust my tool at her. "There's another big tip," I said, pointing to its swollen knob. "For you."

I'm sure she didn't grasp the other meaning of 'tip'

but she grasped my tool in no uncertain manner and
hauled me back to the bedroom by it — where she
once again pushed me back on the bed but this time
dived in between my legs and began licking my erection
as if it were an ice lollipop in the Sahara.

Oh man! If she'd asked me for a tip then, I'd have
given her my chequebook. What that young girl didn't
know about the nerve buds of pleasure in the erect
male organ would have kept a nun innocent. And it
wasn't just her knowledge; she was equipped to use it
like no one else I'd ever met. She had a mouth like
Cheddar Gorge, a tongue like living marshmallow, and
all as warm as the most jaded old roué could wish.

After a while, when she sensed I was about to come
again, she pulled away and flopped down beside me.
"You next," she said breathlessly, bending up her
knees and letting her thighs fall open. She jiggled with
excited anticipation as I eased myself down between
them.

Then sounds of male and female ecstasy intruded
upon us from next door. We paused, listened, and
grinned at each other. When it subsided, Roux called
out, "You've gone very quiet in there, jong. You
finished?"

"Soon," I called back. "Just give me another hour or
so."

He laughed. "I'll give you half an hour. I'll *braai* us
some steaks. Will I ask Gemelle to come back at two?"

"Sure." The glorious complexities of Shara's unique
pussy, now only inches from my face, were claiming all
my attention.

She was like an old-fashioned bourbon rose down
there, all frills and whorls of musky pink — a juicy,

oystery, torrid mishmash of flesh in which the dark recess of her vagina was more often hidden than visible. What a feast it was to explore with the tip of my tongue, questing among those sensual wrinkles, tasting the nectar of her reviving passion ... I found I desperately wanted to hear her moan and gasp in ecstasy once again.

But she wasn't on that wavelength any more, She'd had her jollies, in her own way and her own time, and that was probably *it* for the day. I did everything I knew to seduce her clitoris into rebellion but to no avail; she wasn't going to let me force her into an unwelcome repeat. Of course, like any good sporting girl, she pretended for all she was worth. I got the whole pyrotechnic display of 'little girl lost in erotic wonderland, overwhelmed by sensations, feels earth move beneath her.' Good, too. I agreed to buy it.

"Now you, me, both," she said when she felt I'd feasted long enough, and she flipped about and clamped her lithe young limbs about me in glorious *soixante-neuf*.

After that, when I decided it was useless trying to trick her body into a further ecstasy, I surrendered my own to her consummate skill. And from that time on, things become a little vague in my memory. I remember her kneeling before me on the bed, her hand once again in her fork, splaying those astonishing labia to reveal the way into paradise at last, and her voice calling out an excited, "Go on! Go in!"

And then the indescribable warmth and welcome of her tight, juicy hole ...

And lying full length on her with her adorable young bottom lifted up against me ...

And rolling on our sides and slipping lazily in and out to the accompaniment of moist little smacking noises and sighs of joy from her …

And Shara sitting upright on me, her heels beside my ears, grinning down at me as she jiggled her buttocks to bounce up and down and squeeze me to the point of delirium …

And, finally, lying on top of her with her thighs wrapped round me and her heels in the small of my back, pushing in time with me as if I were not already packing enough meat inside her with each mighty thrust …

And a cry from my throat that brought a shout of, "Jesus, man! You all right in there?" from Roux out there on the stoep. But I only heard him minutes later, in a kind of mental playback as I savoured once more that supreme moment inside Shara, as my tool leaped and throbbed in the hot dark of her belly, spouting every last droplet of sticky my balls could furnish. I could feel the fluid heat of it swelling her vagina and oozing like liquid fire back down around my knob.

Then I collapsed, panting as if the whole planet were about to have its air switched off. She slumped, too, letting her legs and arms fall away from me, gasping, though not so desperately as I was, since most of the final exertions had been mine; all she had to do was let me ramrod away while she held on tight and pretended that earth and heaven were melting all about us.

But we were equally bathed in sweat. So the first thing we did when I landed back on earth was race to the shower. There her gasps of pleasure as the cooling water sluiced her down were genuine at last.

"Now you give me big tip?" she asked, lifting her

hand to give my cheek an affectionate stroke.

"Yes," I agreed. "Good big tip for Shara."

Of course, the inevitable happened when we turned the water off and I started soaping her body. She slumped and looked at me in smiling despair.

"Something for Gemelle," I explained.

Her face said 'Poor Gemelle!' but all she did was grin.

I gave her twenty pounds, which Roux told me later was double what she'd expected. She skipped from the room very happily, and would have skipped all the way back to the dormitory, too, if he hadn't put out a hand and grabbed her by the wrist. "Me next," he said, adding something in Swahili, at which she became all coquettish, grinding her hips and brushing his bare arms with her nipples in a voluptuous, snakelike dance.

Roux was wearing khaki drill shorts a size too small for him. When he eased his erection, I noticed, the tip of his knob was just peeping out between his belly and the leather belt that held them up. Actually, considering the size and power of that erection, I should say *also* held them up, perhaps.

He had barbecued for her, as well — two half-pound fillet steaks each, which we washed down with still Malvern water (truly!) followed by fruits I couldn't even begin to name — descendants of whatever Eve offered Adam in Eden. Then we stretched out in the shade of the thatch and snoozed.

Gemelle turned up bang on cue at two, just as I was nodding off for the third or fourth time. I rubbed my stomach tenderly and said, "Eat too much. Need little sleep."

"That suits me to a tee," she replied as she settled

comfortably near me. "I had a blow-out lunch, myself."

Roux laughed at my embarrassment. "It's only this little monkey who hasn't learned her English yet," he said. "But she'll pick it up soon enough, won't you, eh?" And he chucked her under the chin.

"Shara learn all thing quick," she replied.

"You bet!" Gemelle whispered to me.

I liked her from the start — and not merely her physical charms, considerable though they were. Like Jade in Jo'burg, she was of mixed race, half Chinese, half African. Like Jade, too, she was a real beauty. With her dark skin, her big fleshy breasts, and her pneumatic derrière, Gemelle was predominantly African; but her small, dainty frame, her slender face, her ever-smiling eyes, and her delicate, Cupid lips were all from her Chinese parent. And to lie within three feet of her, naked but for that little square of coloured beads, in the shade of that hot African sun, was to know the tortures of erotic hunger of an exceptionally refined kind — even after an hour or more between Shara's energetically yielding young thighs.

After a while Shara began to snore.

Roux sat up and gave her a mild slap on her bottom, saying, *"Nie, jong mejsie* — that won't do!" And he grabbed her by the wrist once more and dragged her, yawning, stretching, and grumbling, into his half of the hut. Moments later, though, her giggles showed her to be back on all eight cylinders in full sporting-girl mode.

Gemelle raised an inquiring eyebrow at me and tilted her head toward my half.

"Can we just talk a bit?" I asked. "I didn't get much conversation with Shara."

"Sure." She laughed. "We're here for companionship

as well as sex, you know. We could go swimming if you like?"

Her questioning tone and a subtle edge to her voice told me something more than mere swimming would be involved. "Okay," I said.

She stood up and took off her little square of coloured beads. "You can go naked, too, if you like," she told me.

Hand in hand we strolled down over the beach. I learned that she had a university education but no money, hence her excellent command of English as well as her presence at SP. When she had ten thousand put by she was going to open a boutique in Cape Town, where she was born. She was frank in a way no European girl would ever have been. She told me that before she started she thought she would hate the sex and would just have to grit her teeth and bear it for the sake of the money; but actually, although she couldn't say she *liked* it, the business wasn't nearly as distasteful as she had feared. She had a long list of jobs that were more disagreeable, from picking coffee to making beds in hotels. And she enjoyed meeting lots of different people, women as well as men, all in these very relaxed surroundings.

It was a matter of pride to me that I didn't get an erection. I won't say it was completely limp, mind; it was a bit like a horse's when they hang it out to dry. As soon as we hit the water, of course — although the ocean was almost lukewarm — it knew its place, which was snugly inside my body. There it snuggled like a little boy's peepee atop a scrotum that resembled a rejected walnut.

The wind had died back and the surf was now mere

wavelets, hardly worthy of the name. We waded in and as soon as we were waist-deep she launched herself into a powerful swimming stroke. "Come on," she called over her shoulder.

"Sharks?" I asked, seeing no nets.

"They have electronic repellent thingies that seem to work. Hardly anybody ever gets attacked." She laughed.

I swam out to join her.

We stopped and trod water when we were well out of our depth.

"Can you swim underwater?" she asked.

"I used to do it a lot at school. Go under and tweak the girls' toes. I'd be caned for sexual harassment nowadays, I suppose. Sometimes I'd go under and just lie there as if I'd passed out — actually, holding on to the grating over the drain hole — just to scare people."

"Ideal," she said.

"For what?"

"Did you ever wonder what it'd be like to have sex in space — weightlessness and all that?"

I began to get the idea — and so did little peepee down there, who swiftly swelled to a respectable limpness and then, finding no harm in it, sprang to ramrod-stiff attention.

In that sparkling, crystal-clear water she could watch it all happen. "If you haven't before," she said laconically, "I see you're considering it now." And she began breathing in and out fast.

At least, I call it 'breathing in and out fast'; she called it 'hyperventilating,' of course. "Hyperventilate!" she said. "We can stay down longer then."

Already giddy at the erotic prospect, I hyperventilated

until I was physically giddy, too. She saw my head lolling about and, with a gay cry of "Now!" turned turtle and dived — except that I never saw a turtle with such a shapely bottom, nor one that could, in diving, spread such a glorious pair of thighs and give such a stimulating flash of deep-pink oyster on a jet-black beard of hair. And, much as I adore turtle soup, I'd never follow one into the deep with half the eagerness that now sent me in pursuit of Gemelle.

She lay on a bed of water — and in and under a bed of water — a foot or so above the sandy ocean floor. The ripple-filtered sunlight made an ever-changing lattice of fire that shimmered and fluttered over her perfect body. If you think what black fishnet stockings do for a shapely white female thigh, you're one-tenth of the way toward understanding what that sparkling net of gold did for Gemelle down there, as she lay with her thighs wide open, poised over the sandy bed.

She was utterly relaxed, looking as if she could hold out for an hour or two — smiling at me and holding out her arms. The spread of her pussy was like a sweet, tight little sea anemone — as different from Shara's as could be.

I tried to get into a position where I could get stuck into her but she pushed me away, or, rather, pushed my head down toward her open fork. As my mouth reached for her sex she twisted round like an eel and I felt her lips close around my erection — and from then on it became a fight between the two most powerful forces in all living animals: the lust for sex and the need to breathe.

Gravity took care of both, for while I gorged myself on her treasure — and she on mine — and tried to fool

myself that I could stay down as long as any pearl diver,
the buoyancy of our lungs carried us back to the surface,
where we arrived just as the blackness was beginning to
gather in the corners of my vision. But oh, how reluctantly I took my lips away from hers, even as my lungs
forced me to gasp and gulp for the lifesaving air!

"Again?" she said when we had hyperventilated
some more.

And again we went down. And again. And yet again.

"Is it possible to have full sex down there?" I asked
when we surfaced, gasping, yet again. I was discovering
I could stay down a little longer each time.

"Not really," she replied. "The difficulty is ... well,
come down and try it and you'll see."

I got into her all right, though the salt water wasn't as
lubricating as I'd imagined, but the problem was that
our pseudo-weightlessness meant that every thrust of
mine thrust her away from me, so that I could only
enjoy one or two before she became dislodged again."

Laughing and gasping we returned to the surface.

"See?" she asked.

"Yeah. You need one of your feet trapped in those
giant clamshells. Why are those things never around
when you need them!"

She laughed. "You can stay inside me if you *don't*
move," she said.

"Is that much fun?"

"Come down and try it!" She did more things no
turtle could ever do.

When I got down to her she was floating near the
bottom, legs high and wide and arms ready to hug me.
And this time she let me in. As soon as I was snugly
fitted, she clamped her legs around me, grasped my

arms and moved them to indicate that I should swim, and then hugged me as if for her life. I swam, in long, gentle strokes.

The effect was wonderfully erotic. The gentle swimming motion did not threaten to dislodge me down there. And because only I was propelling us onward, I moved first, scooping her forward with me, so to speak — and scooping her with you-know-what. The actual movement of prick in vagina was minimal but the inertia of her body and the resistance of the water gave it a force it could never have achieved in air on a mattress. Not even in air on a water-bed. In short, this was not an old, familiar act transferred to a new setting — nothing so superficial. It was a new sexual experience in its own right, and one that involved nothing kinky or dangerous.

Well, actually, I don't know about its not being dangerous. I was so thrilled by it that I stayed down long enough to pass out. She had much more staying power than me — perhaps because she did this every day and twice on Saturdays. At all events she got me swiftly to the surface and pulled me in best lifeguard fashion to a point deeper than the breaking waves but well within my depth. So, as I recovered consciousness, I felt the comforting touch of sand beneath my feet. "Would you like to try it standing up here?" she asked at once.

"Why not?" I turned away and did a mighty clearing of my nose and throat, spitting and splashing the result into deeper water. "How d'you like to do it?"

"That's up to you," she replied.

"With a super girl like you, I'd even enjoy it with me lying on a bed of sharp nails, so you tell me."

She licked her lips and glanced toward the shore, almost as if she wondered if we could be seen. I did not understand its significance at the time.

"Like this," she said, turning away from me and backing her gorgeous derrière into me. Her hand was already there, helping my fellow into her once more. Then, when he was safely lodged, she stood up straight, leaned into me, and reached her hands back over her shoulders to pull my head beside hers, where she gave me a passionate kiss.

My hands stole around her breasts, where I was delighted to feel her nipples swelling and hardening under my touch. I caressed the whole of her front then, raking my nails as gently as I could from her elbows, up above her head, down to her Venus mound, where I tenderly fondled her clitoris among her limpidly floating bush.

But despite all my efforts and all the novelty of the situation I was too excited to come. When at last she became aware of it she said, "Let's go back to our hut and go to bed."

Our hut — I liked her for that.

The biggest mystery of nudist colonies was explained to me that afternoon: how randy men control their erections when comely, nubile young females are all around them. It is actually extraordinarily difficult to have an erection out in the open air and in full public gaze. I had just been enjoying the most stimulating intercourse with Gemelle; we were walking up the beach with arms around each other's waists; we were going to continue our intercourse in the most agreeable circumstances imaginable; and there were, in any case, only a handful of people about that afternoon. And yet, once again, my fellow hung his head, half stiff and half asleep, all the way there.

We arrived to total silence from Roux's half. In the circumstances, it was deafening.

Gemelle put a warning finger to her lips and disappeared round the side of the rondaavel, returning almost immediately with an aluminium ladder in her hands — a small one that she carried without strain.

When she put it to the dividing wall and made to ascend it I understood her purpose. "Not fair!" I whispered.

She grinned at me. "He watched you with Shara this morning — using this same ladder." She stepped back and invited me to go first.

After that I had no qualms — not moral ones, anyway. "Won't the wall shake?" I asked.

"It's brick up to where I've rested the ladder. Above that it's just reed and stuff. See a little crack there? You can watch them through that."

To see them with both eyes I had to screw my neck painfully on one side. Shara was lying on her right side immediately beneath me. Her right leg was stretched out straight. Her left leg was bent at both hip and knee and her thigh rested on a doubled-up pillow, which had the effect of keeping her vagina wide open whether Roux's cock was stretching it or not.

It was stretching it, of course. He was lying behind her. When I first set eyes on them, his cock — fat, stiff, and gleaming wet with her juices — was lying on the very top of her right thigh, with its tip just nuzzling at the entry to heaven. For a long moment I thought he had fallen asleep in that position — and that she was doing nothing to wake him up again. She just lay there, with the thumb of her right hand lying loosely in her mouth, sucking at it every now and then.

After a while, however, Roux seemed to wake up and to start pushing his meat inside her once more. I never saw a man's cock enter a woman's body so slowly. Well, I haven't seen too many of them do that, fast or slow or medium, come to that; but it was about as slow as a man could move and still claim to be awake. He took a full five seconds to go all the way in; at which point, Shara, who had held her breath most of that time, let it out in a little explosive gasp that must have been highly pleasing to Roux. It certainly put the life back into my fellow!

Gemelle, seeing him grow, whispered, "Is it really that good?"

"See for yourself." I climbed down and held the ladder to steady it for her — or that's my excuse. The vision I gained looking up at her, however, also had something to do with it. And it certainly kept my erection going.

When she came down she carried the ladder back outside. I went and lay ready for her on the bed. As she joined me she snuggled into my arms and said, "Black men have fewer nerve endings in their penises. Did you know that? Fewer than whites. It means they can go on for longer, even if they're poking away like young goats — which is why the white ladies come down here to have them."

"Does that mean black men enjoy it less?"

"How could anyone tell? Who's able to measure? But they *can* go on for longer." Her hand snaked down and closed tenderly round my erection. "D'you want to try what they're doing next door?" she asked. "They've probably been at it half an hour already. And he can go on for twice that again. It's really like what we were doing in the sea. D'you want to try it?"

How could I decline such an amiable invitation!

"Only, I prefer it the other way round," she said. "Lying on my left side. D'you mind?"

"Of course not."

"Of course not!" she echoed, staring at me in what looked like amazement.

"What now?" I asked.

"Men!" she replied. "I'm sure women wouldn't be so nice and so accommodating. If I was paying as much as you are, I wouldn't care if my partner was even comfortable — as long as he served me the way I wanted. Anyway … thanks." And she settled on her left side, wriggling and stretching like a cat until she was settled comfortably. Then she doubled a pillow upon itself and stuck it under her right thigh, bending at the knee so that her foot rested lightly back on her left knee. "You may need a pillow under your left hip," she said. "You may not have noticed but I'm a little broader in the beam than that sixteen-year-old Kikuyu girl!"

She was right. The moment I set a pillow beneath me, my erection rested on the fleshy top of her left thigh, neither drooping nor angled uncomfortably upward, in perfect alignment to slip straight into her.

One small prod was enough to reveal that she was already well juiced-up to receive me. I lay there trembling like a greyhound at the slips.

"Slow, now," she whispered. "As slow as you can."

I had often poked what I considered slowly before but never as slow as that. It had an extraordinary effect because, of course, the feedback from my muscles told me I was moving all the time, so it made her vagina seem enormously deep — and so my tool seemed enormously long in the same proportion. Also, when you thrust your way into a girl at the usual speed, all you're aware of is the uniform warmth and firmness of her vagina; but when you go in as slowly as that, you become aware that almost every millimetre of her vagina has a unique character all its own. There are folds and ridges, rough portions and smooth, tight bands and looser ones, parts that move with you and parts that resist. And you feel them all again on the way out.

Painful though it was, I rose on one elbow and bent sideways, almost double, to watch my fellow pulling out of her. It was glorious to see the way the soft flesh of her inner labia clung to his shaft, as if begging him not to go, and then parted company with little smacking noises, only to cling with equal pathos to the next little bit of him.

I withdrew completely but did not lose contact between my knob and her vestibule. Immediately I began to go in again, for the game was never to hurry and never to stop. She gave out one long, low moan of pleasure to encourage me.

You know how that first thrust up into the yielding vagina of a willing girl — I don't mean the first of your life, just the first of any particular session — you know how it's different from all the others? That first sensation of her warmth and wetness enclosing you? It's never the same on the second thrust and even less so after that — right? Well, let me tell you that when you do it as slowly as Gemelle and I did it that afternoon, *every* thrust has the thrill of the first.

And so we continued with the slowest, most relaxed, most lascivious, most thrilling session I'd ever enjoyed with a sporting girl. After a while time began to lose its meaning and it seemed we had been locked in that easy embrace for ever. I changed position slightly and gripped her lightly round the waist."

"Oh, don't!" she begged.

"Why not?" I asked.

She said nothing. She merely arched her back a little more, offering me another centimetre or so of vagina to penetrate. She let out a little shivery sigh as I took advantage of it. And when I was fully into her I stayed there a second or so and massaged her hips with an almost imperceptible pressure.

"Stop!" she pleaded, arching her back toward me even more.

I ignored her appeal and continued to massage her in that gentle way at the end of each slow penetration. Her breathing became disordered. There were discoloured patches and beads of sweat all down her back. Every muscle in her seemed to lock tight and an almost imperceptible tremor shook her from top to bottom. But there was no gasping for breath, no thrashing of the head from side to side, no cries of ecstasy. If, indeed, it was an orgasm, it was at once the profoundest as well as the quietest and most self-contained one I had ever known in a woman. It happened two or three times more over the hour or so that followed. I was fascinated to see how long I could keep it up, how long I could sustain the feeling that each new penetration was as thrilling as the first. After a time, though, I became aware that, marvellous though it was, I was making no progress toward my own climax. There was no reason to stop, but equally there was no great reason for going on. I began to increase the pace.

"No," she said at once. "Keep going slow. It'll happen. Trust me."

I complied, though with little hope that she was right.

Now she began to make subtle changes of her own, showing what a true professional she was. As I went into her she somehow made her vagina relax and almost, it seemed, suck me in tighter. Then, at the moment when I was in deepest, she tightened it all up again and, one might say, squeezed me back all the way out.

Words like 'suck' and 'squeeze' make it seem a powerful, even violent action but nothing could be further from the truth; it was the gentlest, sweetest, subtlest thing imaginable — and, for that reason, an absolute knockout. After a dozen or so thrusts under her new regime I felt myself on the rim of that vortex which leads to the unstoppable eruption of the male orgasm.

Despite that, I schooled myself not to hurry up again but stuck to the same old rhythm and left it all to her. And when at last I came it seemed that the whole of my body went on fire. It was the most all-over orgasm I had ever known. Of course, I had little left in the way of juice to give her — Shara had taken care of that — but, instead of the pain one usually gets on the third and fourth big, empty orgasms of the day, it seemed that the whole of me had turned to juice and it was all pouring into her through the leaping, bucking knob of my fellow.

A long time later, when I fell back to earth from Cloud Nine, she said, "You can keep me for the whole weekend, if you like. I mean, it *is* allowed."

Two more days and I might have fallen in love with her. Of all the sporting girls I ever knew — in the full biblical sense, as dear old Roux put it — she is the one I regret most having lost touch with. I didn't know then how rare it is to find sex as good as that.

LONDON: Joy and Holly

I cannot close this part of my memoirs without mentioning the strangest encounter I ever had with a sporting girl — chiefly because she wasn't a sporting girl at all. She was my regular girlfriend at the time and had never taken money for sex in her life. It happened shortly after my visit to Surfer's Paradise.

Joy was her name; twenty-two her age; and word-processing her occupation. She had come to our office as a temp. We had taken an immediate liking to each other, and had been going fairly steady whenever I was back in London — which, despite the impression these highly selective memories may have given, was most of the time. She had long since moved on to temp at other offices, so there was no conflict there.

I don't know how it came about but we somehow got to talking about prostitution one evening — about whether men's needs really differ so much from women's that such a vast industry is needed to cater for us. An utterly fruitless discussion, I know, and I was a fool for getting into it.

At some point, I recall, her jaw dropped and she said, "My God, you're not just arguing from the abstract — you know all about it from the inside, don't you! You go with prostitutes yourself."

I could have denied it, of course, but she had that look in her eye which said she'd never let go of this one. So I did the other thing. I said, "Yes. Of course. Why not!"

"Why not?" she echoed, desperately trying to muster reasons. My casual admission had knocked the wind out of her sails. "Aren't I good enough for you?"

Fingers crossed: "Oh, but it's only when I'm abroad — *never* in London."

"Even so." She was getting her breath back now. "You could fuck me on a Sunday …"

"I never 'fuck' you. We make love. I love you. I don't even 'fuck' sporting girls. Animals fuck. With sporting girls I have sex."

"Okay. Don't quibble. You can't deny you 'have sex' with me, too."

"But having sex is just a tiny part of what happens between *us* in bed. Important but tiny. With a sporting girl, however, having sex is ninety-five percent of it."

"Oh? And the other five?"

"The ordinary human pleasure of meeting, of indulging in inconsequential chat — like with a hairdresser or a waitress in a restaurant you go to often. You know."

It all seemed too reasonable to Joy. "But aren't they … I don't know — *awful* women?" She shivered.

"You could meet them away from work and never know it. You probably have, in fact."

"I still can't understand why you do it."

"They want the money. I want the sex. They've got

the sex. I've got the money. Why not?"

"But ... I don't know. So cold and impersonal it seems ..."

I told her then of some of the encounters I'd had, which were far from being cold and impersonal. Jill in Perth ... Marina in Malta ... Jade in Jo'burg in apartheid days ... and so on.

As she listened, her horror dwindled to distaste, then turned to amusement, then to full-blooded interest.

"But I thought they were all man-hating lesbians," she said. "Psychologically damaged for ever."

"Some are, of course," I agreed. "But only a small minority. Most are quite indifferent to the business. One whore in America said that a man's prick waggling around inside her was like shaking a finger in Carlsbad Caverns. She also said she didn't care whether the next man who mounted her was a malformed freak or the world's handsomest film star."

"*That* sounds psychologically damaged to me," Joy said.

"I thought the same — and almost blurted it out to her, too. But then she added that she sometimes had to make love with her boyfriend for an hour or more, as soon as she got home at night, just so that she'd remember what it was really all about."

Joy laughed and said "Phew!" all in one breath.

There was more amazement when we got round to talking about the sums of money involved. She was very thoughtful over the breakfast table next morning. At the toast-and-marmalade stage she said, "Would you do me an enormous favour, Riley? Would you promise not to see me or phone me until Tuesday next week — 'cos I know I'll be free then — and then give me a bell about six o'clock and pretend I'm a call girl and you're making a date with me?"

"You want to know what such telephone calls *sound* like?" I asked in bewilderment.

"No, silly! I want to know what it *feels* like — the whole package. I want you to come round and treat me exactly the way you would if I was a real call girl. Pay me. Tell me what services you require … et cetera."

"It won't work," I warned her.

"It will if you try hard enough," she insisted. "I'll try, too. We'll do the best we can and at least I'll have *some* idea what it feels like. Maybe I'll understand you better then."

That was the bribe, of course, but I should have known better than to fall for it. I really should. But so help me, I agreed.

On Tuesday morning the postman brought me one of those cards you see pinned up in phone booths all over the West End — at least, that's what it looked like when I took it out of the envelope, except that there was a photocopy of a polaroid of Joy in some sex-shop lingerie, showing nipples, pubic hair, and cleft. 'Life's a fiddle,' it said in one of those fancy wordprocessor fonts, 'fancy a pluck?' Her genuine phone number was at the bottom. I hoped I was looking at the only copy of this potentially explosive trade card!

But it certainly showed she meant business — so to speak.

Curiously enough, the fact that she'd gone to such trouble to act the part got beneath my scepticism more than any other trick might have done. I was actually trembling slightly — the way I often do when I dial the number of a genuine call girl — as I punched out her number. It rang once only. Joy must have been hovering right by it. "Desirée speaking," she replied.

"I feel a bit like an old violin, Desirée."

"Fancy a pluck, darling?" She did not giggle. In fact, she sounded disconcertingly like the real thing.

"Depends on what it costs."

"Well, straight business is twenty for ten minutes, or forty for a longer time."

"How much longer?"

"Twenty minutes. I do everything from massage to dominance but no SM. All right?"

"Sounds very good, Desirée. Can you describe the young lady violinist a little?"

Either she had been taking lessons or she caught on very swiftly. "She's nineteen [which was a lie, for, as I've said, she was twenty-two], tall and slim [average height and nicely plump, actually] — busty [no argument there] — blonde, pretty, and very cooperative [again no argument]."

"Could you fit me in in half an hour?" I asked. "The name is Randy."

"Or," she went on, "if you prefer brunettes, Randy, there's another young lady here — name of Holly. She has dark-brown hair and green eyes ... lovely, bouncy bosoms that men just love to ..."

"Okay, Desirée — that's enough. I'll take a shower now and come right over. I'll make my choice then, okay?"

I rang off before I realized I'd forgotten to ask the address. I already knew it, of course, but I wasn't supposed to. However, it was the only slip I'd made in the whole business. For the rest it was beginning to seem intriguingly real.

I chuckled as I drove the mile or so to her Bayswater apartment — that bit about this phantom girl called Holly — very good — but I must warn her she could get done for running a brothel under England's ridiculous prostitution laws.

I really had the shakes as I rang her bell. The doorphone clicked on. "Who is it?" she asked in a husky voice.

"Randy. You remember I ..."

"Come on up, Randy. We're ready and waiting for you."

There she was again — *we!* I really had to tell her.

The door was opened by a girl I hardly recognized. In fact, I didn't recognize her at all. At first I thought it was Joy wearing a brunette wig — and, on closer inspection, contact lenses to recolour her eyes to a divinely smoky green. But what surgeon could have given her those beautiful, shapely breasts and that divinely curved derrière? What crash slimming diet could have left her with so trim a waist? And no hair restorer-colourizer could produce such a luxuriant bush, with its rich chestnut hue. The brief, see-through nightie top and the lacy suspender belt, which supported a pair of sexy fishnet stockings, did nothing to conceal these charms.

"Hi! I'm Holly," she said, taking a pace forward and then back again. She opened the door wider to reveal Joy to her left.

"And I'm Desirée," she said nervously, also taking a step forward and then back.

So they had seen that Chicken Ranch documentary on TV.

"And I'm Randy," I said, stepping over the threshold.

"In fact, I'm twice as randy as I was when I rang half an hour ago. I thought you were joking, Desirée, when you said there were two of you."

"Are you going to choose a girl now?" Holly asked, her voice shivering all over the place. "Or would you like just to sit and chat while you think it over? What would you like to drink?"

They must have seen *Working Girls,* too; the setup was very similar: easy chairs round a glass-topped table strewn with girlie mags for the punters and *Cosmo, Vogue,* etc. for the girls between tricks.

"Just a Coke," I said, sitting down. "This is very cosy."

I smiled nervously at Joy — or Desirée, to get into the spirit of the thing. She smiled rather wanly back. I wondered if Holly's presence had been her idea or Holly's.

"Listen, girls," I said when Holly set my Coke before me. "I may as well come clean. This is the first time in my life that I ever visited a place like this. I don't mean I'm a virgin — God no! I should jolly well think not! But I never … well, you know" — I waved an awkward paw toward them — "paid for … you know. So I was rather hoping you'd, sort of … take me in hand."

Desirée's face fell during this speech. I knew she wanted to step back into Joy's character and tell me that wasn't the bargain at all. *I* was to be the experienced one who'd teach them everything. But Holly was quick to see the point. A sporting girl has to stay in charge of everything that goes on between her and the punter. He may seem to order her about — 'Stand like this … open your legs … suck me off …' and she may seem to meekly obey. But just let him try to tell her to do something that wasn't in the initial bargain — or to do *anything* at all when his time is up!

So when I said that about hoping they'd 'take me in hand,' she cut in at once and said, "Oh, we offer that service, too." She mimed masturbation. "Fifteen pounds. Twenty if you want to grope while we do it — or while one of us does, I mean."

I licked my lips cautiously. Her sudden show of confidence had taken away all my nervousness, too. "Well, that's what I was wondering," I said slowly. "When I said I'm *twice* as randy now, I really meant … I mean, would you both … together, you know?"

They glanced awkwardly at each other. I honestly think it had not crossed their minds when they plotted this little jape. They must have thought I'd have had one of them — Desirée, presumably — and then, after a little rest, the other.

"I don't know," Desirée said awkwardly.

Again, Holly was more positive. "It would cost quite a bit," she warned me.

"I'm fairly loaded," I replied and then giggled. "I suppose that's a dangerous thing to say to girls like you! What I mean is, for something really exciting, I wouldn't mind paying quite a bit. Only it'd have to be *really* exciting — know what I mean? For instance, would the two of you — how can I put it delicately? — give me a *show?* Isn't that what they call it — a show?"

"No!" Desirée said at once. "We don't do that kind of thing."

"Oh, I don't know," Holly drawled. "If the price was right, we might."

I took out a wad of notes — all tens — I always use tens because it looks more than if you count it out in twenties or fifties — and slowly counted out a hundred. "How about that?" I asked.

Desirée's eyes goggled. Her jaw fell slack.

"For a pleasant little twenty-minute show, girl on girl," I added. "And then, for you, Desirée" — I counted out another fifty — "and for you, Holly" — another fifty — "for half an hour of straight sex with both of you in lots of exciting positions. Nothing painful. Nothing humiliating. Nothing too athletic. Nothing kinky. Just tender, loving sex. How about that?"

The twenty little bits of coloured paper mesmerized them — more than a week's wages for either of them, there to be earned in a single hour!

"Including oral?" Holly asked shrewdly. She must really have been *thinking* about this little jaunt.

I nodded. *"Soixante-neuf"* it's called, I think?"

"That's twenty extra," she said.

"Ten," I offered, adding it to the pile. "Two hundred and ten is pretty fair, I think. However, if you don't agree ..." And I started straightening up the notes as if I were going to take them back.

"Two hundred and ten is fine," Holly said quickly. She grinned accusingly at me. "You *have* done this before, you naughty boy!"

I could see I would have to mend a lot of fences with Desirée — or with Joy, rather — when this was over. She was growing resentful not only of the way Holly had taken over but also of the obvious sexual rapport between us, which neither of us could hide.

"Only once," I confessed — and then went on to tell them of my disastrous encounter with Susie in Perth that time.

Joy knew me well enough to realize I was telling the

truth. The resulting sympathy — and the implied challenge to her to succeed where Susie had failed — was enough to put her back in character as Desirée. At which point I gathered up the money, offered it to her, and said, "Let's begin."

We all stood up. Holly took Desirée's hand and led her along the passage to the bedroom, leaving me to follow — and to ogle their near-naked bodies as they walked as slowly and provocatively as possible. My tool, which had hovered between semi-stiff and flaccid up until now, was suddenly stiff as a poker and hot for some action.

"Listen, girls," I said as we reached the bedroom door, "just watching you walk like that, I realize I'm never going to be able to sit still for twenty minutes and just watch. So let's skip the lesbian act and head straight for the open sea, eh?"

Desirée rounded on me. "You mean you want a hundred pounds back?"

"No. We'll just put it to a different purpose — two hours with the pair of you. And I can have as many orgasms as I like. Or can manage. How about that?"

They consulted each other's eyes. Holly, I suspect, had been looking forward to a bit of lesbian fun but, when she saw the relief in Desirée's eyes, she said, "Maybe …"

"I think it's the best offer you'll get tonight," I added pointedly.

"Okay," Desirée said resignedly. "D'you want to make yourself *completely comfortable?*"

Another line from *Working Girls* — even the same hand gestures.

I shucked off my shoes, flung myself full length on

the bed, and rolled on my back. "I don't want to do a thing," I told them. "It's all yours."

They stared at me, then at each other. They grinned and rubbed their hands. They advanced on me as if to say, 'Okay, buster, you asked for it!'

Holly put a foot on the bed, stood on it, took one large stride over me, and jumped down on the other side. And what a magnificent little flash of the promised land she granted me in that brief moment! My fellow down there agreed, as I could tell from the sudden painful surge of rampant flesh against the unyielding cloth and zip of my pants.

She saw it and her deft fingers went to work at once to relieve my distress. Desirée eased my jacket back over my shoulders and started on my shirt buttons. Then, not knowing quite what to do once she had bared me to the waist, she leaned over to kiss me on the lips.

Holly hauled her back at once. "He hasn't paid enough for that," she snapped.

Desirée looked at me in surprise. I winked and nodded confirmation at her.

"If you want something to occupy your mouth," Holly said, "suck this fine upstanding lad while I haul his trousers off him. And you — lift your arse!" She slapped my hip even as I obeyed. She was really getting into the swing of it now.

Desirée, who, as Joy, had sucked me many a time, fell to with a will. Tremulous thrills soon began radiating all through me from my 'fine upstanding lad.'

"That's a lovely fat cock you've got there, Randy," Holly said as she folded my trousers and draped them over a chair. "I can't wait to feel that up inside me. My pussy's all wet just thinking about it. D'you want to see?"

I gulped. "Yes," I managed to croak.

She was standing right beside the bed; her Venus mound, swelling out beneath that rich brown bush, was only inches from my face and, looking up, I could see two jiggly breasts that made my hands itch to hold them.

"Shuffle down the bed, then. Make room for me up by the pillow."

As soon as I had created a little space up there, she knelt with her knees touching my shoulders and the insides of her thighs pressing the sides of my head.

Still suffering the sweetest torture as Desirée continued the good work with her mouth, tongue, and throat down there, I craned my head backward, eager for another glimpse of the promised land. But I gave up trying when, instead, I saw those two fabulous breasts hanging like soft, ripe fruit, *just* beyond the reach of my tongue. The flimsy stuff of her skimpy, see-through top did nothing to obscure their charms.

"Naughty boy!" she chided, bending over and kissing me on the cheek. "Diddum want to see pusspuss straight away? Pussy doesn't like that. Pussy's shy. Pussy's afraid of Bigman Cock …"

Desirée had meanwhile stopped sucking and was now staring in astonishment at this transformation of her friend, who was no doubt a shy, demure young temp during office hours.

"Don't stop, ducky," Holly told her. "He's paid good money for the use of your mouth. Now …" Her hair fell about me. Her breath was like a furnace as she kissed my other cheek and resumed her monologue. "Pussy's

not used to big cocks like Randy's. As soon as she saw
him she went *ooh!*" Her strangled little squeal sent
shivers all down my body. "And she clenched herself
all up tight so's you'd hardly get a *toothpick* in her now.
So if Randy wants to get his Bigman Cock inside her,
he's going to have to get her all excited and relaxed
again, okay?"

"Anything!" I gasped. "Just tell me what to do and
I'll do it."

Her voice went on like velvet in my ear and there was
a soporific, spicy tang in the smell of her skin. "Randy's
got to make pussy think he's small and helpless and no
sort of threat at all, okay? Randy's got to pretend to be
an ickle baby again — and do what babies do."

In case I didn't understand, she drew off the fine stuff
of her nightie top and, as it slipped like thistledown
over my face, I felt the soft, warm flesh of her breasts
brush my lips and cheeks.

"Randy's got to suckle Holly's titties," she went on.
The fact that I was already in seventh heaven, doing
just that, wasn't the sort of thing to stop her telling me
to do it. "Holly just *adores* it when a man with a big fat
cock suckles her titties. It makes her feel all hot and
wriggly inside. And pussy gets all wet and relaxed, so
you'd never *believe* what big cocks she can take in her
stride once that happens. Oh, Randy! That's fantastic!
It's happening already. Pussy's getting ready to yield!
D'you want to know what it feels like?"

And she went down on me — down as far as *my*
nipples, I mean, and started doing things to them that
were out of this world.

Meanwhile Desirée, determined she'd not play
second fiddle to this exciting melody, straddled me

with her knees and got the tip of my tool lodged just a fraction of an inch inside her hole — not so far that she couldn't grab its shaft and waggle it up and down, or back and forth, along the full length of her cleft, from bumhole to clitoris and back again.

Holly, looking up from her labours, saw it and at once set about facing me with a rival attraction — quite literally, for she squatted over me and slipped her hands around, one under each buttock, and pulled her labia apart so that no part of her secret charms remained secret to me. It was the neatest, cleanest, pinkest, prettiest one of those things I ever saw. And, whether my suckling of her titties had done the trick or not, it was as wet and juicy as it was ever going to be. I reached up, grabbed her by the hips, and pulled her down on me.

She joined in the game with a will and mashed and packed and squashed her pussy all over my face until her juices and my saliva formed a spectacular, sexy pulp between us.

Desirée, not to be outdone, sat down abruptly, plunging my erection deep inside her — if one can plunge upwards. She ground and jiggled her hips with increasing frenzy, waggling my ramrod inside her to my mounting delight — and, to judge by her giggles and moans, to hers as well.

Perhaps because their exertions threatened their balance, the two girls leaned toward each other. In fact, they put their arms around each other's necks but I, deliciously blinded at one end and deliciously distracted at the other, was unaware of that. All I knew was that the angle where their bodies touched mine changed. I reached up, hoping to find a breast or two, or three or four, and discovered Holly's pressed loosely against Desirée's, nipple grazing nipple, soft flesh gently crushing soft flesh as they twitched and shook.

The first time I ever got into bed with a girl, when I was sixteen, I reached shyly across the space between us, touched her breast, and shot my load at once. The same happened now in these infinitely more exciting circumstances. My fingers stole up between those four gorgeous lumps and ... wham! wham! wham! Desirée must have felt like a pingpong ball on an erratic waterspout in a fairground shooting gallery.

But, as so often happens when I come quickly like that, I stayed stiff and ready for more; it's as if my balls reckon they've done their bit but every other part of me is complaining it wasn't enough and starts goading me to have another go.

"This isn't working," I said.

"No," Holly agreed. "I didn't come at all."

"Nor me," Desirée put in.

"That's the whole point. You're pros. You do it for money or for love, but certainly not for fun. Let's change the fantasy, slightly. How about this: You're two girls who *want* to go on the Game and I'm your seducer-pimp, teaching you the tricks of the trade?"

Their eyes canvassed each other's and bubbled over in merriment. They liked it.

"Okay," I said, pointing at my erection. "The first thing to know is that *that* dangerous male protuberance should never touch any part of you until it's safely shrouded in a condom. Let's practice that, eh? You'll find some in my coat pocket."

When they started on me, I nearly disgraced myself again. To have ten slender young fingers manipulated by a near-naked girl trying to slip one of those things over your tool while you maul her breasts and derrière in your eagerness to get well lodged inside her is one of life's supreme joys. I got them to repeat it standing up, kneeling, and lying down. Then the best way of all — where I laid on my back and each girl put the rubber into her mouth — rolled the way it is in the packet — and pushed it down my erection with her lips and tongue. I got them to do it three or four times each, just to make sure they'd never forget. (I was already sure I wouldn't.)

Then I taught them how to do a hand job — how they'd do it if there was enough loose foreskin to roll back and forth over the knob ... how they'd juice up their fingers and rub with them if the skin was drumhead-tight all over ... how to support the less sensitive front of it in one hand while they tickled and petted the underside with their knuckles and fingertips ... how to vary the pressure and give an extra little squeeze at the top of each stroke. Also where all the sensitive bits are and which parts are no more erogenous than the average gardening glove. In short, what a young teenage boy may take three or four years to learn in every detail, I taught them inside half an hour — thirty minutes that would have brought on half a dozen orgasms in me if I had still been at the age of my own discoveries.

They were rapt with attention now. I guess they'd started out the evening in the belief that their not-too-serious fantasy would be an extra turn on. Now that I'd converted it into something more serious, they were fascinated to learn things they had never even thought about before. Desirée said she'd always thought that all parts of a man's erection were equally erogenous;

Holly said she knew some bits were more sensitive than others but she'd always thought that the front-top portion — the largest, flattest part of the knob — was the hottest. I didn't need to exaggerate my ecstasy to underline the point, as they stroked and fondled and cuddled and generally fooled about with my plaything.

Then I got them to transfer their new-won science to their lips, mouths, tongues, and throats. And what delightfully apt pupils they proved — which was just as well, since my voice would surely have failed me half-way through any sentence I might have attempted.

After that I thought they should learn a few no-noes, so I sat on the edge of the bed and got them to stand in front of me, facing away, and touch their toes. I suspended the lesson while I just sat there and gloated at the sight. Holly somehow had the ability to see herself as others must see her — specifically, as I was seeing her then. I think she knew exactly how enticing her pussy must appear, being thrust out into view by her pose. So she pushed it that little bit further, clamping her head to her knees, which not only pushed her fleshy outer labia toward my delighted eyes but also unfurled them, causing them to part a little wider — a quarter of an inch or so — to reveal those normally hidden parts, as sweet and pink as before, plus the merest glimpse of her puckered hole.

It was all I could do not to rise to the occasion and unpucker it in one clean thrust. But I braced myself to my duty and taught them the second most important lesson a sporting girl must learn.

I ran my hands over the smoothly provocative curves of their delightful bottoms, round and round, and up and down their thighs, crossing over to feel the insides of their limbs. And they opened their legs wider to give me scope — also giving me, in passing, an even more generous view of those charms that, properly applied, could earn them a life of leisure by the time they reached thirty.

Closer and closer my fingers drew lecherous circles under their buttocks, near their forks. Soon my knuckles were grazing in among their fuzz, picking up juice from their labia. At last, when I could hold myself back no longer, I ran a long finger up and down each warm little cleft, feeling for the openings into heaven. When I found them I pushed those fingers slowly in and even more slowly out again, lulling any suspicions they might have as to my purpose.

Suddenly I gave each a stinging slap on the outside buttock and cried, "Never let a punter do that!"

They gave out strangled shrieks, more of shock than of pain, and rounded on me, asking me what the hell that was for.

I held up the trespassing fingers. "Nails," I said. "Sharp nails that could tear your softest flesh and put you out of work for a week or more. Under a hundred quid *no* man gets anything inside you but his tongue and his prick — rubber sheathed, of course. Over a hundred, he puts on surgical gloves and you make jolly sure he keeps them on."

"But why smack us like that?" Desirée objected.

"So you'll remember the sting of it any time a punter's fingers get near your pussy — and tell him to keep off the grass."

Holly made no objection. Indeed, she stretched herself forward over my lap, bottom-up, and purred: "Smack me again."

I laughed and gave her a playful little thing.

She lashed out at me with her elbow and snapped, "Properly!"

So I did — quite a hard slap that brought a bright pink blush to her blind cheek. She gasped with every show of apparent pleasure.

I said, "Since we don't actually have surgical gloves, and since I'm capable of fingering a girl without damaging the merchandise, we'll assume I'm wearing one, eh?" And, while she was still in the afterglow of that strange pleasure, I slipped my hand into her fork and ran my long finger up and down her furrow, feeling once again for the void at the heart of the universe. I slipped inside and gave her a few loving tickles. Then I whipped my hand out and gave her another sharp smack.

She gasped and fairly squirmed with her pleasure.

Desirée, meanwhile, was staring down at us with a face like thunder.

"You're not supposed just to stand and gawp," I chided. "You either get behind me and cuddle me from behind, or you help add realism to these fake pleasures Holly is simulating."

"How?" She was caught between pique and curiosity.

"Caress her nipples where her breasts are hanging down here." I slipped my hand under and showed her what I meant. "And look as if you're loving it, too," I added when she obeyed rather hesitantly.

I gave Holly's bottom several more slaps — and her vagina several more delicious fingerings — before she rose and flung herself upon me, bearing me back on the bed.

"Fuck this for a lark," she said, giving her hips and

thighs a few expert wriggles so that I slipped right up inside her. "All this pretending! Give me a proper squelch now!" And she went at me like a mad thing, grinding her hips and pumping her buttocks up and down, up and down, until pussy juice ran all over me down there. 'Squelch' was *le mot juste,* all right.

What with the feel of her hot, tight vagina clenched all around me, and the sight of her breasts bouncing above me, begging for the support of a pair of eager, loving hands, and her cries of pleasure ... it wasn't long before I was spermspouting away once again, this time deep inside her.

Honours even.

And so, after a feast of Eggs Benedict, one of my specialities, we returned to Desirée's bed where, while maintaining the thinnest pretence that they were sporting girls while I alternated between naïve punter and all-knowing pimp-teacher, we passed the night in sleep and happy copulation.

In the morning, Joy (no longer Desirée) handed me back her share of the fee I had paid them. "It was fun pretending," she said. "But this is real money."

"Which you more than earned."

"Never!" She shivered. "I've enjoyed the prostitute fantasy all these years and now I know that's all it'll ever be."

I turned to Holly.

"No," she said. "It's different for me. Joy's your girlfriend. I'm not. If I *don't* keep the money, I'm just a trollop who'll screw any man who takes her fancy."

No one was indelicate enough to say, "And if you *do* keep it ...?"

A week later she rang me up at home. Joy was then

temping with a PR outfit at one of the party conferences in Blackpool. "So you're all on your ownio?" Holly said archly.

I cleared my throat. "Wanna make something of it?"

"About a hundred and fifty quid," she replied. "Would you pay me that much to come over and spend the night with you?"

"Where are you now?"

"I can see your shadow on the curtain."

I drew it aside and saw her in the phone box across the street. I sighed. "I'll just have to curb my impatience until you get here," I said.

She was different somehow — even sexier than before, but ... different. More self-contained, as if she had an amusing little secret. I wondered if she'd been moonlighting as a sporting girl for years and was now going to give me a reasoned critique of my teaching efforts the previous week.

Certainly the equipment she'd brought with her did nothing to weaken the possibility. She had a suitcase crammed with enough lingerie for a small sex shop. And there were, besides, a vibrator, a vicious-looking whip that couldn't hurt a fly, cruella masks ... "And these," she said, spilling condoms and rubber gloves across my coffee table. "Tonight," she added, "our fantasy is going to be that you're the owner of a high-class brothel and you're testing me for a position in your establishment. Okay?"

"A horizontal position," I said. The old ones are best, as any sporting girl will confirm.

We left everything in my apartment while I took her out for a meal — not a hasty pizza but a slow, expensive, candlelight affair during which I hoped to loosen her

tongue. I was convinced she was holding something —
indeed, almost everything — back from me. Either she
got her sexual kicks from playing out this fantasy of
being a sporting girl with men who genuinely turned
her on or she had some far more serious purpose
behind her apparently light-hearted offer of one night
of bliss between her admittedly superb young thighs.

Sometime between the entrée and the dessert my
casual probing made her aware that we weren't going
to return to my place until I knew a lot more about her
and her real motives. Then, to her credit, she told me
everything, and with such candour that I had to believe
it was the truth.

She was not, as I had assumed, a temp like Joy, but a
trained social worker with a degree in sociology and
politics from Oxford. From her early teens the subject
of prostitution had fascinated her and she'd always had
the thought that one day she'd be a prostitute herself.
Fear had been the biggest factor holding her back —
plus the fact that her career was going rather well.
However, when Joy had made her joking suggestion
that the two of them should play at being on the Game
with me, it had seemed like Fate saying, 'Now is the
hour.'

Since then she'd become obsessed with her thoughts
on the subject. And now she'd decided to take it one
step further.

"But," I objected, "a life on the Game wouldn't be
anything like that night the three of us ..."

"I know that," she interrupted.

"I mean, you really turned on, didn't you? That
wasn't faking."

"No, that wasn't faking. In fact, *that's* what almost

persuaded me against the decision. I know damn well that prostitutes can't have those feelings at work."

"So what persuaded you back again?"

She smiled nervously, drew a deep breath, and said, "You're going to think this awful. Even now it all seems a bit of a dream."

"What?"

That was when I actually learned she was not just a social worker but one who worked specially among prostitutes. "So I blackmailed one of them — I've got a fair amount of power over them, you know, making reports to the court and probation services et cetera. Anyway, I sort of 'persuaded' one of my clients — as we call them — a funny little kid who's quite romantic underneath her hard-boiled exterior ... I mean, she *believed* the line I fed her!"

"Which was?"

Holly bit her lip like a naughty schoolgirl. "I told her I was expected to do all my work among prostitutes and yet I had no idea of what their life was really like. I said I wanted to change places with her for one day. She works in one of those horrid, dingy little rooms up one flight of stairs in Soho — you know, where there's a light saying MODEL in the window, which the girl switches off when she's doing a punter ..."

"And she believed you?"

"I think so. Anyway, she agreed readily enough. I wasn't alone, of course. There was a maid called Greta there — a sixty-year-old lesbian ex-prostitute who knew twenty ways to disable a man before he could say don't." She fixed her eyes in mine. "Can you imagine what it's like — sitting there in tawdry underwear, with a box full of condoms at your elbow, waiting for men to come trudging up the stairs and use them on you, one by one?"

"Tell me."

She lowered her eyes again. In fact, she kept them shut during most of what she said next. She started in the second person — *you* feel this ... *you* say that ... and so on — as if to distance herself from her story; but when she got caught up in it, she slipped unconsciously into the first person again.

Holly's tale

The cold, hollow sound of those feet! Tramp, tramp, tramp! *What's he going to be like?* you ask yourself. Young, old? Skinny, fat? Easy, critical?

The bell rings and you almost jump out of your see-through negligée. You pick up a condom. Greta takes it from you and puts it down again. She opens the door. He's middle-aged, neither skinny nor fat. Will he be halfway between easy and critical, too?

He's peering over Greta's shoulder, trying to ogle you while she tells him to go into the room opposite. "The young lady will see you there," she says.

That's *you!* The 'young lady'! You never felt less like a young lady. What in God's name possessed you to do this?

In something like a trance you drift out of the little cubbyhole of a waiting room, across the yard-wide landing, and open the flimsy door with the little spyhole in the middle.

He's taken off his raincoat and scarf. He's almost ~~'d~~, short, and rather skinny, except for his little pot ~~;~~ if he was the last man on earth you wouldn't ~~e~~ to have sex with him — but then, you're not going to have sex with him, *he's* going to have it with *you*. Since he's not drunk or obviously diseased, the only one who's going to do any choosing around here is him. Better make him choose in your favour. Tell him your name.

He gets in first: "I'm Trevor," he says, holding out his hand to shake mine.

I shake it. "Holly," I say. It feels absurdly formal. "And this" — I turn to my 'menu,' which some semi-literate girl has scribbled on a piece of cardboard and Blu-tacked to the wall — "is a list of the services I ..."

"Straight sex, please," he says, cutting across me. "Just ten minutes. Three positions. Twenty quid, I believe?" He's already holding it out — a tenner and two fives. "And three for the maid."

"Ah!"

I'm at a loss. I realize I wanted to spin things out — explain *soixante-neuf* and things like that — though what I'd have done if he'd chosen *Dominance* from the list, heaven knows!

"Okay," I say. "You just make yourself completely comfortable" — which means 'get bollock-naked' — "and I'll be with you in a moment."

I sleepwalk back to the cubbyhole. Greta switches off the light saying MODEL as soon as she sees the money in my hand. She takes it from me and gives me a condom. "I'll brew up a nice cup of tea, ducks," she says in a voice laden with fake sympathy. "Give him a minute to get everything off."

I stand there looking at the building site opposite, where a handsome, lean, sinewy young Greek god is looking up at me — or at my window, rather. It's so dingy in here he can't possibly see *me*. He's showing the most gorgeous bum. Maybe if I show myself ...?

I don't dare.

"Okay, my darling," Greta says. "Don't want him going soft on us, do we!"

Another fifteen seconds? Couldn't harm.

Greta squeezes half an inch of KY-Gel onto my finger and pushes me into battle.

I must have been mad to suggest this, I think as I smear it into my cleft.

Maybe there's something I could take that would make me feel nothing — keep me conscious but feeling nothing? Self-hypnosis! I should have bought that book. People do amazing things under hypnosis. Perform brilliantly and can't remember a thing after-wards.

On autopilot I check the time and push open the door.

Omigawd — he's *naked!*

And he's waggling his erection at me like ... what? A stick of French bread. Look at the size of it! He's giggling like it's a huge surprise to him.

Forgive me for saying this but naked men with raging erections are grotesque. Especially when you keep your socks on. It's not how one imagines you — not the way the statues are in the museums.

What if I spew all over him?

I close the door behind me and shoot the little bolt, which is flimsy enough for a bruiser like Greta to bash in but robust enough to deter the casual would-be voyeur — or lost punter.

"Come on, lass!" He points to the condom in my hand.

I'd have forgotten — standing there, staring at his

erection like a hypnotized rabbit before a rearing cobra. I'm never going to be able to fit it inside me.

While I fiddle with it and the condom, he's got his paws all over me, pulling down my bra, slipping his fingers inside my knickers, trying to ease them down. "Time is money," he tells me. *He* tells *me!*

As soon as he's sheathed, he spins me round and pushes me onto the bed, which is part covered in a big towel with a little one in the middle. "Kneeling," he says. "Like dog and bitch."

My bra is hanging by a strap and my knickers are still round one ankle but he's already found my hole with his knob. Thank heavens for the gel. I'm sure I'd be bone dry without it. True prostitutes start juicing up at the crinkle of money but I'm not there yet.

In he goes — wham!

I thought I'd never fit that monster in but it doesn't even reach the top of my vagina, which is a huge relief. So is the fact that I can *feel* nothing. I don't mean the contact. Of course I can feel that. But no sensations. No pleasure. No pain. Just contact — like a stranger standing next to you in a crowd.

Thrust-thrust-thrust … He's going at it like a stud in a porno movie. Still no *feeling*. He fumbles for my tits but is too excited to hold them — grabs my hips instead. The bed is going bonk-bonk-bonk against the wall. Beyond it a customer is going upstairs to Sandra in the room above. It must excite him to hear the bonk-bonk-bonk.

"Lie flat," Trevor gasps.

I obey and he fits himself back inside me in a flash — and goes on piling it into me, in-out-in-out … faster than you'd think a human could move. Now he can grope my tits more easily — and does so. Still no feeling. I wonder what sandwiches to send out for at lunchtime.

"On your back. Knees up!" He sounds like a dying man.

Please God, don't let him have a coronary until he's on the stairs going down!

He has to fiddle his knob into position for the first stab.

And don't let him lose it now, either!

Wham! In he goes again — and this time he does just hit the top of my vagina. It must be the different position.

Bonk-bonk-bonk — still just the physical contact. No feeling.

Suddenly he stays rammed tight, right up me, holding his breath. Then he gasps, pants, giggles, as I feel his erection bucking and leaping inside me. I imagine I can feel the gushes of semen hitting the top of my vagina and I picture his cock like a squat howitzer, firing and recoiling in the warm dark down there.

Over his shoulder I check my watch. Seven minutes! Twenty quid for seven minutes of that! There are some things about men that women will never understand!

Holly went on to describe the remainder of her day but in far less detail. That first encounter was clearly etched on her memory — her baptism of fire as a sporting girl. She started work at eleven that morning and continued until six that evening, when another girl and her maid took over — seven hours during which she *did* eleven more men. Four of them were like Trevor, wanting ten minutes of straight sex — wham, bang, thank-you, ma'am! Two more were basically the same but with a little oral first; she said my 'orienteering' around the mysteries of the male priap was of inestimable help.

One paid forty quid to talk to her for twenty minutes. His wife had 'gone off' sex and had agreed to let him buy it elsewhere. He wasn't sure ... maybe next week he'd get undressed. He talked mainly about disappointments in life. Holly almost cried when he'd gone.

Another wanted dominance. He put on an old-fashioned housemaid's uniform and she scolded him while he cleaned up the workroom. Greta said he was the headmaster of a public school.

Another got her to tie him to the bed with nylon stockings, which he supplied, while she straddled him and rode him like he was a bronco.

Another wanted *soixante-neuf* — and, again, my little tutorial was invaluable, she said. The man told her he'd never been sucked off so superbly; she remembered to tell him she'd got pretty excited, too, and hoped she hadn't drowned him with the flow of her juices.

And the final man of the day was the young Greek-god building worker from the site across the road.

"He was even more gorgeous naked and close up," Holly said. "The only one who didn't look grotesque when he waggled a rampant tool at me. I actually tried to turn on with him but I couldn't. He wanted ten minutes but I told him he could have twenty for the price of ten because I didn't want another punter turning up at five to six and making me late. Even then I couldn't raise a flicker of erotic feeling for him. It was *nicer* than with any of the others. More relaxed and friendly, I mean. But that was all."

She announced this last achievement as a kind of

triumph. Whatever she had intended to accomplish by this crazy experiment, she had obviously succeeded beyond all her expectations.

"And when did all this happen?" I asked.

"Yesterday afternoon."

I just gawped at her.

"Honestly," she said.

"And you want to spend the whole night with me? What can you prove that you haven't already ..."

"No, no — it's different with you. After I failed to get any feeling with that Greek god — I mean, when I got home and had an hour-long soak in the tub — I began to panic, thinking maybe I'd lost it for *ever!* So I thought I must find someone I really can turn on with, who can remind me what it's all about."

"But he was out, too?"

"No!" She grinned and punched me lightly. "You! I thought at once of you."

"But you want me to pay you as well."

"That's only to keep both of us mentally and morally square with Joy."

I sighed. "There are some things about women that men will never understand!"

We went home and, of course, had a marvellous night of sexual gluttony in bed (and on it, and half on it, and under it ...) all night long. In the morning I discovered what it was *really* all about. I don't mean she didn't enjoy our night together but that wasn't what she was really after.

"You've got a big exhibition at Olympia next week, haven't you," she said; it wasn't a question.

But my answer was: "Yes?" I asked guardedly.

"Your company's exhibiting there?" Now she was

asking. "You get a lot of important customers from overseas?"

"And from the UK, too."

"And I guess some of them ask you to find them girls?"

"Not only that. They expect me to pay the girls, too."

"D'you think I could give them as good a time as the girls you usually hire?"

Wow!

She was, of course, way above the class of the girl (not girls) I usually hired, but I couldn't afford to pay her what she was truly worth.

"Be honest," she said, on tenterhooks.

I decided to give it a try for once. "You're so far above my usual class of girl, Holly, that I couldn't begin to make the comparison. D'you want to know the truth? Can you take it on the chin?"

She gulped and nodded — and held her breath.

"You could charge from two grand upwards for the sort of night you've just given me. If I was to play fair by you, I couldn't possibly afford the fees you ought to charge for satisfying my sort of customers."

She pondered these words a good long while; she was certainly no creature of impulse. "Okay," she said at last. "But if *I* decide it — if I agree to work for whatever you usually pay ..."

"Why?" I interrupted her.

"Because it's the next step up the professional ladder for me. From a Soho 'model' to a three-star-hotel call girl in one week! It's worth it to me. And who knows where it might not lead?"

I felt bloody sure she knew exactly where she wanted it to lead.

"I can give you three appointments for Sunday," I told her. "Four for Monday. And at least two for Tuesday — maybe plus three more if they put some business our way."

"Nine men," she mused. "Maybe twelve."

"An hour each for a hundred a time. They can do anything they want as long as it's not painful to you. Or just too disgusting. If they want longer than an hour, they pay the extra. They don't know what I'm paying you but I'll give the impression it's at least two hundred, so you can set your own charge accordingly."

"And if one of the Sunday or Monday ones wants me back on the Tuesday?"

"Up to you — as long as you fulfil your contract with me."

She shook her head and gave a slightly bewildered smile. "I keep getting this feeling of unreality. We're talking about it so calmly."

I gave her arm a squeeze. "That's because it's just another business." I laughed. "I wish *your* business held exhibitions at Olympia!"

She joined in. "And madams and brothel owners would jet in from all over the world and they'd expect the exhibitors to pay for air-conditioning consultants to visit them privately in their hotels to discuss their ventilation problems!"

To finish her story: That same quick wit stood her in good stead during the week of our exhibition. Not only did she service all my customers superbly, she got one of them to show her the next rung on the ladder to fame and fortune — or to fortune, anyway.

"You know Herr Müller?" she said when it was all over.

"Have done for many years."

"He told me of a fabulous *maison de plaisir* — as he called it — in Vienna where he thinks the madam would be very interested in offering me a position. I know!" she added hastily as I drew breath to butt in. "A *horizontal* position! I've heard it. What d'you think?"

"I think I should help you make a video to send her," I replied.

We had fun making that, too.

I met her by the merest accident about eighteen months later, admiring the horses at the Pont Marly in Paris. I took her out to dinner, after which she took me back to the most luxurious apartment I'd ever been in. Its *pièce de résistance* was a four-poster bed whose mattress and frame were furnished with a dozen motors that did the most amazing things for a couple *in flagrante delicto*.

She woke me the following morning with a kiss and she whispered into my ear, "I usually charge two and a half K for a night like that."

I froze for I fully expected her to add, 'But I'll let you have it for half-price!'

"But," she said, "I'm the one who ought to be paying you, Riley, for if you had not suggested it that day — remember? — I doubt I'd ever have had the courage to aim so high."

I said I'd take it in used notes of low denomination.

She dangled her full, luscious breasts over my face, brushing my cheeks and lips with her nipples, and murmured, "You'll take it like this or not at all."

I didn't grumble.

Cremorne Gardens

Anonymous

An erotic romp from the libidinous age of the Victorians

UPSTAIRS, DOWNSTAIRS . . .
IN MY LADY'S CHAMBER

Cast into confusion by the wholesale defection of their domestic staff, the nubile daughters of Sir Paul Arkley are forced to throw themselves on the mercy of the handsome young gardener Bob Goggin. And Bob, in turn, is only too happy to throw himself on the luscious and oh-so-grateful form of the delicious Penny.

Meanwhile, in the Mayfair mansion of Count Gewirtz of Galicia, the former Arkley employees prepare a feast intended to further the Count's erotic education of the voluptuous singer Vaźelina Volpe – and destined to degenerate into the kind of wild and secret orgy for which the denizens of Cremorne Gardens are justly famous . . .

Here are forbidden extracts drawn from the notorious chronicles of the Cremorne – a society of hedonists and debauchees, united in their common aim to glorify the pleasures of the flesh!

FICTION / EROTICA 0 7472 3433 7

EROS IN THE FAR EAST

ANONYMOUS

Recuperating from a dampening experience at the hands of one of London's most demanding ladies, the ever-dauntless Andy resolves to titillate his palate with foreign pleasures: namely a return passage to Siam. After a riotously libidinous ocean crossing, he finds himself in southern Africa, sampling a warm welcome from its delightfully unabashed natives.

Meanwhile, herself escaping an unsavoury encounter in the English lakes, his lovely cousin Sophia sets sail for Panama and thence to the intriguing islands of Hawaii – and a series of bizarrely erotic tribal initiations which challenge the limits of even her sensuous imagination!

After a string of energetically abandoned frolics, Andy and Sophia fetch up in the stately city of Singapore, a city which holds all the dangerously piquant pleasures of the mysterious East, and an adventure more outrageous than any our plucky pair have yet encountered . . .

FICTION / EROTICA 0 7472 3449 3

A selection of Erotica from Headline

BLUE HEAVENS	Nick Bancroft	£4.99 ☐
MAID	Dagmar Brand	£4.99 ☐
EROS IN AUTUMN	Anonymous	£4.99 ☐
EROTICON THRILLS	Anonymous	£4.99 ☐
IN THE GROOVE	Lesley Asquith	£4.99 ☐
THE CALL OF THE FLESH	Faye Rossignol	£4.99 ☐
SWEET VIBRATIONS	Jeff Charles	£4.99 ☐
UNDER THE WHIP	Nick Aymes	£4.99 ☐
RETURN TO THE CASTING COUCH	Becky Bell	£4.99 ☐
MAIDS IN HEAVEN	Samantha Austen	£4.99 ☐
CLOSE UP	Felice Ash	£4.99 ☐
TOUCH ME, FEEL ME	Rosanna Challis	£4.99 ☐

All Headline books are available at your local bookshop or newsagent, or can be ordered direct from the publisher. Just tick the titles you want and fill in the form below. Prices and availability subject to change without notice.

Headline Book Publishing, Cash Sales Department, Bookpoint, 39 Milton Park, Abingdon, OXON, OX14 4TD, UK. If you have a credit card you may order by telephone – 01235 400400.

Please enclose a cheque or postal order made payable to Bookpoint Ltd to the value of the cover price and allow the following for postage and packing:

UK & BFPO: £1.00 for the first book, 50p for the second book and 30p for each additional book ordered up to a maximum charge of £3.00.

OVERSEAS & EIRE: £2.00 for the first book, £1.00 for the second book and 50p for each additional book.

Name ....

Address ....

....

....

If you would prefer to pay by credit card, please complete:
Please debit my Visa/Access/Diner's Card/American Express (delete as applicable) card no:

Signature .... Expiry Date ....